A Place Called Grace

By Fran Driscoll Roberts

Ruth,
Nice meeting you.
Enjoy!
— Fran Roberts

Text copyright © 2016
Fran Driscoll Roberts
All Rights Reserved

Scripture quotations: New International Version (NIV) Holy Bible, New International Version. Copyright © 1973, 1978, 1984, 2011.

To the God, family and friends who love me. THANKS

Chapter 1
Psalm 27:10 When my father and my mother forsake me, then the LORD will take care of me.

Sheanna knew she wasn't supposed to get out of bed, but her stomach was twisted in painful knots. She had to find something to eat, even if it meant taking a beating from Cullen. She waved the flies away from her face, and silently rolled from the mattress to the floor, listening for the sound of his stomping steps in the hallway, or the rattling click as he unlocked the padlock that kept her inside, but all was still.

Cullen was never happy, unless he was screaming or swinging his brick-like fists. He was skeleton-thin, with blackened, broken teeth, and smelled like sweat and beer. He seemed to take singular pleasure in hurting people, then trying to make them think that they had asked for the pain. Sheanna often spent nights crying silently on her mattress as he raged at her, calling her names she didn't dare repeat. Then he would suddenly go to sleep, and she would have a few hours of peace.

Mom would cry and kiss the top of her head saying, "Be a good little girl, Sheanna," then curl up next to the beast, as if he was a regular person.

The moon shone brightly through the tattered towel that was their curtain, and Sheanna tiptoed across the tiny studio apartment to the refrigerator. She opened it gingerly. No light. No outline of a leftover piece of pizza or jar of jelly. Nothing. A tear coursed down her cheek as Sheanna ran her hand around the inside of the warm, musty-smelling box, and her tummy contracted again. It hurt, and nobody cared. Sheanna crawled back on her mattress and peeked out the window at the trashy street below, where teenage boys hung around, selling their wares and playing screaming music from rusty cars. Sometimes, a pretty girl would walk by, and then get into a car and speed away. Sheanna wished she could speed away. Anywhere there was food.

"Granny LouAnn has food," a little voice whispered inside her head. "She's only three blocks away."

Sheanna pictured herself running the three little blocks to the townhouse where Granny LouAnn lived. She also pictured the wrath of Cullen, and looked down through her threadbare nightgown at the scars and yellowing bruises that lined her legs. He said that she could never, ever go back there or he would break her legs next time. He said that Granny had lied about him to the police, and Mom agreed that Sheanna was too little to walk three blocks alone. Mom said someone might grab her and do terrible things to her, but nothing had ever happened before. Besides, Cullen would beat her no matter what, so Sheanna decided she was going to go. Anything would be better than the hunger that sliced through her stomach.

    Sheanna pawed through her mom's pile of clothes, looking for something that wasn't too dirty or smelly. Finally, she found a thick t-shirt with only one small tear in the sleeve, and no sweaty smell. It hung like a dress on Sheanna's tiny body, but it was better than nothing. She looked at the window Cullen had nailed shut, the one that led to the fire escape; then she tiptoed past the grimy mattress. Sheanna bit her lip, flipped the broken lock and slid open the window on the back wall. She pushed her body into the window and placed a tiny foot on the narrow ledge that would take her to freedom. The bite of the chilly April air deadened her toes, and Sheanna wished she had some shoes. Cullen had thrown her new ones from Granny outside when they caught her last time. She pressed her back against the rough bricks as she slid along the tiny ledge and held her breath as she swung her leg around the corner, then pushed off and dropped onto the fire escape as silently as she could. She didn't want any trouble from the neighborhood kids, who often were as cruel as Cullen. She glided down the stairs, keeping one eye on the street, and one looking for pieces of glass or pointy rocks. Broken glass hid in the grass and littered the streets between the apartment and Granny's porch. She stepped carefully, her aching stomach urging her on. Soon she was sprinting through the back gate and down the alley as fast as she dared.

    "Please, Jesus," Sheanna prayed silently. "Granny said you would protect me. Please don't let Cullen get me. I'm so hungry."

    Thunder shook the air, and Sheanna jumped a little, then she picked up her speed. She was already cold, her feet were wet, and she didn't know how much longer she could stand it. Her teeth chattered, and the icy raindrops and cold air sliced through her arms as she ran. It felt like forever before she saw the little apartment her Granny called home, with its cheerful yellow light, and tiny porch full of potted plants, which she somehow kept alive in the Wisconsin cold. With the last of her strength, Sheanna threw herself at the door, pounding her tiny fists as hard as she could manage.

"Granny! It's Sheanna. Please open up, Granny!" she called as hot tears flowed down her cheeks.

"I'm comin' child." LouAnn sounded close to the door, as if she had been expecting her.

Sheanna almost fainted with relief when she heard the deadbolt turn and saw the sweet face smiling down at her. She threw herself into Granny LouAnn's arms and squeezed as tightly as she could.

"I was so scared, Granny. So hungry. He put a big lock on the door, so I couldn't come see you."

"Shh, I know, Baby. I knew there was a good reason you didn't come. It's all right now. Come on and get something to eat, and we'll get you into a nice hot bath. We'll fix you right up, She-she."

Sheanna wiped her feet on the braided rug and quickly washed her hands as Granny shuffled to the refrigerator and pulled out a quart of milk, a brick of cheddar cheese and a thick package of sliced ham. The tiny woman with bright ice-blue eyes carefully poured a tall glass of milk with her shaky hands and handed it to Sheanna.

"Drink up, while I fix you a warm sandwich."

Sheanna tried not to gulp the rich, cool drink too quickly. She knew that she had to take it slow, or her stomach would hurt even worse. She took a drink, then set down her glass, and reached for an apple in Granny's fruit bowl. She bit into the aptly named red delicious, her tongue darting to catch all the juice. The elderly woman set the sandwich in the microwave for a few seconds. Soon it steamed on the plate in front of her, while Granny slipped a fleece blanket over the girl's shoulders.

"You're like ice, girl," she whispered, and then she winked. "Next time, take three t-shirts before you run away."

"They were nasty, Granny," Sheanna said, her big aquamarine eyes wide with the memory. "I hate that sweaty smell."

LouAnn muttered to herself, "Brinne should be whipped for how she's 'raising' her only child, and that sorry boyfriend of hers is no friend. He's barely human."

She turned and ran her hand lightly along Sheanna's arm.

"I'm going to fill the bathtub, She-she. You look like you could use a bath, and I still have your footie pajamas from last time."

Sheanna grinned. They were pink, fuzzy and warmed her from her neck to her toes. Granny used special shampoo to take the itches away, and her soap smelled like flowers. Then Granny would brush her hair until it shined like gold, and read her Bible stories until she fell asleep in a nice warm bed. In the morning, there would be scrambled eggs, toast with jelly and real orange juice. If she was real lucky, it would be days before Mom and Cullen would come and get her. Maybe this time they would think she just disappeared and leave her alone.

"Honey," Granny LouAnn said, with a very serious look on her face, "how would you like to go see your Aunt Beth and Uncle Phil down in Mississippi? I've been dreaming of going home since your dear Pappy died, and I want to take you with me. They have a huge house right near the beach, and you'll really love it there. You'll have other kids to play with, and you will never, ever go hungry or be hurt again, I promise."

"But I thought you said I had to stay with Mom and Cullen or you go to jail. Why can't we just stay here? Just don't answer the door when they come knocking. That's what Cullen does."

LouAnn traced her fingers over the thin scars that crisscrossed Sheanna's legs. Then she pulled a small disposable camera from her purse and started taking pictures of the welts on the girl's legs, then her arms and neck. Sheanna knew to keep very still so the pictures wouldn't be blurry.

"Cullen is a terrible man. I tried doing it the legal way, and it just got you hurt worse and locked in. I've known men like him before, and they only get meaner. What if there was a fire?" LouAnn shuddered. "Now I'm going to do it my way-- if you want to. Besides, your Uncle Phil is a police officer, and he will help me find the right people so we can keep you forever."

The smile that lit up Sheanna's pixie face was the answer LouAnn was looking for.

"Finish up, baby," she said as she marched toward the phone. "I'm gettin' us a ride home. We've got plans to make."

Chapter 2
Prov. 20:6 "...But who can find a faithful man?"

"They are still remodeling this doggone library." Leah whispered into her cell phone, fearful of Mrs. Finley's wrath as she stepped between the two-by-fours. She ran her hand through her unruly black curls in frustration. "Shay, what was that book again? I've looked everywhere, even back by the new construction, and I can't find anything by Alison Murphy."

"Told ya to write it down. *Aestival's End* by Alison Murphy. Are you in the right section?" Her best friend Shay's voice crackled through the phone.

"Yes, I've tried the fiction section, new releases and I'd even ask Finley if she wasn't busy with a preschool class with a zillion questions. I found a Marguerite Murphy, but no Alison. Why can't the book club pick something simple to find, like Charles Dickens?"

"I promise it's worth finding," Shay scolded. "Keep looking. I'm not bailing you out this time."

"You know I'm not big on romances." Leah frowned and headed for the "Inspirational" section. "My first day off in two months, and I'm wasting it at the library."

"Really? Weren't you just talking about some fine-looking construction worker? Maybe you'll find more than a good book on your day off."

Leah snorted and peeked over at the man with the kind face and the golden tan as she inhaled the sweet smell of cut wood. "Not just any construction worker, the boss."

"How do you know that? Have you been spying?"

"No, I just heard one of the guys asking him how to frame up something."

"So how long have you been watching him? Guess your New Year's Resolution isn't going to last much longer."

"I've been walking around looking for that crazy book long enough to know his whole life story if I was nosy like you. He doesn't say much, but he's a babe. Hey, I found that book. It was in the 'Inspirational' section. Thanks for the directions."

"Go say 'hi' to him."

"I'm looking at him right now, and that's as close as I'm getting. You know I've been cursed with a man-repellant personality. I'm a nerd with scary hair that does taxes for a living. But if you're ready to dump Landon, he's tall and has the greatest deep voice. Josh Turner for sure. You should see the muscles in his arms. Perfect tan, too. Oh, great, he's looking over here."

"You're talking too loud, silly."

"It's this cheap cell phone," Leah whispered fiercely. "Oh, now you've done it, Shay. He's walking over here."

"Call me when you get home," Shay laughed.

"Traitor," Leah said to the dead phone.

"Hi, can I help you find something?" the man asked.

"You don't look like you work for the library," Leah looked up at him, holding her phone in front of her like a shield.

"Oh, don't let the clothes fool you. I spend a lot of time in the library."

His baritone voice rolled toward her, and Leah could feel her heart beating in her throat. "I was just looking for this silly novel for my book club, but now I've found it. It's not that important."

"So, you're not married?" he grinned, a mischievous glint in his golden brown eyes.

"Married people don't read?" she looked up at him with her best innocent expression, as she slipped her phone into her purse.

He smiled and looked down at her naked left hand. "If a married woman is looking for a romance novel on her day off, her husband isn't doing something right."

Leah laughed and flushed. "I'm not married—well, maybe to my job— but that doesn't really count."

"Can I show you what we've been doing? I know a lot of people are tired of the pounding and sawdust."

Leah felt her cheeks warm and wondered how much of the conversation he has heard. "Sure, and if there's any way you can make that great smell hang around after you're finished, that would be nice, too."

"There's nothing like the smell of freshly-cut wood and new books."

"True, but you'd better watch out for Finley. She *hates* talking in the library."

"I've met her. She's not so bad."

"You've never had to sit through one of her classes!"

Two men looked up from their hammering, and stared at the

couple. Leah felt her cheeks warm slightly again.

"Guys, this is…sorry I didn't get your name."

"I'm Leah McPhillen." She stuck out her hand to shake theirs and the older man slipped off his dusty gloves and gently shook her hand.

"I'm Jason, and this is my brother Clint. Okay if we stop for lunch now, Boss? I have to run pick up a prescription for my wife."

"Fine with me. I thought we'd knock this out faster, but we still have a couple of hours before we can turn it over to the sheetrock crew."

The shorter one, Clint, waved at Leah then wiped sweat from his bald head. "See you later, Miss."

She gave a little wave and looked at the rows of wooden frames that lined the new addition. "It looks good. These meeting rooms will be so nice once they're finished."

"We had a problem with the guys who ran the plumbing and had to redo this whole section. It's been quite a job."

"But it sounds like you're almost finished now. I know how it feels to have a mountain of work that never ends. Job security is nice, but I'd like to be bored every once in a while."

"I know the feeling. But I'll bet it would be a nice break for both of us if you let me take you out on Saturday night. I can't promise boring, but maybe relaxing?"

"Are you always so direct?" she asked, staring into his stormy eyes, not quite brown or green, with golden flecks.

"I don't believe in wastin' words, Ma'am," he drawled in his musical country accent.

"You will have to pass the Trooper test."

"Trooper test?"

"He is my best friend, and a wonderful judge of character. He adopted our family about two years ago, and he pre-screens all my friends."

"What do you mean, adopted your family?"

"One day this old black German Shepherd with incredibly huge ears just showed up in our carport. He was half-starved and beaten. His nose was all dry and scratched up. We didn't think he would last a week. But now he's fat and sassy, and plays like a puppy. You'd never know he'd been abused."

"We had a couple of dogs like that in Rattlesnake Bayou over the years. People just drove out to the country and dropped off their pets. I never could stand to see a skinny dog."

The tenderness in his voice went straight to her heart, and Leah smiled. He looked like any other contractor in his baseball cap, paint-stained jeans and heavy work boots, but there was something intriguing about him. She looked up into his face and tried to read his bottomless brown eyes.

"I may be persuaded to go out with you," she said slowly, "but I don't even know your name."

"I'm Michael, Michael Charbonneau." He handed her a business card. "Just in case you want me to fix something one day."

"Pleased to meet you, and I'm sure I'll have something that needs fixing sooner or later."

She stuck out her hand to shake his.

He took her hand and held it for a moment. "Let's go sit outside by the fountain for a few minutes and talk. The guys are all on lunch break by now, and I didn't bring anything to eat."

"There's a nice little place across the street. The food is good, and I could use some coffee," she blurted, gently sliding her hand out of his. "Let me just check out this book, since I wasted an hour trying to find it."

I just asked him to lunch! I can't believe I'm doing this, Leah thought. *I'm twenty-four years old, and I feel like I'm fourteen.*

Michael nodded and followed her to the checkout desk. Leah couldn't help but notice that Finley's sour expression almost disappeared when she saw Michael. Wow, he even had the power to charm the wicked witch of the South.

Leah looked him over as they walked into the hot Mississippi sun and across the street to The Oyster Buoy, wondering what it was about him that made her blood race. There was a kind spirit about him that made her want to know him more, and his deep, quiet voice sent little electric pulses through her arms. Was it because she'd overhead one of the workers thanking him for 'coming to get things straight on his day off'? Maybe it was the contrasts-- the light brown-almost blonde hair that curled slightly around the edges of his cap, his innocent-looking face, and the well-muscled body of a man used to working hard, with those exotic stormy eyes that kept changing color from golden brown to almost black. Whatever it was, she was breaking all her rules and enjoying it.

The girl at the cash register smiled and said, "Just sit anywhere, Y'all," so they took a small corner table near the fish tank. It was Monday, so the restaurant was only half full, and Leah was happy for the quiet. The front of the restaurant was a series of huge plate glass windows, which usually offered a pretty view of the well-landscaped town square, and the occasional shopper strolling toward the gift shops. But today was especially humid for April, and most of the patrons were sitting in the back, where it was cool. Leah watched the colorful fish darting in and out of the greenery, trying hard not to stare at the man who sat painfully close to her.

Leah let her gaze sweep the room. "I don't know why, but I just love it here."

"I've heard that this place is almost a hundred years old." He glanced up at the crown molding.

"Something like that, and maybe that gorgeous woodwork is part of the charm. The service is great, and the shrimp and grits is wonderful, so they pretty much have it all here."

"I love the crab claws," Michael said, barely glancing at the menu.

"Oh, so you have been here before," Leah said, biting her bottom lip slightly. "We usually send a kid from the office for the special, but I like the buffet, most of all."

Leah wasn't really hungry, and now she wished she'd just kept her mouth shut. *Yes, I eat everything and lots of it.* She looked at the waitress who was about sixteen and skinny as a newborn deer.

"That's a good idea, Leah." Her name sounded good rolling off his tongue. Michael looked up at the waitress, who was setting down two glasses of ice water. "We'll have the buffet, and keep the coffee coming."

Oh, good, another caffeine addict, she thought. *This is getting spooky.*

"What's the matter?" Michael asked.

"You're the only person I know who drinks coffee *before* eating lunch. Except me, that is."

"Momma got me started drinking coffee when I was about five or six— heavy on the sugar and light on the cream. I've loved it ever since."

"I had to sneak it, but me too. Except the sugar part. Where did you grow up?"

"Slidell 'til I was thirteen, then Rattlesnake Bayou, now Mobile. How 'bout you?"

"I've lived in Ocean Shores pretty much all my life. I love this little town-- being near the Gulf and knowing everybody's business," she said, using her favorite line.

Michael laughed and picked up his plate. "C'mon, let's get some of that fried catfish while it's hot."

Leah followed him to the buffet, thinking he was pretty smart for letting that one go. She'd tried to bait him, and it didn't work, unlike her last disastrous date-- another friend of Shay's from work. It seemed logical that a math teacher and an accountant would get along, but the only thing they'd had in common was that he was as set in his ways as she was. Thankfully, the date ended quickly, and she'd refused any more mercy-date offers from friends and family. Men usually spelled disaster, especially those she cared most for, so Leah decided that for now her dog was enough companionship and concentrated on saving for her dream home. Trooper kept her warm when it was cold, was fun to play with, and she could trust him with her life, so she contented herself with that. And she was happy, usually.

Leah watched as Michael heaped the food on his plate while she made herself a chef salad. She licked her lips as she dropped some crab salad on the side.

"Please tell me you're going to eat some real cookin' and not just rabbit food," he teased.

"Oh, I'm just getting warmed up," Leah sassed back. "You'll see. They cover the dessert bar when I come in."

Why did I say that? Leah thought. *I have lost my mind.*

"I don't believe that," he said, his eyes locked on hers. He was standing so close it made her feel like a thin stream of ice water was running down her spine.

"Their peach cobbler is the best," she said in some soft Southern belle's voice.

His eyes bored into her for one long second, and then he went back to heaping food on his plate.

Thank goodness, Leah thought. *There's a lady behind me shoving her plate into my back. I guess she's in dire need of some croutons.*

Leah looked back at the woman, who turned out to be an

elderly lady trying to balance her tray on a walker.

"Would you like some help with that?" Leah asked, setting down her salad plate.

"Thank ya, darlin'," the woman crooned. "I'll just have a little French dressing, and a scoop of that crab salad."

Leah loaded her plate, and slid it onto a nearby table. The woman thanked her and patted her hand as she sat down.

Leah looked up to see Michael staring at her with the funniest expression on his face, and the butterflies flew out of her stomach and into her chest. She smiled at him, wondering at her reaction. He was just a guy-- a cute guy, but just a guy.

One little look and I'm blushing? Leah thought, as she retrieved her plate and self-consciously walked to their table.

Usually, she was content to be on her own, but sometimes Leah had wondered why there was no one for her. She knew part of the problem was her living at home. Since her daddy's motorcycle wreck and months-long recovery, she was too nervous to be too far away from him. Momma had terrible arthritis, which crippled her right hand, so Leah took over many of the household chores. Plus, she had her own office, home cookin' every night, and she was saving for the most beautiful antebellum home on the next block. She caught herself picturing Michael on the front porch in a sleeveless t-shirt and cut-off shorts, helping to put up a porch swing. Then she chided herself for being so silly.

She watched Michael as he finished the last of his catfish, then the chicken and dumplings, and quickly drained his coffee.

He smiled sheepishly under her stare. "Guess I was hungry. Do you want something else? I'm going to see if there's some chicken-fried steak left."

Leah smiled and made herself eat a bite of the crab salad. "I'm fine."

She watched him walk back to the buffet, and noticed other women in the room were watching, too. Leah knew she wanted a strong man, but it was so hard to find a man that was strong on the outside but not full of himself. Michael seemed different, somehow. His voice sounded like music to her. There was something in his tone that was almost tender when he spoke. She flushed as he caught her staring again.

She made herself eat her salad, though her stomach was too

busy fluttering to notice.

"That was real nice of you," Michael said, nodding at the older lady's walker as he stirred a large hunk of butter into his grits. "I didn't even notice her."

"Oh, bless her heart, she was having a rough time. Anyone would have helped her."

"So, what do you do when you're not helping out little old ladies?" He leaned forward, his dark eyes holding hers.

"I'm a tax accountant," she said with a grin.

"You don't look like any accountant I ever met," he smiled back. "Please don't say you work for the IRS."

"Not in my worst nightmare. My thick glasses and pocket protector are at home. I only wear them during tax season or in the office." She tried to tear her eyes away from his, but was hopelessly caught.

"That's good to know. You really shouldn't hide those pretty brown eyes. They have just a little touch of red, like cherry wood. I'm sure you've already figured out that I'm a carpenter."

"You look like one. Do you work for the city?"

"I was just helping out a friend. Clint calls me 'Boss' but it's his company. He's had a hard time keeping good help. I usually work over in Mobile. You've heard of Charbonneau Woodworks?"

She hadn't, and she wished she'd taken a closer look at his card before slipping it into her purse. "Family business?"

"Don't tell anybody, but I'm it. I have a couple guys that work with me, but I don't have any family to speak of," he said, his eyes looking just a little sad.

"Our family is spread all over this country like a bunch of gypsies. I do have one brother here, and Momma and Daddy, of course. There's Paw-Paw and quite a few cousins up in Sardis Lake, but except for family reunions every few years, McPhillens are pretty hard to find. I've already told you about my best guy, Trooper."

"I'd like to meet him," he said, as if they'd known each other for weeks instead of minutes.

"So, even though you know how much I like to eat, you still want to take me out on Saturday?" She clamped her lips together, sorry her mouth just rattled on, spewing embarrassing comments.

"I've been waiting for you to say 'yes' for almost a half

hour."

Leah giggled, a high nervous alien sound, and took a pen from her purse. She drew a rough map on her napkin. "Just go down Ocean Shores Drive here to the Gulf. Go left on Beach Road two blocks and then left on Vista Bonita."

Michael had slid his chair right up next to hers. The nearness of him was so overpowering she could barely breathe.

"You can't miss it," she'd assured him, with a mischievous grin. "It's a yellow house with white trim, and an Ocean Shores Police car in the carport."

He didn't even look surprised.

The explosion of brick and shattering glass broke the spell. A dark blue pickup truck was sliding through the plate glass windows. It skidded on its side and then flipped over, smashing tables and chairs like toothpicks as it slid through the restaurant in a heart-stopping tangle of metal and wood. Leah dove out of the way, bouncing off the fish tank and crawling around the counter behind the desserts. She buried her face in her arms and listened in horror as screams tore through the room, followed by blaring sirens wailing in the distance.

She didn't even notice that Michael was beside her until he grabbed her hand and helped her up. She stared at a small piece of glass, which stuck out just below his eye.

Michael reached up and snatched it away, and a fat trail of blood wound its way down his cheek and began to drip onto his shirt. Leah reached across the dessert bar, and came up with a handful of napkins.

"Here, press this against it," she whispered, looking around at the destruction.

A skinny teenaged boy howled in pain as he crawled out of the passenger window of the upended truck, joining the horrific sounds of those who hadn't gotten out of the way fast enough. His arm hung at a strange angle, and blood seemed to cover him, from his swollen, bruised face to his bare feet. Leah grabbed another handful of napkins, and ran to help staunch the flow of blood. Michael was pulling smashed chairs and tables away, working his way toward where the lady with the walker had been sitting.

"Don't touch my arm," the boy pleaded as Leah climbed toward him. Tears and snot ran down his face, mingling with the blood from several huge gashes above his misshapen eye. His left ear seemed to be hanging from his head at an odd angle, like it was partially torn off, and his shoulder looked like hamburger.

"I won't hurt you. I promise. I'm just gonna press this against your forehead and see if we can slow down all that bleeding. You're pretty cut up, and I don't want you to bleed to death before the ambulance gets here."

Before Leah knew it, several cops surrounded her, including her daddy, wearing a look as dark as a February thunderstorm.

"Are you okay? What did you see, Leah?" he asked.

"I'm fine." Leah swallowed hard, trying to collect her thoughts amid the screams of the wounded and the smell of burned rubber and blood. "I-I don't know what caused it. There was just a huge crash and a lot of people were screaming," she stammered, and pointed to the teenaged boy slumped on the floor next to her. "That boy was in the truck. He passed out a few seconds ago. I think it was from the pain when I tried to clean up that arm, but the blood was spewing everywhere. I have a tourniquet on his arm near where the bone is sticking out. Don't know where the driver is, but I'm fine, Daddy. I just feel like I'm going to puke right now, and I want to go home."

He nodded, and gently cupped her arm. "Go on, girl. We have enough witnesses, and the ambulance is on its way." He pointed toward the side door.

Leah bent down to retrieve her purse, and stumbled out into the hot sunshine. She breathed in great gulps of fresh air, willing her stomach to stop contracting as she wiped the blood from her hands with a tissue. She walked slowly, willing the nausea to be gone, forcing herself to put one foot in front of the other. She only remembered Michael as she crossed the library parking lot, but he was nowhere to be seen, and nothing on earth could make her walk back into that nightmare.

"I hope they're okay, God," she whispered as she forced her shaking hands to find her car keys at the bottom of her purse. "And if it's not too much to ask, please let Michael be as nice as he seems."

Chapter 3
Ez. 18:32 "For I have no pleasure in the death of anyone who dies, declares the Lord GOD..."

Leah watched in horror as her father's face flashed across the television screen, accompanied by the sound of several protestors screaming the background.

"Officer Liam 'Phil' McPhillen has been placed on administrative leave pending the outcome of an investigation into a high speed chase, which left one fourteen-year-old dead, fifteen-year-old Jacobi Ray Jackson in critical condition, and several others seriously wounded. On Monday, April 25th, Officer McPhillen noticed two teens in a blue '97 Chevy Silverado during school hours and allegedly instigated a high-speed chase through the heavily trafficked shopping district. The resulting crash all but destroyed the landmark Oyster Buoy restaurant, and killed Robert Maximus Holmes, of Saucier, Mississippi. Lawyers for the family maintain that this chase was unwarranted, and the injuries and death that resulted from it lay squarely at the feet of Sergeant McPhillen."

The reporter flipped her platinum blonde hair from her shoulder and assumed her trademark smirk, which made her look like a fish about to swallow a minnow. "Calls placed to the Ocean Shores police department have not been returned, and the results of a preliminary department investigation have not yet been released. This is Patti Petrowski on the case for WWMS-News, Biloxi."

"Patti Polyester gets it wrong again!" Leah snapped at the television, as if the pasty-faced girl with perfect blonde highlights could see her ire. "How can delinquents tearing up the town be the fault of the police department?"

Beth McPhillen snatched the remote and clicked the television off. "You don't need to watch this right now, Leah. Daddy's going to be home any minute from Hunter's football game, and I do not want him any more upset than he already is."

"Momma, you know Daddy has never been this torn up about anything. That girl has everybody all riled up, and she doesn't care who gets hurt. The phone calls, the hate mail-- they're calling him a killer right to his face! The world has gone crazy."

"Those kids are young and upset. Phil understands that, but this story is bloody and juicy and the media has it like a dog with a soup bone. We have to stay strong. The other boy may not live either, and that's what they're buzzing around waiting to see. It's just hard."

"As if Dad wouldn't do anything to help anyone—but Petrowski will do what it takes to make a name for herself including trying to find a scandal where there is none. She's been getting away with it her whole life. I wish she'd just move away and go haunt some other town."

"You two have been at each other's throats since sixth grade. Why do you even watch her if you know it's going to upset you?"

"Opposition research. I knew it would only be a matter of time before she'd try to make a criminal of one of the nicest guys in town. If she only knew that Daddy spends more time changing tires and helping find lost kids than anything else, she'd shut those fish lips of hers. One day I'm going to knock her out on camera and give her something worth shouting about!"

"Leah, I know you're upset, but you know that vengeance doesn't accomplish anything. The Lord has this handled. The prayer group is on it. Just be patient, and you'll see something good come out of all this."

"That's why Hunter was up early spraying half-dried egg off the front porch? The prayer group has never been able to undo Patti. She's like a plague! You know Patti's had it in for the police department ever since they took her driver's license for refusing to pay her parking tickets. She thinks she's above following the rules because of who her family is. Everybody knows it."

"If everybody knows it, the story will die, and Daddy will go back to working sixty hours a week protecting and serving, instead of helping Hunter coach his football team. Just let it go."

"I don't think so, Momma. This has already made it to the national news. They don't care about the facts. They're just parroting Patti Pea-brain."

"I know. I've been praying about it," Beth sighed. "I wish you'd trust Almighty God and do the same. It's the best thing we can do when the mud gets knee deep."

Leah bit her lip to keep the words from spilling out of her heart as she unconsciously glanced at her mother's gnarled right hand. *"Sometimes God doesn't answer, Momma. Sometimes bad things keep happening."*

Leah walked back into her bedroom. It was actually a mother-in-law suite, which had housed her great-grandmother Michelle before Leah was born. After the motorcycle wreck that had put her father in intensive care for two months, Leah had converted the space into an office and bedroom, first to help nurse her father, then to give her parents a tax advantage after she'd decided to stay home and save her money.

The tiny kitchenette was normally unused, and piles of folders were stacked next to the sink. There was a dorm-sized refrigerator that held several diet Dr. Peppers and any restaurant leftovers she wanted to hide from her brother, Hunter, the human garbage disposal. Several boxes of Great Granny Michelle's belongings still lined the wall next to the oven, and two old guitars rested on stands next to her bed. Leah walked to her desk, where piles of unfinished "extension" tax returns awaited her attention. She loved that Mr. Alexander let her work at home after the Friday morning staff meetings. She got a lot more done without the phones ringing and the air blasting arctic temperatures throughout the office. Plus, Momma's house just smelled better, like freshly cut flowers and lemon Pledge, instead of ammonia and onion rings. Lunch always tasted better, too.

Leah usually kept her phone off when she was working, but a tiny chime told her she'd just received a text message. It was Shay.

Just saw Ur hunk at the library unloading wood. Nice muscles. ☺

Leah smiled in spite of herself. Just one more day until the big date. Michael had called that morning to confirm. He'd looked up her home phone number in the phone book; they were the only McPhillen in town. Leah had been pleasantly surprised to hear his deep voice that morning and wondered what color his eyes were today. They had seemed to get darker when they talked about the past, and had golden flecks that glimmered when he stood in the sunshine. She lifted his business card up to her nose and inhaled the woody scent. Why was this guy still single? Leah made herself stop daydreaming about the man because there were too many unknowns. She could tell that he really loved working with wood, and that the men he worked with respected him. But was that enough? Was she setting herself up for yet another disappointment? Shay hadn't just happened to see him at the library. Leah figured she went to check him out for herself. Technically, teachers weren't allowed to leave school at lunch without special permission from the principal—and hers was no prize. Shay had gone the extra mile to watch her back, as always.

Does this mean you're checking out my date? Leah texted back.

The scar tissue on Leah's heart was massive, and the worst thing was that every time her heart was shredded the knife came out of nowhere. There was never any warning or time to prepare. Leah had been blindsided again and again, both figuratively and literally. Shay had helped her keep her eyes open and her heart protected, and she knew there would be plenty of input from her friend on whether he was worthy of a second glance. But Leah had to admit she was impressed that Michael was serious enough to look up her phone number when he was going to see her in just twenty-six hours, not that she was counting down. Of course, a lot of unbalanced teens that hated her daddy had looked up their phone number too, and harassed them unmercifully. They had to unplug the house phone before going to bed. It went both ways.

"Momma, we're home," Hunter called from the front porch.

"Take off those muddy shoes before you walk on my clean floor," Momma answered. "Supper is on the table."

Leah grinned as she walked toward the kitchen, picturing Hunter and Daddy removing their shoes carefully and shaking the orange dust off their clothes before daring to come into the house. If cleanliness was next to Godliness, Beth McPhillen had a room pretty close to the Lord's throne.

"What's that stench?" Leah yelled as she heard Trooper barking and the screen door slam. "Smells like old sweaty socks that have been marinated in wet towels."

"Daddy, Leah said you stink," Hunter tattled. "I think she needs to cut the grass."

Leah couldn't resist her younger brother's challenge. She walked to the table.

"You're the one who had to cut the grass when you were bad. Besides, I wouldn't mind driving Daddy's new zero-turn lawn machine. Did your team lose again?"

Hunter laughed and grabbed the tennis ball from Trooper's mouth. He opened the screen door and threw it across the yard, bouncing it off the back gate with little effort. Trooper barked again and sped off toward his toy. The elderly dog still played like a puppy at times, his limp barely noticeable.

"We won big today, in more ways than one."

Hunter was proud of his job helping coach the football team at the Junior college, and he'd arranged a scrimmage against the high school varsity football team as part of their post-season Championship celebration. Students bought tickets for five dollars each to raise money for the scholarship fund, and Hunter had bragged that they sold out in two days. It didn't hurt that every high school student with a ticket got out of class fifteen minutes early either. It seemed the whole school took advantage of that little perk.

It also didn't hurt that half of the girls in town were in love with Hunter's Caribbean blue eyes and black wavy hair, and the guys knew that the junior college team's quarterback would probably be drafted into the NFL long before his senior year. Football season was never over in Ocean Shores, Mississippi. People started to speculate about next year's championship team just minutes after the championship was won. If it wasn't football season, there was training and football camp and conditioning and scrimmages. Hunter was a natural athlete, talented in every sport he tried, but football was by far his favorite. He called it a chess game with muscle. He would still be the star quarterback himself if he had his way, but the McPhillen luck had taken him out early—a compound fracture of his throwing arm had ended any chance of him playing in the big leagues. So now he was an assistant coach, working on his Criminal Justice major.

"Of course we won. Last year's championship team wasn't about to be creamed by this year's championship team. With admission and concessions, we raised over $5,700.00. Daddy was a great defensive coordinator. Oh, and Toby Lipschitz asked if you were dating anybody."

Leah pictured the wide receiver with the missing front tooth and screeching voice. "As much as I'd love to be Leah Lipshitz one day, I'll have to pass. Besides, I happen to have a date tomorrow night. Oh, and I forgot to mention that I'd rather kiss a Komodo dragon than Toby Lipschitz."

"So, you do think about kissing Toby? I knew it."

Leah ignored the comment and looked at her father, whose

face was still bright red and dripping sweat. His smile told her it had been a good day for him too.

Beth put a wet washcloth on the back of her husband's neck, and planted a tiny kiss on his cheek. "Liam McPhillen, when are you going to realize that you can't run around in this heat like a kid?"

Phil grabbed his wife's hand and kissed her palm. "We won, baby. It was a beautiful thing. Hunter's coaching is up there with the best of 'em. I think we'd better be careful or we'll lose him to Tulane or Mississippi State."

Leah bit down on her lip at the mention of Tulane. Today seemed to be the day for tearing scabs off of old wounds! The pain rose up from her chest, stinging her eyes with hot tears.

"I'd better get back to work," she said, grabbing her plate and fleeing to her office.

Chapter Four

Proverbs 4:26— Ponder the path of your feet and let all your ways be established.

"Leah, I need to ask a huge favor." The lines around Momma's mouth were deep, her cheeks flushed, and she looked angrier than she ever had.

"Sure, Momma." Leah hung up Trooper's leash and stared into Beth's blazing brown eyes, wondering what had gotten her so flustered.

"Leah, do you remember your baby cousin, Sheanna? You know, Brinne's girl? They were at the family reunion a few years back with Great Aunt LouAnn." Momma sipped from her coffee cup, then glanced out at the cheerful, sunny afternoon.

"Yes, that baby had some chunky legs! She had the prettiest green eyes and long dark eyelashes. I remember carrying her around everywhere until Brinne said it was time for her nap."

"That's right. You did take quite a shine to her. Well Ms. Brinne went and got hooked up with another no good snake of a man, and LouAnn is going to get Sheanna out of there before they beat or starve the poor child to death."

"Isn't it illegal just to take her, Momma?"

"You let me worry about that. Your Daddy's got some friends who're going to help us with the legalities, and I know how to handle Sheanna's mother when the time comes. She's only twenty years old, and she's already had enough trouble for a lifetime, let me tell you. I need you and Hunter to drive up to Milwaukee in the truck, pack them up and haul them back down here. I know you have this date planned, but we have to move quickly or that Cullen will do something terrible. The trip is over nine hundred miles, and I'll show you the fastest way on the map. Daddy and I would go, but with that court case coming and all the troubles, I need to be here—and to get the guest room ready for Aunt LouAnn and that poor little girl, bless her heart."

"Why Hunter, Momma? I'm better off bringing this tough doggy here. Hunter's got classes, and he's not much of a city driver. I know he'll get lost in Chicago. Why don't you let me take somebody who is stronger, who I can share the driving with?"

"Such as?"

"Shay. She's strong as an ox and a good driver, too. If we have any trouble up there, she knows how to handle herself in the city. She's from New Orleans, you know."

"The drive will take two full days. I hardly think Shay would miss work—"

"She never takes her sick days. I know she can get a substitute easily. She drives that old beat-up truck of hers like lightning, and she's taken all those self-defense courses. That time we went to the New Orleans Zoo, she zipped through those city streets around three parades and got us to I-10 in no time flat."

"That's what you get for going to New Orleans on St. Patrick's Day." Beth shook her head, worry lines easing slightly.

"We didn't even think about the date. It was Saturday, and the weather was so nice, we just had to get out and do something different. Besides, the point is, Shay's a great city driver, and I know she'll do it."

"Well, I'll call her and see what she thinks. You'll be taking Daddy's truck, not hers. But don't you girls get sidetracked on any explorations when you get up there. You'll have to load up Auntie's stuff quick because it's a very long drive, and the neighborhood isn't very safe. Don't let Aunt LouAnn do too much, because she'll try, and keep an eye on Sheanna. The little thing has basically raised herself, and she probably won't be too happy about having y'all boss her around."

"I won't boss her around, Momma. I'll be careful," Leah grinned, and ran to her room to pack a bag. Her boring life had suddenly gotten very interesting. First, meeting Michael, the crash, and now a road trip! But how would she tell Michael without sounding like she was trying to get out of their date? Leah felt her insides pinch together as she tried to think of the kindest way to ask him to wait a few more days. She decided the truth was the best way. If he didn't believe her, he wasn't the guy she thought he was anyway. Her mouth suddenly dried up, and Leah found it hard to breathe as she looked up Michael's number on her phone and hit "send". She breathed a sigh of relief as she got his voice mail, the chicken's best friend.

"Michael, it's Leah. I know how this sounds, but I need you

to trust me. I have to go out of town for a family emergency. I'll be back in a couple of days. I promise we'll go out whenever you want, but I have to leave today. I have to help my little cousin. I'm so sorry. Text me if you forgive me. If not, I'm still glad I met you. It's certainly a day I'll never forget."

She left her cell phone number and hung up, hoping that Michael believed her and wasn't insulted at the short notice. But there was nothing she could do either way.

Within an hour, Leah and Shay had their bags in the back seat of Phil's new truck, his gold credit card, great aunt LouAnn's address and phone number, and $200 emergency money.

Leah scratched behind Trooper's head. "Watch over 'em, boy," she said softly. "If the punks try to egg the house again, bite 'em in the pants."

Leah kissed her parents goodbye. "I promise I'll stop and rest if I get too tired. Don't worry about us. I have the cell phone if I need you."

"Shay, you don't overdo it either. And don't do anything that's going to call attention to yourself with that custody mess. I'd feel terrible if you lost your teacher's license because of me," Momma cautioned. "Aunt LouAnn will have everything packed up and be waiting for you girls, whenever you get there. Just get to Milwaukee and back in one piece."

"Yes, ma'am," the young women dutifully replied, then giggled as they jumped into the fine F-150 king cab. Neither girl had ever driven anything so new, or been so far from home, but they couldn't wait to get started.

"I called Tony Alexander and told him what's going on in case you're not back in time for work on Monday, so don't worry about that," Daddy added. "It's not like the IRS is going anywhere."

Leah hadn't even thought about it. She'd be doing a lot of quick computing next week to catch up, but she wouldn't trade this chance for anything. She had a special hatred for people who hurt kids. Some of the "cop" stories Daddy had told her made her blood boil. Now she was getting a chance to help one of those poor kids, her own cousin, and she couldn't wait.

As the miles passed between them and Ocean Shores, Leah and Shay settled into a routine, stopping every couple of hours to get cokes and snacks and to switch drivers. They were too wound up to sleep, and arrived at the first Illinois tollbooth at 1 a.m. Leah was driving, and merging in and out of the lanes was harrowing. The Illinois drivers switched from lane to lane at eighty miles an hour like there was no speed limit and cameras weren't overhead. It seemed there was a tollbooth every couple of miles, and the tolls were not cheap. Thankfully, Phil had left a cup-holder full of change for them, and they furiously dug for quarters—several times. Less than an hour later, they were near Milwaukee, looking for the Hope Road exit, and they easily followed the written directions to LouAnn's apartment. Leah was too tired to search for the parking lot, so she backed the truck up the curb to LouAnn's porch, and the two girls got out of the truck, complaining at the biting chill in the air. Neither girl had thought to bring a heavy jacket, and both regretted it.

"Aunt LouAnn, open up," Leah called out, as she banged on the door. It was nearly 3 a.m., and she was ready to lie down. The adrenaline had finally worn off, and she was beat.

The door opened quickly, and soon they were in the cheerful apartment, glad for the warmth of the room, and the smell of fresh bread in the air. Leah looked into the piercing blue eyes of her tiny, sinewy aunt with a mass of iron gray hair piled on her head.

"I couldn't sleep last night, so I baked a little," LouAnn said softly, as she pointed the girls to her overstuffed couch and love seat replete with brightly colored pillows and handmade quilts. "Can I get you girls something to eat or drink?"

"No, ma'am," Leah said. "I drank so many cokes I think I'll bust."

"Me too," Shay said, tossing her ponytail holder into her purse and shaking her long brown hair loose." I'm Shay, by the way."

LouAnn shook her hand and smiled. "I've heard stories."

"Then you know I'm the good one."

Leah pushed her friend's arm, trying to throw her off balance. "Not really."

Shay and Leah kicked off their shoes and slipped under the quilts. Leah curled up on the loveseat since Shay was four inches taller.

LouAnn tucked them in, planted a tiny kiss on each girl's head, and whispered, "Goodnight, girls. Sheanna and I are just in the next room if you need anything."

They settled in to sleep, almost as quickly as their heads hit the pillows.

The smell of brewing coffee and sizzling bacon woke Leah and Shay late that morning. They yawned and stretched, blinking the sleep from their eyes.

"Wake up, sleepyheads, it's almost lunch time," Sheanna piped, pulling on the comforters. "You already missed church and cartoons and everything."

"How are you, shortcake?" Leah asked, rubbing her eyes. She looked at the beautiful little girl with thin blonde pigtails poking out of her head like antennae. She tried not to frown at the girl's toothpick arms and legs and the veins showing on her gaunt face. Her eyes were the most beautiful pale aquamarine cat eyes, framed by thick brown lashes, and they flashed with anger at the nickname.

"I'm not a short cake. I'm Sheanna," the tiny girl scolded, fists on her hips. "Don't you know me, Cousin Leah?"

"I knew a cute, chubby baby girl. You sure your name is Sheanna?" Leah teased.

Shay threw a pillow at her friend. "You're so mean."

Sheanna ran over to Shay and put her arms around her, "I like you. Your hair is so long. Is that a weave or is it real?"

Both girls laughed out loud.

"It's real," Shay said as she pulled her hair back into a ponytail.

"Come and eat," Aunt LouAnn insisted. "We've got a big day ahead of us, girls, and no time to waste."

"Oh, my favorite," Sheanna cooed. "Scrambled eggs and bacon again!"

The small black folding table was laden with bacon, biscuits, jelly, fresh fruit, and heaping bowls of sausage gravy and eggs.

"Drink up all this milk," LouAnn said, as she poured four tall glasses slowly, trying to keep her shaky hands steady. "We can't bring it with us. Cooler's slap full."

A sharp knock sounded at the door, and Sheanna spilled her milk all over the table. Then she ran from the room as silently as a cat.

"I'll get it," LouAnn said, striding toward the door with one hand outstretched, the other in the oversized pocket of her apron.

Leah grabbed a roll of paper towels and started to wipe up the mess, and Sheanna slipped into the bedroom, slamming the door behind her.

"Ma'am," a tall, muscular man wearing a crisp blue shirt stood at the door. "You can't leave that truck parked on the front lawn. It's against the rules."

"We'll be moving it in about an hour, sir, if that's okay. I'm moving out, and I don't get around too well."

The man frowned. "Okay, you got one hour."

"Who is that?" Shay asked.

"Security. They make sure that nobody messes the place up. Actually, the manager keeps it pretty clean around here, so I can't complain."

"How can you stand the cold up here?" Leah asked, remembering the chill that had sliced through her just hours before.

"Oh, you get used to it," she grinned. "My husband, rest his soul, loved ice skating and skiing. When he passed away, I just thought about what I'd lost, instead of what I had back home. I was a wreck at the reunion, but I remember how you loved this girl, Leah. I'm so glad it's you that came to get her. I tried going through the proper channels here and waited for things to get better, but they haven't."

"Why doesn't Brinne have that guy locked up?"

"I wish I knew, honey. This little doll has seen more misery than a child should have to bear. I hope this will wake Brinne up and bring her back to us—away from the so-called 'party' life, which is no party from where I'm standing. But now, we're going home."

"Are you sure this is the only option?" Leah asked. "I'd hate to visit you in prison, Aunt LouAnn."

"I'll explain along the way. Thank you, girls, for coming to get us. Sheanna deserves to be a child, to go swimming and fishing. I'm so sorry that I didn't have the guts to do it before." A sob tore from LouAnn's throat.

Leah put her arms around the tiny woman, and kissed the top of her head. "I'm sure you did all you could. The family grapevine never lies. We'll get that truck packed up in no time."

LouAnn nodded, wiped her eyes and said, "Coast is clear, Sheanna. Come back out and finish this food. We're leaving in one hour!"

Sheanna peeked out of the door suspiciously, and then scampered to the table carrying a spotted, floppy stuffed animal. "It wasn't Cullen?"

"Who's Cullen?" Shay asked.

Leah kicked her under the table.

"Ouch, what was that for?"

"Cullen is mostly why we're here," Leah said.

"He hurts me," Sheanna said, setting down the stuffed cheetah and putting her tiny foot on the table. Several round scars at the bottom of her feet made the girls gasp.

"Cigarettes," Sheanna whispered.

"What?" Leah growled. "Oh, I hope he shows up here."

Sheanna's eyes grew wide, "No you don't. He's mean."

"Momma's pistol is in my bag. We'll show him who's mean," Leah said.

Shay threw a warning look at Leah and picked up the stuffed animal. "Sheanna, who is this little guy?"

"Her name is Spot. She protects me and Granny LouAnn. She's a great attack cat, and her favorite food is biscuits, too."

"If you girls don't hush and eat, we won't be done in time," Aunt LouAnn scolded. "I don't want that security guard to come back again."

The girls quickly cleaned their plates, and LouAnn washed up the dishes, wrapped them in newspaper, and slipped them into a box marked "kitchen".

"The other boxes are in my bedroom," LouAnn said, as she folded up the chairs and stacked them beside the front door.

Leah and Shay quickly loaded the boxes from the bedroom, while Aunt LouAnn folded up the quilts and bedding and Sheanna carried out the folding chairs.

"We're never going to fit the couch and bedroom suite in the truck," Shay said.

"I have a friend coming to get them later. Her furniture should have been thrown away years ago, and she has four kids. Leave the front porch light on. That's her signal to come get them. Good thing is, it's May 1st, so they expect a lot of moving around here. Nothing will seem out of the ordinary unless Cullen shows up before we leave. He's mean as a cottonmouth and twice as dangerous."

The older girls traded looks. LouAnn didn't have much, but just like Momma, she was always willing to give something away. Unlike Momma, she was a fighter. Leah appreciated that. If Cullen did show up, he'd have quite a catfight on his hands.

"Sheanna, go brush your teeth, and put your toothbrush in our suitcase. We're almost ready to go."

Sheanna bounced away, chatting to Spot.

"Wow, Aunt LouAnn, you're really prepared," Leah said.

"I don't know when Ms. Brinne is going to decide to come get this child, and I don't want to be here when she does. Sheanna wasn't exaggerating about Cullen. I have a pistol, too, and there's nothing I'd like better than to put one between that man's eyes. What he did to that child proves he's nothing but a rabid animal that needs to be put down. He makes his drug money by cooking meth and taking 'glamour' shots of that baby. He sells them to perverts like himself, which is why he's careful about how he hurts her."

"And the police do nothing?"

"He's good at hiding what he is. But I've waited and planned. Me being locked up won't help Sheanna when Brinne picks the next abuser. And she will. Her momma, my daughter, died young, and we thought her husband was a fine man. In those days nobody talked about things, so it was a long time before I knew what sorry trash was raising my grandchild. A couple of the relatives tried to pay him off to let them adopt her, but he thought Brinne was his, like his dogs or his boat, and he wouldn't let her go. The man hated females, even his own child."

"So if Brinne's father abused *her*, why wouldn't she protect her daughter?"

"Wish I knew, but every man she chooses is just like him. Being a teenaged mother didn't help her any. It's going to stop here. I didn't step in and help poor Brinne, but I can help her daughter. No matter what, I'm getting this girl to safety. I just hope none of us ends up in jail because nobody would protect this child."

Leah squeezed the elderly woman's hand and blinked angry tears from her eyes. "Me too. I'm with you, Aunt LouAnn."

"Me three," Shay said, a huge box in her arms. "Let's get outta here."

Thirty minutes later, the truck was fully loaded and LouAnn

took one more walk through the tiny apartment. She placed an envelope with the name "Brinne" on the counter, and handed Sheanna a small neon pink backpack. She opened the refrigerator and removed a jar of apple juice and a large paper bag from the top shelf.

"Sandwiches for the trip on freshly-baked bread, apples, and homemade chocolate chip cookies," she explained. "Let's go."

"I'm driving first," Shay called out.

"I'm riding shotgun," Leah countered. "I need my beauty rest."

"That's for sure," Shay giggled. "You look pale as the vampire zombie from the planet Wreck."

"See how my best friend treats me?" Leah made a face.

Sheanna exploded with laughter as she climbed into the tiny booster seat. "I'll stick up for you, Cousin Leah."

"I'm glad somebody loves me."

Soon they were back on the highway, headed for the Illinois toll way. As they neared the first toll, a lady in a small, rusty Chevy cut right in front of the truck, and Shay swerved, almost hitting the retaining wall.

"You rotten heifer," she snapped, as the vehicle fishtailed back into the lane.

"Be careful, honey, there are cameras everywhere," LouAnn cautioned. "Just drive carefully, and let it go. There's a hundred more like her before we get to Missouri."

"I couldn't catch her if I wanted to," Shay said, as she dropped her money into the basket and tried to merge back into the regular lanes of traffic. Suddenly, Sheanna started bouncing up and down on the booster seat.

"I gotta go, Granny. I need a bathroom."

"Okay, honey. We'll find one."

Without thinking about it, Shay floored it and began to frantically look for the nearest exit. Sure enough, red and blue lights flashed in the rearview mirror seconds later, and the sound of a siren tore through the cab of the truck.

"I'm sorry, girls. This is Illinois. A state trooper every mile," Aunt LouAnn said, shaking her head.

Shay pulled over to the side, shifted into park and jumped out of the truck. "I'll just explain it to him."

LouAnn tried to stop her, but Shay was already bounding toward the officer, her long brown hair flying behind her. Leah looked out the back window in time to see the officer back his car up about twenty yards and start yelling at Shay over the loudspeaker.

"Ma'am, return to your vehicle. Now. Return to your vehicle."

Shay tried pointing at the truck where Sheanna was still bouncing up and down on the seat, but the officer would hear none of it. He repeated the announcement again.

Shay slapped the side of her leg and returned to the cab of the truck.

"Shut off the vehicle!" the officer screamed when he finally approached the driver's side window.

Shay glared at the short middle-aged man with a slight paunch, beady eyes and a pushed-in face like an angry bulldog, but she did as he said.

The state trooper was still yelling at Shay, "What were you thinking? Don't you know any better than to charge a police car?"

"Don't you know when a little girl bounces on the seat; it means she has to use the bathroom? In Mississippi, our officers aren't afraid of young women and old ladies!" There was no mistaking the anger in Shay's voice, and Leah prayed that they wouldn't be going to jail already.

LouAnn pinched Shay on the side of her arm, and Leah bit back the snort that threatened to erupt from her mouth. She could tell Shay was furious, and hoped she didn't do anything crazy. Leah knew that they usually took teacher's licenses away from women with a record of assaulting police officers. The kidnapping thing probably wouldn't help either.

The officer peered into the back seat. "You just passed a rest area at the first Illinois exit. Why didn't you stop there? Also, you don't have her belted correctly into that child seat. That's another violation."

Leah looked at Sheanna, who had turned as pale as death, and squeezed her arm. "We'll fix it, officer."

Shay bit down on her bottom lip and resolutely handed the officer her driver's license and insurance card. Her face was beet red, and her chest was heaving with anger. Leah hoped he'd walk away soon, or Shay would probably get herself another ticket.

Finally, he finished yelling at her, and walked back to his car.

"So, the guy doesn't notice we're from out of town and don't know where all the rest areas are? Guess that Mississippi tag doesn't scream 'visitor'! Open your door, Sheanna," Leah said. "I'll take you into the tall grass and you can go potty."

"No, I can't go in the grass. There's probably snakes in there, and that mean man will yell at us again. He might— he might take me if I get out!" Her voice rose to a shriek.

Leah forced her voice to a calm, soothing tone, "You don't have to go in the grass, but it's going to be a few minutes until we can find a gas station, honey. Are you sure you can wait?"

"I-I can hold it," Sheanna whispered, her eyes filling with tears. "I can't go outside. He'll take me away. I know he'll take me away."

Thankfully, the officer wrote the two citations quickly, and returned the truck before Sheanna had an accident.

"If you choose not to appear in court, you can send the payment to the address shown on the citation. Call this number in ten days to find out the amount of the speeding fine."

Shay was still biting her lip hard, forcing herself to nod her head as the officer barked out the information. Then she signed the papers on his clipboard, and he handed her back her license and insurance card.

"Be careful, girl, or you'll get sideswiped," Aunt LouAnn said as Shay pulled into traffic once again.

"He'd probably write me another ticket if that happened."

Then, finally, LouAnn pointed to an exit sign, only half a mile to the next gas station.

"Hold on, Sheanna. Only a minute or two more," Shay said, setting the cruise control at exactly the speed limit so there would be no more interruptions.

Leah looked out of the back window and noticed that the state trooper was following them. Her mouth dropped open as he exited behind them, and followed the truck to the gas station.

Had Brinne made a complaint already? Her phone hadn't broadcast an Amber alert. Were they all about to be arrested?

Leah prayed silently that they wouldn't. She wiped her sweaty hands against her pants and hoped her mother's prayer team was on the job. It was Sunday, after all.

"LouAnn, what's the plan if he tries to take Sheanna?" she whispered.

"No plan. If he wants her, we're done. I'm sorry, girls. This was the only option I had left, and I think we're done for."

Shay pulled right up to the gas station entrance. Forcing herself not to look back at the officer, Leah grabbed Sheanna's hand and walked as quickly as she could to the restroom. At least if they were going to be arrested, this little girl was going to have dry pants. Leah quickly shot a text message to her dad.

"Is there Amber Alert 4 Sheanna? Being followed by an Illinois State Trooper. Shay got 2 tickets from a crazy man with a gun."

She was shivering and sweating at the same time, hoping that the sick feeling in the pit of her stomach was just her overactive imagination. Moments later, Shay walked in and tossed the truck key to Leah.

"You're driving until we get out of Illinois," she said with disgust.

"Okay. Don't worry, Shay. When Daddy gets my text, he'll call. I'll tell him the whole story and he'll fix it, unless we're about to go to jail for kidnapping. It scares me that someone that high-strung has access to a gun. That guy has the disposition of a cobra and the warm cuddliness of a porcupine."

"No kidding. I thought police officers had to pass a psychological evaluation or something. What a short fuse! I know I'm tall, but all 130 pounds of me 'charging the police car'! What am I going to do? Flip it over? Really."

Leah shook her head. "You look like a model, not a criminal. I think he was mad because you have nice legs and perfect hair."

"Well," said Great Aunt LouAnn as she walked to the sink, "he's probably just stressed out. Maybe his wife just left him or his dog died."

"Why do you think he followed us here?" Leah asked.

"I hope it was just to make sure we weren't lying to him. He seems kind of control-freakish to me. I've been watching him. He drove off soon after you went through the door with Sheanna," LouAnn said. "Hopefully, he's really gone."

"Thank goodness," Leah breathed. "I'd hate to miss another date with Michael because I'm in jail!"

"A date?" Sheanna squeaked.

"Yep, cousin Leah finally found a good one," Shay said.

"Well, we'll see about that," Leah said. "Right now, let's get a move-on for Missouri."

"Then Arkansas, Tennessee, and Mississippi," Shay reminded her with a groan.

"Oh, it's not so bad in Daddy's truck," Leah said. "I have my CD collection for entertainment. I love driving it, and we haven't lost any of Aunt LouAnn's things yet, so I'd say we're doing just fine."

Leah didn't know where Sheanna got the energy, but the child was in constant motion. Shay had let her play a couple games on her phone, which was good for about thirty minutes of silence, but Sheanna was full of questions and made a game of climbing from the back seat to the front seat and back again.

Shay finally sighed loudly and said, "Sheanna, will you sit still if I tell you the true story about the pirates and gypsies in my family?"

"Real pirates?"

"The realest. My daddy comes from a long line of great thieves and hopeless vagabonds."

"Wow, I wish I could sail with some pirates. I would find the treasure and buy my mom a whole island of her own."

"Sit in your seat and put Spot where he can hear, too. It's a great story."

Sheanna scrambled back into her booster seat, tucked Spot under her arm and put her finger in her mouth.

"There's an island off the Gulf Coast that they used for prisoners during the War Between the States. It was a terrible thing for my great-great-great grandfather, Jean LaBouche, when the Union troops showed up. They were a regiment of black soldiers from New Orleans, and they knew the same conjurings that had made LaBouche very rich. They also had to keep the Confederate prisoners busy so they decided to have them dig holes until they hit water and then fill them in."

"Conjurings?"

"Dark magic. It helped LaBouche know which ships had treasure and which to leave alone. It also helped him bury the treasure where nobody else would ever find it. And now, on his island, there were others who could conjure. He knew that he didn't want to draw more Federal troops down on his head, but he didn't want to risk that the treasure he had worked so hard to steal would be dug up and stolen from him."

"Did he sneak the treasure out at night?" Leah asked.

"No, he knew it would be safe if he could just scare the New Orleans troops into thinking that the island was full of haunts and keep them inside the walls of the fort."

"Haunts?"

"Ghosts. Many of the soldiers knew of the dark power that could be turned against them, so LaBouche started small. A chicken head and pig entrails in the right place, a bag of snakes dropped over the wall at night, and the eerie howls of strange night creatures was how he got the soldiers focused on breaking the bad mojo instead of tormenting their Confederate prisoners. One moonlit night he knew that his message had been received by the right people when he heard the chanting and saw the salt being spread across each entrance to the fort and LaBouche felt much more secure. But he had an enemy in his camp who wanted the treasure even more than he did."

"Oh no!" Sheanna whimpered.

"The enemy was his own first mate, a man he had trusted and known since he was a young cabin boy. LaBouche happened to see him sneaking into the fort as he was putting chicken feet and dead toads near the well. He followed him, and heard as the man whispered to a sentry that the magic was not real. LaBouche's well-thrown knife stopped the traitor from saying any more, and he quickly removed the body when the sentry ran to find help. He dropped a handful of dead toads for good measure into the spot where he'd erased the traitor's footprints and hustled into the tall grass carrying his former friend slung over his shoulder. He reached the longboat in record time, and quickly rowed away from the island to the small cove where his ship was docked. LaBouche waved an 'all clear' signal at the ship's sentry and tied up to the ladder. His first thought was to cut off the mate's head and display it as a warning to the Federals, but he didn't want the other soldiers to believe that the traitor had been a real man. So he decided to let the sharks have most of the body. It didn't take him long to remove the left arm and the tongue from the body, as well as his prized knife;

then he silently slipped the traitor's body into the Gulf."

"Why didn't he take the knife out right away and clean it on his sleeve?" Leah asked.

"He'd left it in the body so there would be less blood to track."

"Just like CSI," Sheanna said.

"LaBouche was a clever man. He stowed the arm and tongue under the seat and climbed up the rope ladder to get a few hours' rest. He wouldn't be getting much sleep the next night, either. Then they would have to shove off for a while. His men were not the patient sort, and he wasn't sure when he'd be able to retrieve his treasure."

"So what did he do the next night?" Leah asked, hoping that this story wasn't already too gruesome for the little girl.

"Voodoo. He wrapped the tongue tightly in seaweed and left it at the back gate, hoping the sentry would find it. There was no more effective way to say 'keep your mouth shut' than a tongue that has been bound. Then he buried the arm, hand up, in the sand near the beach. It wasn't close enough that the tide would take it, but it was far enough in that it may not be found for a while. That was what LaBouche was hoping for."

"Why wouldn't he want it to be found?" LouAnn asked.

"He wanted it to look like a skeleton by the time they found it, like his body had been pulled to the netherworld and only the arm had been left. That's how they take care of traitors in New Orleans."

"She's asleep, Shay. You did it," LouAnn whispered.

"Thanks to the pirate LaBouche and his buried treasure," Shay whispered back.

Sheanna's little nap was soon over, as the questions began to pour out of her again.

"Why is it so flat here?" she asked about fifteen times as they passed through the Illinois farm country. "Did God stomp down all the hills? Why aren't there any apartments? Do the people all fit in those little houses? Who took all the trees away? Why is that giant windmill not turning and all the other ones are? Is it broken? Can we get Dairy Queen for supper? Is it suppertime yet? I like McDonald's too. Can we get McDonald's for supper if there's no Dairy Queen? Oh, look Granny. The Po-po's got that lady pulled over."

"It's policemen, dear," LouAnn corrected. "We're not going

to talk like Cullen."

"I'd get a spanking if I cussed like him. Is it that police the same man that was so mean to Shay? He looks skinny, so I guess it's a different man. Why do they wear those hats? Don't those big hats get stuck on the top of the car when they sit down? Don't they get bored sitting in a car all day? I don't like this strap on me. Can I take it off? I promise I'll sit still this time. When Cullen takes my picture I sit very still, and he tells me that I look gorgeous. The swimsuits itch, and I just can't wait to wipe off all that nasty lipstick. Don't you think lipstick tastes terrible? I hate little, tiny swimsuits too. Granny LouAnn bought me a mermaid swimsuit that I really liked, but Cullen threw it away. Do you like to wear pink? I light bright pink."

LouAnn and Shay took turns answering Sheanna's questions as best they could, but the little girl never seemed to run out of them. Dark clouds started to fill the sky and Leah hoped that they would only have scattered showers as the weatherman had promised. As they entered Missouri the sky turned even darker, and swirling clouds made mini-tornadoes in the dirt. Leah sent up a prayer that if there were any tornadoes trying to form that they would stay in the sky where they belonged. LouAnn rummaged through a paper bag, pulled out two cookies and a small carton of chocolate milk and gave them to Sheanna.

"Here, baby. Have a little snack, and then we'll rest our eyes a little."

"I'm not sleepy, but I love chocolate chip cookies. What's your favorite cookie, Shay?"

"Christmas cookies with sprinkles."

"I love butterscotch cookies," Leah chimed in.

The smell of chocolate made Leah's stomach growl as Sheanna enjoyed her treat. LouAnn handed out cookies to Leah and Shay who accepted happily. Everything grew quiet for a few minutes and soon Sheanna's breathing grew deep and steady once more.

The next few hours passed quickly, and Shay, Sheanna and LouAnn slept a good part of the way. Leah drove as fast as she dared, but kept watching for state troopers. Something made her feel like she was being followed, even though the traffic was moving along at well over the posted speed limit. The state trooper's angry shouts had sent chills down her spine, and there was a pickup truck that looked like it was following her. It was the strangest blue color, almost silver, and it had been behind her for hours. Was Cullen following them somehow? It also seemed like there were just too many police cars sitting in the median. Had the uptight trooper heard Sheanna's frightened cries and figured out their secret? Leah hoped not, as she sped down the rainy roads headed toward safety. She relaxed a little as she was welcomed into Arkansas, and she fought the urge to stop and use the restroom. Every mile closer to home was a mile away from Sheanna's tormentor. Besides, once everybody woke up they could get gas and cokes and switch drivers. At least the rain had stopped.

Shay took over driving once they reached West Memphis, Arkansas and she did a great Elvis impression as they crossed into Tennessee. The Memphis traffic was surprisingly light, and Leah's feeling of being watched faded with each passing mile. When LouAnn announced, "Mississippi, Sheanna! We made it," the tension seemed to flow out of all of them in waves. Leah dozed until the screeching of the brakes and the sight of a large deer racing toward the truck startled her awake.

"No!" she cried, as Shay turned the wheel hard and spun the truck into the median. The deer bounced off the side of the truck and continued across the highway, causing two other vehicles to swerve off the road.

Sheanna screamed as if she'd been stabbed and scrambled into her granny's lap, burying her face into the woman's chest. Her pitiful sobs made Leah's heart hurt, but she feared what would happen when the police showed up. She glanced at Shay, looking for injuries, but her friend was already opening her door. Leah had to throw herself against her door a couple of times before it would open. She hoped it would close again or they weren't going anywhere.

LouAnn comforted Sheanna as Leah and Shay jumped from the vehicle to survey the damage. Leah groaned as she looked at the huge dent in the passenger front panel and the two flat tires partially submerged in the muddy construction zone. She started to sink into the orange ooze and she wondered if her father would be more upset about the muddy floor or the dented door. She finally decided that the two flat tires would probably win the prize.

"How will we get home now?" Shay asked, shaking her head.

"Did you notice what the last town we passed was?" LouAnn

called from the back seat. "My brother lives near Sardis Lake, but I don't know his phone number."

"Momma will know it!" Leah cried, pulling her phone from her pocket. "We can't be that far south. I'll bet he can help us."

"We're close to Sardis Lake," Shay said. "I'm not sure how close, but I remember seeing the sign. Is your daddy going to kill me, Leah?"

"Probably."

It wasn't long before Leah's grandfather, a lanky, wrinkled octogenarian with a twinkle in his blue eyes, affectionately known as 'Paw-Paw' was pulling them out of the mud and onto the more sturdy shoulder. The bed of his truck was full of tools, tires and assorted junk, and he and the teenaged boy with him soon had two inflated, albeit bald, tires mounted on the F150.

"I'm your cousin Dale," the boy said, shaking everybody's hand. "Marge's boy."

Leah nodded and walked toward the truck, trying to remember what Marge looked like. It had been a long time since she'd seen this particular branch of her family. It was hard for them to get away and visit the Gulf Coast when they had a farm to run, and Liam McPhillen was such a workaholic that he rarely took more than a day or two off at a time.

"We'll take her home and fix those tires up. Might have to pull out that dent or she'll rub. It won't take but an hour or two. Follow me, gal!" Paw-Paw said.

Leah did as she was told, and spent the next twenty minutes praying furiously as he led her through twisty, dark dirt roads that kicked up gravel and looked much too small for the large truck to navigate.

She breathed a sigh of relief when his familiar cottage came into sight. Her Uncle Bud was sitting on the porch swing with his long-time girlfriend Whitney, and the dogs ran around in circles, barking while two gray tabby cats glared at them from the porch steps.

"Welcome to Paw-Paw's farm, Sheanna," LouAnn said. "You are going to love this place. I bet Uncle Bud will show you his horses before it gets dark."

Sheanna's eyes were wide with excitement, and the questions began to pour out of her once more.

"What's that smell? Do the dogs bite? What are we having for supper? I never ate food way out in the woods before. Do they have ice cream?"

"The dogs don't bite, and Paw-Paw will tell you their names in a couple of minutes. Right now the men have to get working on the truck's tires or we'll never make it home tonight." LouAnn patted the girl's head and helped her slide to the ground.

Leah threw her car keys to her cousin and followed LouAnn into the house. The mosquitoes were feasting on her, and she did not want to be covered in itchy red welts for the next week. She thought of Michael and decided to send him a quick text.

"Hit a deer. May be killed when I get home. Hope I can still make our date."

It only took a minute for Michael to send his reply. "Death is no excuse. I'm picking you up Saturday @ 6 no matter what."

"Even though I'm bad luck?" she countered.

"You're only bad luck for deer."

She didn't bother to explain that Shay was the actual driver. She just wanted Michael to know how things were going, and that surprised her. He hadn't even met her dog, the best judge of any man's character, and here she was giving him updates.

Leah flashed a compassionate smile at Whitney. She was a pretty woman, full of laughter and good sense, but she could do so much better than Uncle Bud. The man's one true love was the outdoors. He'd been dating Whitney for seven or eight years, and according to the family grapevine hadn't even once mentioned marrying her. But she came over every weekend, rain or shine, bringing him food and companionship. Leah couldn't understand why she did it. Uncle Bud was a good man and okay looking but not worth waiting seven years for. You could only eat so much wild game stew and hear so many fishing stories before it got old. But Whitney kept coming back, and the look in her eyes told everyone that she loved Bud. Leah hoped that one day she would love a man enough to get that sparkle in her eyes and pink in her cheeks whenever he was near. Maybe some day.

"Hi Lee-ah," Uncle Bud drawled. He did have a pretty, country accent.

"Hi Uncle Bud. How's the fishing?"

"When you eat what I caught for supper, you gonna love it."

"You'll never believe it, Leah," Aunt Marge called from the kitchen. "We're having 'gator tail tonight."

Sheanna gasped. "We're eating a alligator?"

"Gator tail is good eatin' child," LouAnn said. "Been a long time."

"It isn't the season, is it?" Leah asked.

"No, but the law wanted this particular 'gator far away from the tourists, so I got special permission. He ate Sheriff Clarke's dog, you know."

"I didn't know," Leah said, impressed. Sheriff Clarke was strictly law and order. He must have really loved that dog.

Bud stood up. "Guess I'll go lend a hand with those tires. Heard you ladies have a long way to go tonight."

Shay sidled up to the group. "I already called in for tomorrow. Don't put yourselves out for me. Those kids can stand to have a substitute for a day or two. I have so many sick days I could take off for the rest of the school year and not use them all."

Leah grunted. "I'm surrounded by worker bees. No wonder I never take time off."

Sheanna piped up. "You could retire like Granny LouAnn and do nothing all the time."

The group laughed.

"She already does that," Bud teased. "Hunter keeps me in the loop."

"Hunter is too busy chasing football titles and girls to know what I do."

"Granny says the girls chase him," Sheanna added.

Leah had to admit defeat. "That's true; they could change his name to 'Hunted' any day. Girls buzz around him like flies. Now let's go in and get something to drink. I'm thirsty."

"Beat you to it," Aunt Marge said, pushing open the screen door with the tray full of ice-cold sweet tea in mason jars.

Paw-Paw called to Leah from the yard. "Sorry, gal. The tires I got don't fit, and there's nothing more I can do tonight. Y'all are gonna have to bunk with us."

Leah looked down at Sheanna to see if the girl was upset, but she seemed to be fine. She had introduced Spot to the dogs, the cats and one small frog. She was currently looking for a cricket that chirped somewhere nearby.

"No complaints here," Leah said. "I haven't had one of Aunt Marge's fine biscuits in way too long."

"And Whitney brought her chocolate pie," Bud bragged.

Whitney jumped up. "I have some blueberry jam in the car, too. Please take some home with you. You know how your Momma loves it."

Leah could never remember a time that she left one of her relatives with less food than she came with. Her whole family just loved to give things away to people. Their friends were the same kind of good people. Leah watched her sprint to her little Ford Fiesta.

"Uncle Bud, are you ever going to marry that woman so I can call her Aunt Whitney?"

"Call her what you want. She'll answer."

"You're incorrigible."

"Thank you."

"I'm incorrigible too," Sheanna piped in.

"No," LouAnn corrected. "You're my sweet little She-She."

"Can I sleep with you tonight?"

"Of course. You're my little bedbug, and I wouldn't know what to do without you."

Paw-Paw yelled from the kitchen. "Why you standing out there sweating? Y'all come in and eat. Food's getting cold."

"You don't have to tell me twice. Y'all can wash up over there." Bud pointed to a sink near the side door.

Sheanna ran to the sink and proceeded to douse herself and everyone nearby with cool water. Nobody had the heart to correct her because she was so full of enthusiasm for even the simplest pleasure. From what Leah knew, eating three meals in one day was a huge treat for the child. It made her insides twist with anger.

Leah couldn't help but notice the joy on Sheanna's face as she bit into her fried chicken leg or the quick hands that hid at least three biscuits in her pink bag under the table. Leah took only one bite of Whitney's rich chocolate pie before she pushed her plate over to Sheanna.

"Do you have any room left, Sprite? I can't finish this."

Sheanna scooped out the chocolate filling with a spoon before sliding the plate back.

"Granny says it can melt down in the cracks."

"I believe it will," Leah agreed. Then she made quick work of the pie that was left. It really was the best dessert she had ever put in her mouth.

It was only a few minutes later that Sheanna's head began to droop. Her beautiful long eyelashes fluttered as she struggled to keep her eyes open.

"Take the green room, LouAnn," Paw-Paw said, nodding toward the back of the house.

LouAnn scooped the girl up as if she weighed nothing and walked away with her. Leah followed, carrying the pink bag and Spot. Something told her that Sheanna would not be happy to be parted from them.

LouAnn soon had the girl tucked in, and kisses followed. Sheanna kept touching a different part of her face and saying, "You missed a spot," and LouAnn happily complied until Sheanna finally slept. LouAnn tiptoed out, but Leah stood there watching her cousin breathe. *How could anyone hurt her, Lord? Why was this allowed to happen to such a sweet, little doll?*

Leah put a feathery kiss on Sheanna's forehead, and hoped that every day would be a happy one from now on. She pulled out her phone and sent an update to her parents, then sunk down into the couch to watch Aunt Marge whip everybody at cards.

The next thing Leah knew, sunlight was streaming through her window and a rooster was crowing. She was on the couch in the living room, her head on a throw pillow and a flowered sheet twisted around her legs. She inhaled the scent of pancakes and stretched, listening for the happy chatter of the cooks making breakfast. The cabin was strangely silent, and a shiver ran down Leah's spine. Something was wrong. She sat up and glanced out of the back window. Paw Paw was walking at the edge of the field near the woods. He seemed to be shouting. Leah kicked off her sheet and jumped from the couch. *Cullen hadn't found Sheanna already, had he? How did he get past the dogs?*

She slipped on her shoes and went to join the search. Dale met her at the side door.

"Uncle Bud tracked Sheanna to the cypress swamp. You'll need boots. Check the front closet."

"Sheanna was alone?" she asked as she slipped large rubber boots over her tennis shoes.

"Far as Uncle Bud could tell. I knew I should've listened when she kept buggin' me about huntin' gators. She didn't believe that their eyes glow red, and she said that she was going to prove that I was lyin'. I told her I'd take her another time, but I guess she woke up early and decided to see for herself." He held the screen door open for her.

"Gators?"

"Yep, doncha remember? That's all she could talk about last night before supper. She even tried to sneak my gator tooth necklace into her bag. LouAnn woke up early this morning and just about had a fit. Can't believe you slept through it all."

Leah steadied herself against the side of the house and mentally counted off all the things that she hoped that Sheanna never learned about Mississippi the hard way: fire ants, alligators, poisonous snakes, panthers and wild boars. And that was just off the top of her head. She never dreamed that the girl would have the guts to wander off by herself after she'd cried about snakes in the tall grass in Illinois. But Paw Paw's field was recently cut, and huge circular bales of hay dotted the landscape. Maybe it was only tall grass that she was afraid of. More importantly, where was she now?

Dale and Leah jogged across the field toward the cypress swamp. Leah couldn't keep up with him because of her clunky boots, but she hoped that Uncle Bud had already tracked the little girl down and was bringing her back in one piece. *How did I sleep through all the commotion this morning?*

Whitney's little Ford pulled into the yard, and she was blasting her horn and yelling something. Leah turned and hurried back. She knew that something had to be wrong for the quiet woman to make all that noise. Dale was already at the woods, and didn't even turn around.

"Hey, I got Sheanna!" Whitney yelled. "Leah, I found her!" She blasted the horn again several times, trying to let the men in the woods know that all was well.

She lifted the mud-covered child out of the back seat. Her bare foot had been bound in white gauze and the shoe on the other foot looked like a pile of orange dirt.

"Fire ants got me, Leah," Sheanna whimpered. "It itches so bad!"

"You better hope that Uncle Bud doesn't tan your hide for

this. You scared us half to death. Why did you run off?"

"I just wanted to see a real gator like everybody else. I got lost, and I lost my Tweedy sneaker and--" Sheanna burst into tears.

Whitney shook her head as she whisked the girl up the stairs and into the house. "Bud's not gonna do anything. When he sees that cut on your foot and the fire ant stings, he'll know you been punished more than enough."

"Will she need stitches?" Leah asked.

"I don't think so. I think she just got tangled in some brambles. It's not that deep, just thick. I want to put some more vinegar on the fire ant stings when we get a better dressing on the cut. I need the first aid kit from the back bathroom."

"I'll get it," Aunt Marge said. "Some superglue will keep the vinegar from stinging."

Sheanna looked very worried, but remained silent. It seemed she had been trained not to comment on pain. Anger churned in Leah's belly.

"I'll start the bath," Whitney said. "There's LouAnn."

She nodded at the side door where LouAnn stood trembling. She strode across the room, her cheeks crimson, her face pale. "Never go anywhere alone again, She-She. You're too little, and there are too many critters that could hurt you."

Human and animal, Leah thought.

"I'm not little. I take care of myself," Sheanna whispered.

LouAnn sat next to her. "You used to take care of yourself. Now you got a whole bunch of people to watch out for you, so let us do our job. Your job is to be a little girl."

"Do you think we could go look for my Tweedy Bird shoe? It's stuck in the mud."

"Maybe Uncle Bud has it," Leah offered, as she carefully unwrapped the dressing from Sheanna's foot. Thousands of red bumps from fire ants went from her ankle to her toes. "He can find anything."

"I hope so. I don't have any other shoes."

"I bet Aunt LouAnn has something else that you can wear."

"Not with Tweedy on it."

LouAnn sighed. "We will go shopping as soon as we can. Let's just get you cleaned up first."

Leah scooped the girl up and carried her to the bathroom,

where a huge mound of bubbles greeted the little adventurer.

"Whitney, you are amazing," Leah said, as she watched her give the girl a spoonful of Benadryl.

Sheanna squirmed from her arms and almost fell into the tub. "I love bubbles!"

"I'm going to call off the search so we can get that truck running," Leah said, as she watched Whitney pull the last few twigs from Sheanna's hair.

"Your dad is not going to be happy about that poor truck. It looks even worse in the daylight."

"Good thing Shay was driving. Hunter would never let that one go."

"You're right about that."

***

After a huge brunch and many goodbyes, Leah drove the final four hours home. Sheanna slept most of the way, and it was a quiet drive.

Soon they were pulling into the driveway, drained but strangely charged.

"Just after two p.m., pretty good," Shay complimented her friend as she slid Sheanna's sleeping form out of the car and started to carry her toward the house.

Leah grabbed her phone and texted Michael, "Home sweet home. Date back on."

Shay winked at Leah. "You certainly keep him well informed."

Leah stuck out her tongue.

"I'll help you with her," Phil called. He jumped off the front porch and took Sheanna from Shay.

Sheanna's eyes fluttered open, widened, and then Sheanna began twisting and screaming, and Phil almost dropped her.

"No, don't take me! No, don't take me away from Granny LouAnn!" Her little fists beat against Phil's chest.

"It's the uniform," Leah shouted. "She doesn't know who you are, Daddy!"

Phil held the girl away from him a bit and soothed, "Sheanna, I'm your Uncle Phil. I am a policeman, but I'm just getting ready for work, Sugar. I'm not going to take you away. I promise."

He just kept repeating himself calmly until Sheanna stopped squirming and screaming, though her face had gone stark white and tear trails left jagged red lines on her cheeks. LouAnn jumped from the truck and raced toward the frightened child.

"Hush, baby. It's Granny LouAnn. I'm sorry I didn't warn you better. Uncle Phil is a police officer, but he's not here to take you away. Shush, now. It's okay. He's going to help us, remember?"

Sheanna scrambled into her arms and clung to her, shaking and hiccupping.

"C'mon inside y'all," Beth cried from the front door. "No need to wake the whole neighborhood."

"Remember your Aunt Beth? You used to send her some of your drawings on her birthday and at Christmas." LouAnn asked Sheanna as she walked up the front porch steps. "She makes the best blueberry muffins you'll ever eat."

Phil opened the tailgate of his truck and slid two overstuffed boxes out of the pile. Leah bent down and petted her dog, which was licking her like a steak Popsicle. "And this big guy is Trooper. He's the smartest dog east of the Mississippi."

"Oh, I never had a real dog before," Sheanna whispered, lowering her hand toward the long slurping tongue. "Why are his ears so big?"

Leah laughed. "We don't know. Maybe he's part donkey?"

Sheanna's breathing was returning to normal, and some color rose in her cheeks.

"I made coffee," Phil said gently, setting his boxes on the kitchen floor against the wall. "Anybody thirsty?"

"Your coffee will keep them from sleeping," Beth said gently. "How about some hot cocoa, ladies? I heard it was awful cold up there."

Sheanna nodded her head, "With marshmallows?"

"Of course. Is there any other way to drink cocoa?" Leah quipped.

Shay came into the house carrying LouAnn's oversized suitcase and a small neon-pink backpack full of Sheanna's things. She dropped them just inside the door and collapsed on the couch, rolling herself up in the gold and black afghan.

Soon Sheanna was topping her piping cocoa with

marshmallows, and Phil placed a small kiss on the top of her head before strapping on his gun belt and reaching for his helmet. Beth and LouAnn sipped peppermint tea, and Shay's deep steady breathing told them that she was fast asleep on the couch. Leah could barely keep her eyes open, but homemade cocoa with marshmallows was worth waiting a few moments for, so she blinked her dry eyes and forced herself to stay awake as she blew on the steaming brew.

Phil kissed his wife. "I'll see y'all later. Hunter and I put most of the boxes in the carport, but I have to get to work now."

"Work? I thought you were on the overnight shift," Leah said as she brushed her hair.

"I have to testify in court today. Remember that big meth bust last year? The lawyers finally let it come up. Guess the drug money's running low, and they are ready to move on to the next gangster."

"You taking Hunters' truck?"

"No, that truck's at the shop getting a new tire and headlights."

Leah dropped the hairbrush. "What happened now?"

"The kids again. My truck doesn't look too bad next to his. There's a guy that's only a block from the courthouse who'll take a look at it for me. One of the guys will run Hunter up to school."

"Bye, Daddy," Leah mumbled, blowing a kiss into the air. "Hope your case is okay."

"Me too, believe me. I hate when the lawyers decide who gets locked up and who gets to walk around free. They don't live where the bad guys prowl."

Hunter appeared behind him, "Do you mind if I drop you off at the courthouse and take the truck instead of it going straight to the shop? I have an exam tonight and have to go hit the books."

Phil shrugged. "Just help me get the last of the boxes unloaded. I don't want Aunt LouAnn's belongings messed with by any of our new 'fans'."

"Did anything else happen while we were gone, Daddy?" Leah asked, trying to keep the irritation from her voice.

"Just a few phone calls. Hunter, court starts in thirty minutes so we'll have to move it."

"It's lunch on the go, then. This test is going to be a bear."

"It won't do you any good," Leah smiled mischievously as she took the steaming mug of cocoa from her mother's tray of goodies. "You have to *read* the books to get the information."

"Ha ha. I did read them. Now I have to get the pertinent info into my brain. I have four hours to get it in there or I'll never finish my criminal justice degree. Nice to meet you, Sheanna. By the way, I'm cousin Hunter, future sheriff of Andrews County and football coach to the stars." Hunter patted her on the head and reached for a handful of biscuits.

Leah snorted and almost dropped the hot cocoa in her lap.

"Don't worry, Sheanna. Your cousin Hunter does have a future working with the public. I hear they need baggers at the grocery store."

Hunter was slathering blueberry jam all over his remaining biscuit. "You're just jealous that my education is paid for because I'm such a superior athlete."

"I just wish you hadn't been hit in the head so much. It would help if you lived in the real world with the rest of us."

Hunter ignored the comment and sprinted out of the door trying to catch Phil, his overstuffed backpack slung across his back. Sheanna's head was nodding, and Beth scooped her up.

"Let me show you where you and Aunt LouAnn can take a nap."

"I get to sleep with Granny LouAnn?" Sheanna squeaked.

"Today you will. We do have a room for you, but it's not quite ready."

Leah's eyes went wide, and she tried to keep her voice steady, "Sammy's room, Momma?"

"Yes, dear. It's about time we started to get some use out of it. They'll be in the guest room until I can finish painting, and then Sheanna will have her own room."

"Where are Sammy's things?" Leah whispered as a knot formed in the pit of her stomach.

"In boxes in the crawl space. Daddy and Hunter worked all day yesterday, and we've got the room almost done. We even found a border with hot pink stripes that doesn't look too 'girly', since that's what LouAnn told me that Sheanna liked. Daddy repainted Sammy's dresser white, so it'll be more welcoming for a little girl. It's just about dry."

Leah chewed on her lip as she absently walked toward her room. She never dreamed that Momma would pack up Sammy's things and put them in the crawl space with the spiders. Sammy hated spiders, so how could he use his stuff when he finally returned? It seemed that now she was the only McPhillen who expected him to come back to them one day.

Chapter 5
Proverbs 14:33 – Wisdom rests in the heart of him who has understanding, but what is in the heart of fools is made known.

"Ouch!" Leah quickly set down her coffee cup, and turned on the cold water, hoping to ease the burn the steaming coffee had just blessed her with. She ran her hand under the soothing spray as she listened in disbelief to the News-at-Noon special report.

"We have just learned that the family of Robert 'Bobby Max' Holmes has filed a civil suit in the district court for several million dollars against Sergeant Liam "Phil" McPhillen, the police officer whose reckless car chase allegedly resulted in the death of a fourteen year-old boy on April 25th. A second teen is still in critical condition at Ocean Shores Infirmary."

The reporter put on her best solemn face and continued, her voice dripping with cynicism. "Although McPhillen was cleared of wrong-doing by the *local* police department, sources claim that the family is hopeful that they will receive some justice in civil court."

The camera cut to the courthouse entrance and Bobby Max's weeping mother, who had just exited the main entrance surrounded by lawyers and family members. Leah felt the heat rise in her cheeks as she stared at the woman's skin-tight dress and perfect hair and wondered how somebody so distraught had managed to keep her hair perfectly coiffed in 100% humidity.

Patti of the poison pen just wouldn't let it go! Leah stared at the "Live from Andrews County Courthouse" caption and the heavily made-up Ms. Petrowski, this time wearing a salmon-colored polyester suit, which made her sallow skin look even more like sweaty buttermilk. Leah hoped she could get down there before the news crew packed up and left. She had a few choice words for her former classmate.

"I'll give you something to report about, Patti," Leah snarled, as she dried her hand gently with a towel, and reached for the burn cream that Beth kept nearby.

Shay rolled from the couch, snatched up the remote control and turned the television to mute.

"Leah, your Momma and Daddy have enough going on without you getting yourself locked up. How would they feel if they

Place Called Grace 51

had to bail you out of jail on top of everything else? We're supposed to be low profile for the next couple of months, remember? Think about it, Leah. Patti's time will come. There are dozens of women in town who would like to beat her sorry tail. It doesn't have to be you. Plus, what if your dad is still at the courthouse? You think he wants to come outside to a circus?"

Leah looked at her friend and bit her lip. She was making sense, but that didn't make it any easier to hear. It would be foolish of her to knock Patti out with witnesses and cameras all around. There had to be another way to express her displeasure.

"You know, I don't think I heard her say the word 'allegedly' in that whole diatribe. Think I'll call her boss and threaten a little lawsuit of my own."

"That's not exactly what I had in mind."

Leah grabbed her phone and furiously typed, looking for the news station's phone number. "It's that or a beat down. She's had it coming since she fabricated that story in the high school newspaper about you supposedly stealing the answers to the Geometry II final exam. Now she tells lies to the whole Gulf Coast instead of the high school. How could you have ever been friends with that thing? Why does the sludge always rise to the top?"

"You really need to learn to forgive, Leah. Your Daddy always says, 'A little grace can save a lotta hurt' and he's right. Patti does enough to hurt herself daily. She doesn't need any help."

"Some people need forgiving, and some need a kick in the pants. Patti Polyester is the latter."

"You're not kicking anyone's pants," Beth McPhillen fumed, walking into the kitchen with a basket overflowing with laundry. "Come help me fold these."

"Yes, Momma," Leah said glumly, putting down the phone book and feeling like she was sixteen again.

"Is Daddy's court case done?" Leah asked as she furiously folded towels.

Momma waved her hand at the television. "Another continuance, somehow. Hunter brought him home a little while ago, but he's taking a short power nap. He didn't sleep much last night, since all this mess dredged up the prank phone calls at 3 a.m. again. Somehow they got his cell phone number this time. He's working third shift tonight on the motorcycle, since the bosses thought it would be less easy for folks to recognize him through the helmet and harass him."

On the motorcycle! Now Leah understood why Momma was out of sorts. At least in a cruiser he had a steel frame protecting him, and that gave them great comfort.

An image of Patti's news truck running her father off the road flitted across Leah's mind. Patti was ruthless and sneaky. There was nothing Leah would put past her. She knew Momma had never liked it when Phil was on the bike-- too many cops had already been killed or seriously injured by careless drivers, and her dad had been one of them just three years before. That wreck had shaken the entire family to the core, and Leah never wanted to feel hurt like that again.

Phil had asked to be reassigned to a patrol car once he was well enough to pass the physical fitness test and return to duty. He assured the family that he was in no rush to ever go through that kind of pain again. Momma accepted it with her usual calm, but Leah had nightmares for months. She hated that she woke up crying like a little kid in the middle of the night. In fact, she hated crying period. The sight of her big, strong father unconscious, ghastly pale and near death in the ICU was one that seared itself into her brain and took a long time to file away. Too many times had a guy she loved suddenly been removed from her life, and those scars were deep and still painful, but almost losing her father had rocked Leah's world like nothing else had. She lost her job and thirty pounds in the weeks following the crash. The man who hit Phil's motorcycle had been so high that he sustained only minor injuries, but they'd had to cut him out of his car.

Leah just kept telling herself that the tragedies were over, and her Daddy would be okay. Phil McPhillen had beaten the odds and survived. Not only had he survived, he was in better shape than most men his age by the time he had finished the long months of rehabilitation. If he got hit in a patrol car, he reminded the family that there was a steel frame to protect him, so the chances of such a serious injury were very small. They weren't going to lose any other family members.

Leah had to believe that because her poor heart couldn't take any more men she loved being ripped away from her. Her best childhood friend, her first love, her big brother—all had been spirited away without warning. Surely she had lost enough for one lifetime.

She also knew that her father missed the wind in his face and the maneuverability of the bike. But Beth and Leah had gotten their way this time. On a motorcycle, it was just him, some leather, and a whole lot of road. Daddy had promised that his days on a motorcycle were over, except for parades and funeral processions, which were slow moving and relatively safe. But life had jumped in and changed all of that.

"Leah, why don't we go to Mobile today and take Sheanna shopping? She needs new shoes, socks and a couple of pretty dresses for church. Don't let me forget hair bows either. She can't wear the same dress week after week. I hope we can find a decent swimsuit, too," Beth said with a slight tremor in her voice. "The one from Ms. Karen's box of clothes is too big for her, and I want to take her to Preston's Bayou for her birthday dinner this weekend."

"Oh, Momma, she'll love that. She's so tiny for her age. I don't know where we'll find something to fit her. Where is the little sprite anyway?"

"She didn't sleep too well either. Last I saw her, she was curled up next to Aunt LouAnn, thumb in her mouth, sleepin' like a baby."

"Poor little thing. All this TV drama had me forgetting what she's been through. I can't even imagine how horrible her short life has been. Let's take her out for ice cream after we find her a swimsuit. I bet she'll love one of Ted's famous double scoop sundaes with extra whipped cream and cherries."

"That's a great idea, Leah. Maybe Aunt LouAnn would like to come along, too. Those sundaes sure brightened your days enough times. As soon as they wake up, we'll go."

Hunter laughed, "You two will have Sheanna as fat and sassy as Leah in no time."

"Well, she's already smarter than you," Leah retorted, sticking her tongue out at her brother. "Don't you have some girls to stalk or a football game to lose or something?"

"I've been sitting around here, waiting to see if I have to keep Patti Petrowski from pulling out all that wild black hair of yours. My test is in thirty minutes, so I guess I'll hit the road. I just needed to get this notebook since it has most of the answers in it."

"Oh, somebody took notes for you?"

"Honestly, I don't think you two will ever grow up," Momma sighed. "I'll be able to show you how to make that tomato gravy in just a few more minutes, Shay. This is the last load of laundry for today."

Leah looked at her friend, who was sitting on the couch matching socks.

"Shay, what about *your* Momma? Is she going to be disappointed to miss out on all this fun?" Leah snickered.

Shay put on her best British accent. "My Momma wouldn't dare wreck her nails. As head loan officer at the bank, she has to look 'just so'."

Both girls broke out into giggles, as Leah scooped the folded clothes off the kitchen table. Shay's Daddy was from the Louisiana swamps, as backwoods bayou as they come, and her Momma was such a priss-- wouldn't break a nail for any reason. She spent more time making them perfect than most people spend on their hair, makeup and clothes together. Gemma's manicures always included special designs on both pinkies, and she used expensive cream on her hands so they wouldn't get age spots and spoil the effect. It was almost impossible to imagine Ms. Perfect even marrying into a family of moonshine runners and gypsies, but that was exactly what she'd done.

The girls were just finishing putting up the last of the linens when the doorbell rang, and Hunter went to get it. A short time later, Leah heard him talking softly into his cell phone, but there wasn't anyone at the door. Hunter was asking for Officer Dardan, Daddy's best friend and partner, affectionately known as "Dan".

"Hey, Dan, it's Hunter. Dad took a nap after that court mess, and I need your help," he said in a half-whisper. "There was a box at our front door. Someone just rang the doorbell and took off. It says 'Killer' on it. I know it might be a prank, but I wanted to make sure. Things have been so crazy lately."

Leah held her breath, and looked over at Shay, who was at the stove, stirring the gravy under Momma's watchful eye.

"I moved it out by the road next to the mailbox. No, I won't touch it again," Hunter said softly. "No, it's not ticking or anything. Come quick, please. Everyone is at home, and I, uh, don't want anything to happen."

As much as Leah wanted to run to the door and look, she didn't want to get everyone all upset again. A little voice inside her said it was probably just a sick joke, but that word, probably, made her heart thud in her chest.

When would this all end? she wondered. Why was it Daddy's fault that some punk kid stole his neighbor's truck and went joy riding instead of going to school? Why couldn't the kid just pull over instead of flying down Market Street like a maniac? That kid killed himself. It wasn't Daddy's doing. He broke his friend up pretty badly, too, not that anyone seemed to remember poor Tyler, confined to a body cast until further notice.

But, Leah thought, *I guess you can't sue a teenaged boy for a million dollars, and attacking a fourteen year-old kid won't win a reporter any prizes. So let's go after the guy that's spent his life protecting our town. Yeah, there's an idea.*

"What are you shaking your head about, Leah?" Shay asked. "Don't you think I'm doing this right?"

"I'm just thinking. I am positive you are doing it right because Momma would fix it if you weren't. When it comes to food, there's Momma's way and the wrong way."

Sheanna shuffled into the room in her pink Tinkerbelle pajamas. "I'm hungry, Aunt Beth," she whispered.

"Do you want some tomatoes?" Leah teased.

"I want cereal," again in a whisper. "Please?"

Leah reached over and lifted Sheanna up to the shelf so she could pick out her favorite kind. They cleared a small spot at the table, and soon Sheanna was happily munching frosted corn flakes, watching the cooks create their masterpiece. Great Aunt LouAnn joined them a few moments later, looking small and pale.

"Did I miss something?" she asked, eyeing the steaming biscuits on the table.

"I think this is how breakfast buffets were invented," Leah said.

"Smells like it," LouAnn quipped as she poured a huge cup of coffee.

Leah made a mental note to mention how much different she looked to Beth. In Milwaukee, LouAnn had been the picture of health, moving heavy boxes like one of the girls. Now her color wasn't good. The feisty little lady looked frail and sickly. Something was very wrong, and one long trip couldn't take that much out of a person, could it? Maybe they both could gang up on her and get her to see the doctor.

Leah was cleaning the table when she heard the sound of a very large boom, like fireworks had gone off right next to the house. The windows rattled and she sprinted to the front porch in time to see their mailbox going up in flames and Hunter lying on the grass in the front yard. She ran toward him, but stopped short when she realized that he was covered in something that smelled terrible. The side of Dan's cruiser was similarly decorated.

"Are you okay?" she asked her brother.

"Don't say a word." He pushed himself up from the ground and stalked past her, pieces of something brown and very smelly dropping from his clothes as he jogged toward the garden hose.

Leah didn't see any blood, and Hunter wasn't staggering at all so she figured that he hadn't been too close to the box when it had blown up. She wanted to go to her brother, but the persistent ringing of the phone pulled her in another direction.

Shay was at the side door talking to Dan, whose face was redder than his hair. Aunt LouAnn was in the shower, and Sheanna was already dressed in a cute pastel blue shorts set, a matching bow in her tiny pencil-thin ponytail, watching cartoons as she waited for their big shopping trip to Mobile. Leah knew that she had somehow missed all the noise or she would be hiding somewhere instead of calmly sitting on the couch. Leah wiped her sweaty hands on her shorts and grabbed the cordless telephone.

"Hello?"

"Is the killer there?" a menacing whisper demanded.

"What?" Leah held the phone out to see the number on the caller I.D. It was an unknown caller, of course. Leah walked out to the back porch.

"I want to talk to the killer. Is he home?"

"Why don't you come on over? I'll show the killer. His name is Mr. 357. Come visit me, you punk!"

Leah stormed into the house, slammed down the phone, waited a few seconds, and then took it off the hook. She knew that was only good for a few hours until the battery wore out and calls could get through, but it was better than nothing.

She turned to see Momma standing in the hallway, hugging

the laundry basket against her like a pillow, shaking her head slowly.

"What is wrong with people?" Leah asked, suddenly exhausted. "Don't they have any common decency? Why would any grown man play silly games with the phone-- are we all in high school now?"

Beth shook her head and looked at the floor. "Shay just told me that the box was full of dog excrement. I guess that caller wanted to be sure we got the message. Dan's hosing Hunter down in the back yard right now. He's got about fifteen minutes to make it to the junior college for his test. When it rains it pours, but I'm so thankful he's not hurt."

Leah looked out the back window where her brother stood bent over in his blue boxer shorts, shivering as the cold spray washed the last clumps of fecal material from his hair. "I think we need to change this phone number, Momma. And maybe move."

"No sense in makin' everybody learn a new number just 'cause some kids are playing pranks, Leah."

"That prank could've really hurt somebody! Look at our mailbox. It wasn't a kid on the phone. It was a man, and he asked if Daddy was here. His voice gave me the creeps."

Leah decided she probably shouldn't have invited him to 'come on over' to their house. He may already be outside, or come lurking in the dark, waiting to introduce himself. Leah shuddered as she pictured what her rash words could do to her family.

"I think we should get a younger dog, Momma. Or borrow one of the police dogs. I'm sure Daddy could get one from somebody."

Leah felt guilty, like she was saying Trooper wasn't good enough.

"A puppy? I never had a puppy," Sheanna squealed from the next room.

"We'll see, honey. Right now, I'm going to give these clean clothes to Hunter and fix your Uncle Phil a plate of biscuits and tomato gravy, since we'll be eating in town. He will be up in a few minutes. Nobody say a word about the box or the mailbox until he eats something. He'll hear about it soon enough."

Momma stood up on her toes and planted a kiss on her daughter's flushed cheek. "Why don't you help Shay finish washing up those dishes?"

"Yes, Ma'am," Leah said. "Are you comin' to Mobile with us, Shay? We're going to Ted's for supper. Turtle sundaes are still your favorite, right?"

"Oh, you just said the magic words, Leah! If you're treating, I'm getting a double turtle sundae with extra pecans," Shay giggled.

Leah rolled her eyes. "It's sick how much you eat and never gain an ounce."

"I'd rather be curvy like you, so quit complaining."

The girls hurried to finish the cleanup. Hunter raced past them to the shower, and Leah had to force herself not to comment as he went by, leaving a trail of wet footprints. She knew that he'd been humiliated quite enough for one day, and that he was going to have to take his big test without having studied his notes. Her brother had a long fuse, but when he was angry it wasn't pretty.

LouAnn jumped right in and helped dry the dishes.

"Has Brinne called at all?" she asked Beth.

"Not a word."

"It's two days until that baby's fifth birthday and her momma doesn't even know she's gone. It breaks my heart."

"We'll make sure her birthday is great," Beth said. "We're going to Preston's Bayou that morning and Phil's annual chicken burn is that night. The girl will have presents coming out of her ears. Half the police force is already in love with her."

"Everyone except her own parents. Who is Sheanna's daddy?" Leah asked.

"We aren't positive, but we're pretty sure it was the criminal Brinne dated before Cullen. His name was Darby Reich, and he is the one who got Brinne started on the methamphetamines. He was in prison for a couple of years after Sheanna was born, but when he got out he disappeared pretty quickly. Addicts don't have money for child support, you know. Plus, there was the statutory rape charge. Brinne was only fifteen when Darby got her pregnant, and her daddy beat her within an inch of her life when he found out. He put the word out that Darby was a dead man if he ever had the guts to show his face. That's when Brinne moved up North with Aunt LouAnn and Uncle Red, and Darby's wife divorced him. It was a big mess."

"Where is Brinne's dad?" Shay asked.

"Biloxi or thereabouts. He's a dealer at one of the casinos last I heard. The law never seems to catch up with *that* one either."

Phil walked into the kitchen. "Never a cop around when you need one, right?"

"You're better than me, Daddy. There would be a lot of unsolved murders of bad guys if they let me have a badge and a gun."

"Then I'm glad you don't. Visiting my children in prison is not on my list of things I want to do. But digging into these biscuits and gravy—that is a definite plus. Thank you Beth, my darling. You are the best cook east of the Mississippi, or anywhere, for that matter."

Beth kissed his cheek. "The girls and I are going shopping for church clothes for Sheanna. You want me to pick up anything for you?"

"I'm good, my darlin'. You girls have a good time."

"When you finish breakfast, you may want to take a look at the mailbox and give Dan a call." Beth's gift for understatement was epic.

"Will do. See y'all later."

"Last one to the car buys dinner," Beth called, and the girls flew out of the house like a shot.

"I was planning to treat you all tonight anyway," said Aunt LouAnn, as she shuffled out behind them. "Y'all need to stay close. Sheanna scared me half to death when she took off down the block this morning."

"Aw, I just wanted to pet that little puppy." Her lip quivered slightly.

Beth bent down and took the little girl's hand in hers. "You have to stay with us, Sheanna. Mobile, Alabama is a lot bigger than Ocean Shores, Mississippi, and I really don't want to lose you. I would never forgive myself if anything happened to my sweet little She-She."

"I'm not sweet!" Sheanna protested.

"Of course you are, Sprite," Leah chimed in. "And we're going to sweeten you up even more in a little while. What's your favorite kind of ice cream?"

"Vanilla with crunched up Oreos."

"Well this place is so good it will make you forget all about that."

LouAnn snorted. "You hear this girl? Like she can make us

forget our favorite treat."

"You have never been to Ted's, Aunt LouAnn. You're going to love it."

On the way to Mobile, Leah's phone started to play Stevie Ray Vaughn, and she knew it was Michael.

"Hey, are we still going out Friday night?" he purred in his low silky voice.

"You can see me today if you want to meet us at Ted's in a few minutes."

"I can't today. I have to finish this job by six o'clock or we don't get paid."

"Okay, but you're missing out. I'm buying. We're going to get Sheanna some new dresses, too. I know how you men love shopping."

Michael laughed, and her heart skipped a beat. "I just wanted to check up on you and see how y'all are doing. Sounds like it's all good."

"So far. Sheanna's doing great, and the rest of us can't help but be wonderful."

"Is that a fact?"

"Yes sir. As much as I love our daily chats, I have about eight perked up ears surrounding me, so I guess I'll let you go."

"Okay, I'm counting down the days to Friday. Don't go on any more rescue missions without me, or you'll miss out on some fantastic food."

"You don't have to worry about that. I do think there's a little blonde here that you're going to fall in love with, though."

"I like dark-haired girls with chestnut brown eyes."

"Girls? How many are there?"

"We'll talk about that on Friday. I'm hoping there will be one."

"How many are there now?"

"None, but I'm hoping to change that."

"Goodbye, Michael."

"Goodbye, Leah McPhillen. See you soon."

Chapter 6
Prov. 3:31 – Do not envy the oppressor, and choose none of his ways.

Cullen punched the wall, enjoying the pain that coursed through his arm. It helped him think, and he had a lot of thinking to do.

He looked down at Brinne as she slept on the mattress, thick black tear-trails dried on her cheeks, and it made him want to choke the life from her pale skinny throat. She was no help. All she was good at was crying these days.

He wasn't about to let that little snot get away with leaving them, but he had a cash problem. There wasn't any. He needed a gun and a car and there was nobody who'd trust him with either. Brinne was no help, a worthless rag doll. He should've dumped that load a long time ago. But her daughter, now there was something to behold. That little cat-eyed beauty kept the bills paid, and would fetch a great price in a year or two, but he had to get her back. When he came home and found the brat gone, he searched the usual places, but LouAnn had surprised him. The old bat grew a spine and took off with the kid. At least she was stupid enough to leave Brinne a letter to let him know where they were. Like he was scared of some old cop. Now he just had to get down there and get his property back.

The last group of the brat's pictures had been sold online a week before, and it kept him in cigarettes and spending money, but once she was old enough to rent out he'd be flush. Brinne didn't bring in much money anymore, now that her teeth were going bad. The clientele was getting poorer and wanting more for their money. His ticket was the snot; it was the only reason she was still alive.

Cullen pulled up a list on his phone and contacted some of the people who bought his pictures. Surely one of them was from the Gulf Coast area. He'd make it sound like they'd be paid well for putting him up for a few days—if he could convince them he wasn't working for the cops. He'd never cared who he was dealing with before, as long as they had the cash. Would anybody believe him? Soon enough it would all come together. It always did.

Cullen laughed softly at the irony of it. How had those he so despised become so important to him?

It wouldn't take much to get the girl alone, he knew. She was used to wandering around whenever she got it into her head, and he was great at making himself blend into his surroundings. Sometimes being the little guy that nobody noticed was a good thing—a great thing. Now all he needed was to find a contact in Mississippi, and hit a gas station for some cash. And maybe one of those Cash Advance places. They didn't have any security to speak of. He'd been watching for a long time, knowing he couldn't squeeze much more money from Brinne. He mentally scoured the neighborhood for a decent car, something common and not too old. LouAnn's apartment complex. Several of the old women there had cars that were not used very often, so it may be days before anybody was even looking. He kept his eyes open, always looking for something better. It was a gift he had. That and taking pictures.

"I've got nothin' but time," he whispered as he headed out the door.

Chapter 7

***Prov. 17:11** An evil man seeks only rebellion; therefore a cruel messenger will be sent against him.*

Phil got up at his usual 4 a.m. and put on his usual pot of coffee, then set out for his three mile run. That was not usual. Phil had slacked off the past year, trimming his workout to two miles, then one, telling himself that he didn't need to overdo it at his age. But since April 25th, he called all his decisions into question. Was he making bad choices, just coasting through the day without thinking things through? Had he unnecessarily escalated things, as some people seemed to think?

As he ran, Phil replayed the scenario that had haunted him for weeks over and over in his mind. The media had it wrong. Another officer had spotted the boys in the truck—a friend of the family who knew they were skipping school and had no business driving anything larger than a bicycle. When Randall called it in, Phil had been only a quarter of a mile away, headed back to the police station to meet with another officer about a domestic violence case. The boys had already been spooked at the sight of the first squad car, and the old truck had been screaming down Market Street at about seventy miles an hour, trying to make it to the bridge. It seemed that they thought if they made it out of town they'd be safe. No one was behind them when they almost took out a letter carrier crossing the road. That's when Phil hit his lights and turned to follow the truck. It wasn't long before the fourteen year-old driver tried to turn left without slowing down and ended up destroying the Oyster Buoy and two futures. Or was it three?

Was it time for him to retire? He had his years in, and then some. Maybe he could work security at one of the shipyards. He would hate that, he knew, but maybe it was better than killing kids. That's what the bloggers on the WWMS website had dubbed him, "Phil, the Killer, McPhillen" or "Killer Phil" for short. What a great catchy name for a guy who had always lived to put the bad guys away. Was he now one of the bad guys? Many folks thought so. That little Patti never did forgive him for busting her graduation night party—complete with plenty of drugs and underage drinking.

She thought that since she lived in the "good" neighborhood she could do whatever she wanted. Unfortunately, her parents agreed, and started a letter-writing campaign against the Ocean Shores Police Department. Thankfully, his friends and neighbors wrote their own letters; his dear Beth enlisted the help of Mothers Against Drunk Drivers, and the uproar quickly died down. This time, though, a child had died, and most of his friends didn't have all the information. He was sworn to silence until all the court business was over with, and again relegated to a motorcycle, which Beth hated. The alternative was a desk, the place he hated more than any other, until the latest uproar died down.

Why are you still a beat cop at your age, Phil? The little voice inside his head chided. *Because you love being outside in the sunshine more than anything. You always loved the adrenaline rush. And what did it get you? Your oldest son is somewhere in New York City, pretending he never knew you; your daughter thinks she's Rambo, and your youngest son is you made over. Is it time to give it all up, Lord? Show me the way.*

He ran along the concrete abutment as the brilliant pink and gold sunrise broke over the water, his belly bouncing up and down, his muscles protesting. The sweat streamed into his eyes and he quickly wiped it away, willing himself to keep putting one foot in front of the other.

The sound of his cell phone broke through the screeching of the gulls and his wheezing lungs. It was a tune he hadn't heard in a very long time. He stopped jogging and took a few deep breaths before he answered it.

"Hey man, what you been up to?" Phil tried to sound rested and confident.

"Well, that's what I'm calling you about. I understand you have a little time off comin' to you," his former partner Robbie's voice sounded carefully controlled.

"I do. Right now I'm mostly warming a chair, and you know how I love that." Phil laughed a bitter chortle.

"Do you remember that little strawberry-blonde girl we found after the Hurricane a few years back?" a slight tremor was in Robbie's voice now.

"The one from the river?" Phil's hands were instantly sweaty, and he almost dropped his phone remembering the sweet-faced child. "The girl with the strange tattoos, and no foam in her lungs."

"That's the one."

"You found out who did it?" Phil was hopeful.

"No. I think we found her sister yesterday. Same condition."

The air whooshed out of Phil's lungs as if he'd been punched in the stomach. "No," was all he could say.

"She's got a matching tattoo, and they can't blame this one on Hurricane Katrina. If you can take today off, I'd like to bounce some ideas off of you."

"My pleasure. I'll meet you at Los Lobos Coffeehouse in an hour."

"Sounds good," the phone cut off.

Phil jogged quickly toward home thinking of his former partner. Robbie never was much for long goodbyes. Even when he'd left the Ocean Shores P.D. to join the Andrews County Sheriff's Department, he didn't have much to say. Phil had always figured the little girl's case had something to do with it. Robbie had always had a soft spot when it came to injured kids. The other guys kidded him about it, but his intolerance toward those indicted for cruelty to children often got him reprimanded. One time, it almost got him killed, but Phil shook that thought out of his mind. It was too painful. As he crossed the front yard, Phil took his cell phone and dialed.

As Phil rounded the corner of the house, he didn't notice Leah rocking on the back porch.

"Yes, Ma'am, this is Sergeant Liam McPhillen. I'm running a pretty good fever, and I'm going to have to take the day off. Yes, Ma'am, I will. Goodbye."

Leah rushed into the house. "Daddy, has this case gotten that bad? I never thought—"

"Don't jump to conclusions, girl. I have to help a friend. You remember Robbie?" he said as he spooned two teaspoons of sugar into his coffee mug.

"Sure. He was the best-looking partner you ever had. I used to dream that he would ask me to marry him so we could all be one happy family."

"You are wrong for that," Phil snorted, shaking his head. "I'm going to tell him you said that."

"Sure, Daddy. Now you'll go tell him I've always had a mad

crush on him. He's got the best dimples, and I love his Texas accent. If I wasn't dating Michael, you'd be looking for a way to lock me in my room." Leah sipped from his coffee cup and made a face. "Ugh, too sweet."

He smiled. "You got that right. Two cops in the family will be quite enough."

"So what are you helping him with?" she asked, pouring herself a fresh cup of coffee with a generous splash of milk.

Phil tried to sound nonchalant. "It's an old case we worked. Something new has turned up, and he wants me to take a look at it."

"None of the sheriff's deputies can help in out?"

"None as good as me."

"But why would a deputy sheriff be working a case from Ocean Shores?"

"Guess I'll find out in a few minutes. Now let me get a shower, or I'm going to be late."

"Can I come with you?"

"I don't think it's a good idea, honey."

"Daddy, I want to help. If it's important enough for you to miss work—"

"Not this time, Sugar. Besides, you've been complaining all week how far behind you are on your own work."

"You got me. I do have a truckload of work to catch up on." She pouted and shuffled toward her office. But the slamming screen door told her that her pitiful gait hadn't had the intended effect. She wouldn't be hearing any of Rob's great stories today.

Soon Phil was driving his truck north, his blood pumping as he reviewed the case in his mind. His old notebook lay on the seat beside him. He didn't write in it often, but this case had shaken him like no other. He had written everything down from the day they had found the body to the day they finally had to consider themselves beaten and move on to other cases. There was little evidence and the police department was overwhelmed with crime at the time. The aftermath of Hurricane Katrina hadn't helped them any with this case. The streets had been lined with ruined furniture, and piled with putrid debris. Flies were everywhere, and the heat made it difficult to breathe. Many people literally had nothing except what the Red Cross brought them, and some tried to rectify the situation by taking from those who did have food or water stored. Gasoline was like gold. It seemed ridiculous to the police that some people were running around stealing TV sets and CD players when there was no electricity, but they did. Domestic violence exploded as the oppressive heat made short tempers even shorter. Several dead bodies from Bay St. Louis and New Orleans washed onshore, which had to be identified, stored and eventually returned home. It was very difficult to get gasoline, but the drug addicts managed to get their drugs of choice, and had to keep stealing or prostituting themselves to feed their habit. But of all the ugly things they had seen after Hurricane Katrina, the face of that little girl had haunted Phil and Robbie more than any other. They often sat and threw ideas at each other, trying to figure out who she belonged to and how she had ended up snagged on a branch in the Pascagoula River, which ran through Ocean Shores.

No one fitting her description had been reported missing in Mississippi, Alabama, Florida or Louisiana. Her autopsy, when it finally had been performed, had shown no foam in her mouth or lungs. She hadn't drowned. Most haunting of all, her tiny body had several strange scars. There were ligature marks on her right wrist and ankle, and red welts crisscrossed her back, as if she'd been recently whipped with a very thin willow branch or switch. There were several thin, triangular scars on her buttocks, as if someone had repeatedly poked her with a small paring knife, just deep enough to cause pain. There was a small bald spot on the left side of her head in front of her ear, as if she'd nervously twirled her hair until it came out. Yet her face was unmarked, and her long reddish-blonde hair had been French braided into two pert pigtails that were fastened with glittery ponytail holders. But the strangest thing was the tattoo on the inside of her left wrist. It was two conjoined black hearts with three tiny pink hearts surrounding it, and it wasn't fresh. What kind of monster would tattoo a young child? What did the hearts mean, and why in such a sensitive place? Was the torture a part of why she was dead, or just for some sicko's pleasure? Why didn't anyone care that this six- or seven-year-old girl was missing?

As he pulled into the parking lot, Phil looked for the Andrews County Sheriff car. There it was, facing the highway, under the oak tree. Robbie was hunched over, juggling a stack of file folders as he pushed the door open with the tip of his black and tan snakeskin boot. Roberto Colazzo, the youngest of six boys, was

Place Called Grace   68

raised on a cattle ranch near Austin, Texas, and from his belt buckle to his boots he never left any doubt about where he came from. He was well over six feet tall, with a stocky build and a voice as smooth as butter. He nodded at Phil and grinned as he stood.

"It's been too long, Buddy. Way too long."

"Here, give me some of those," Phil commanded, showing the lone journal in his hand. "I can tote half that load."

Robbie deposited half of the files into Phil's waiting arms and slapped him on the shoulder playfully. "You put on a few pounds this year?"

"Them's fightin' words," he snickered. "Us Mississippi boys don't take mess from y'all Texans."

"Much as I'd love to throw down, we'd better get inside and get started on this stuff. My shift starts in six hours."

Phil raised an eyebrow. *What exactly did Robbie have in mind?*

The men walked into the cheerful cottage and admired the murals that were painted on the interior walls. It was a forest scene, complete with howling wolves and a full moon shining off a lake. The place always smelled of brewing coffee and warm, buttery biscuits, and the pretty waitresses made excellent tips form their mostly-male clientele. Los Lobos Coffeehouse did serve food— breakfast from 5 a.m. to 3 p.m., every Monday through Saturday. The prices were reasonable and there was always plenty of food on the plate, so there were rarely two open tables at the same time. The two men seated themselves at a small booth at the back of the restaurant. Phil faced the rear exit, and Robbie faced the front entrance. A cute blonde with a step as bouncy as her ponytail and deep dimples came to take their order.

"Coffee, y'all?"

"Yes, Ma'am," the two officers agreed, as they ran their eyes down the menu.

Los Lobos made wonderful steak and cheese omelets, Phil remembered, and he licked his lips in anticipation. It really had been too long.

Soon the steaming mugs were placed in from of them, and they placed their orders like two friends having breakfast instead of two men preparing to go through gruesome files of a horrific crime. Correction, two horrific crimes.

"I'll have the steak and eggs over easy, cheese grits and hash brown," Robbie said. "Extra onions in the hash browns, please Ma'am."

"I'll have a Philly cheese steak omelet with fried grits and wheat toast," Phil said, watching Robbie for any sign of disdain.

Robbie chortled, "You really think the wheat toast is going to make up for all that grease?"

"I hope nobody has to ride with you later after all those onions," Phil threw back at him. As soon as the waitress was out of earshot, he leaned toward Robbie and said, "Now, tell me about the tattoo."

Robbie grimaced and slid a picture toward his friend. It was a little girl's left wrist, and it had two intertwined black hearts, with two small pink hearts above them.

"She's nearly the same age as the first body was, maybe a little older. But only two pink hearts?"

Maybe there are two hearts instead of three because one of the little hearts stopped ten years ago."

Phil nodded grimly. It made sense. That meant there was possible another tattooed child out there, waiting to be killed.

"Okay, let's figure the time line. Nine years ago, there were three children. Were they all girls? The pink would suggest it. One was possibly eleven, and two were an unknown age, but likely between one and six years old."

"That's what I figure," Robbie agreed. "Plus two adults—two black hearts."

"So the little girl is killed, and her body is dumped in the river, and that leaves two kids. But now we find another little girl with the same tattoo, so maybe there is still one child in that house who could be the next victim."

"I hope she's grown, and has gotten far away. Maybe she's ready to talk. We can work that angle. How many tattooed kids can there be in Mississippi? Wouldn't the schools report it?"

"You'd think so. She could be home schooled, or they never registered her in the first place. Lots of teens could get away with tats on their wrist. It's easily covered, but maybe our girl is still a pre-teen. How do we identify her?"

"That's where I'm hoping you can help me. You can call the sheriff's departments in the neighboring counties, and here's a list of tattoo parlors. Just focus on the area between here and Hattiesburg. A tattoo like that would have to stand out."

"So why do you need *me* to call them?"

"The sheriff doesn't see the connection. He says that the Hurricane Katrina case is long dead, and should stay that way. He says we don't have time to chase ghosts, that anybody could have tattoos these days, and that we have no proof of a crime until the DNA evidence comes back."

"Doesn't he realize that those lost weeks could cost us many leads?"

"Obviously not. One more thing, the girl had her hair braided the exact same way as the first one. She had the same strawberry blonde hair, and the M.E. says there was no foam in her throat or lungs. She didn't drown. The rape kit turned up two different kinds of hair—so the two black hearts could symbolize two men. But then how are they getting the little girls, and why aren't the disappearances reported? It's sick any way you cut it."

"Any ideas on cause of death?"

"Maybe a blow to the head. Maybe she was poisoned. I'm still working on a couple of theories. She was found two days ago at Preston's Bayou by the grounds crew just after sunset. Of course they weren't going to broadcast it, and were as cooperative as possible."

"So that's how you kept it quiet." A shudder went through Phil as he realized that he had dropped his son and a friend there just hours before the body was found. If they hadn't seen the storm coming, he would have been there. He racked his brain trying to picture the other families he saw that day. Were there any little red-headed girls running around the beach? He didn't remember any. Nothing seemed out of the ordinary. Just regular families enjoying the sunny day.

"One more weird thing, she had the ligature marks on her right wrist and right ankle, just like the other girl, but this body was in much better shape—no whipping or scars on the buttocks. She wasn't in the water very long; we figure she can't be from too far away. She may even be from Andrews County."

Phil shuddered at the thought of someone that evil living in their county, swimming in their river, driving their same roads, maybe eating at the same restaurants. He knew from experience that there was plenty of suffering to go around, but what had happened to these two precious little girls made his blood run cold. And who was the second black heart? Surely the girls' mother had some sliver of compassion for them. Maybe she was a prisoner too. Sometimes fear was a terrible jailer. But Phil felt sure that if they could find her in time, heart number three could keep beating.

"Okay, Robbie. I'll do whatever you need me to do. Show me what else you have, and I'll get right to work on it."

Chapter 8
Proverbs 16:24 Pleasant words are a honeycomb, sweet to the soul and healing to the bones.

That Friday, at exactly 6:15, Michael pulled up in a maroon 1957 Thunderbird convertible.

"Well, he's early Momma. That's a good sign. At least there are no reporters out front," Leah sighed, as she peeked through the curtain.

"I think they'll let up until the court date now," Beth said. "That Holmes woman is banking on public outrage, and people will get tired of the story if they overdo it too much."

"I think they've overdone it quite enough," Leah sniffed.

Beth nodded and rocked, as her good hand furiously crocheted a new gold and black throw for Sheanna's bed. Phil and Hunter had already gotten the poor little thing all worked up over their favorite NFL team, the New Orleans Saints, even though they hadn't won a Super Bowl since 2009, and Beth was happy to help them.

"Momma, look at Daddy and Hunter gushing over that car," she said, embarrassment pinking her cheeks as she peeked out the window.

"Boys will be boys," Beth said softly, as she looked admiringly out the window. "Your Daddy had a car like it once, if I remember correctly."

"Sheesh! What is it with guys and old cars?" she asked, as she clipped on Trooper's leash and led him toward the door. "I better get out there before they run my date off."

"You're bringing the dog?"

"I promised I'd introduce him to Trooper. 'Bye Aunt LouAnn. 'Bye She-She."

Beth just shrugged and walked her out the front door, as Sheanna stood on tiptoe and peeked through the lacy kitchen curtains.

"Have fun, dear," LouAnn chirped. "Don't do anything I wouldn't do."

Leah rolled her eyes. That was a feisty old thing if she ever met one—like Momma with a pitchfork.

"Are you okay out here?" she asked Michael. "I know these nosy things are about to run you off."

"This is my baby," he'd said proudly, as he ran to open the car door for her. He reached in and pulled out a beautiful white rose surrounded by baby's breath and wrapped in green tissue. "The truck just wasn't right. Mind if we go to this little place I know in Mobile?"

Leah breathed in the delicate scent of the rose. *How sweet,* she thought. The bud had just started to open, and she knew it would be around for a while. She hoped Michael would turn out to be a keeper.

"Sure." She nodded, embarrassed that everyone was just standing around grinning like the ugly duckling had finally turned into a swan. So, it was her first date in ages. So, instead of sitting in his chair cleaning his gun, Daddy was practically embracing this almost-stranger. Could she help it that she had the worst luck in the world, and that most "tough guys" were so into themselves that she didn't see any point in ruining a perfect relationship?

Leah pulled on the leash. "This is *my* baby, Trooper. Doesn't he have the biggest ears you've ever seen?' she giggled.

Michael reached out and let him sniff his hand, then gently rubbed his graying chin.

"Good boy. Are you a good dog?"

Trooper licked his hand, and Michael scratched between his ears.

Leah winked at her mother, and handed her the tissue-wrapped flower and Trooper's leash.

"He's the best dog we ever had," Beth said, as she led Trooper toward the house. "You kids have fun."

Leah waved goodbye and blew a kiss as they backed out of the driveway. Then she stared down at her hands as B.B. King sang the Blues from the radio.

He passed tests number one and *two. Trooper and the folks seemed to like him.*

"Should I change it?" Michael asked.

"No, I really love the Blues." She looked through her purse for a ponytail holder. No use in looking like Medusa after the wind got a hold of her hair.

"Me, too. Blues or Country."

"I usually listen to Christian Rock, bluegrass, blues or classical—it depends on my mood—mostly Christian contemporary."

Leah looked at him trying to gauge his reaction. She had promised herself long ago that she wouldn't waste her time dating a guy that wasn't a Believer, and she prided herself on being able to decide whether a guy was worth a second date within the first fifteen minutes. Of course, Shay said this was technically their second date, and Leah noticed that Michael still had a small scar under his eye from the piece of glass that had embedded itself there the day of the wreck. He also had scratches and fading bruises on his arms from the destruction at the Oyster Buoy. Was that some kind of divine warning, or were those kids just unlucky enough to "borrow" the neighbor's truck on the wrong day?

"I didn't think you were the rock-n-roll type."

"Oh, what type am I?" she'd teased, twirling her ponytail with her fingers.

"Something beautiful, but not too wild. Country, with Bluegrass overtones, and eyes the color of a chestnut mare." He flashed her a mischievous grin.

"Well, you're not even close. I was a quite the head-banger my first couple of years of college—first taste of freedom and all that. I wore black all the way down to my leather boots, drank way too much, and almost flunked out. My oldest brother, Sammy, was at Tulane, too. He was such a talented musician. You name it; he could play it. He got us so many good jobs. I could see we had a bright future coming, almost switched my major to music. Then one day, he just up and left me. I was so angry that I kind of lost it for a while. My poor liver took quite a beating that year."

"That's pretty standard for college, isn't it?"

Her mouth just kept on going, like she had to tell him everything all at once. "Sammy was gone to New York City, and I felt like I was completely alone in the world. I knew Momma and Daddy were disappointed with the life I'd chosen, and there was no way I was comin' home with my tail between my legs. But then Shay introduced me to this Pastor that was like nobody I'd ever known before. He wasn't the polished guy in a pressed suit with the perfect hair, and for some reason that appealed to me."

Michael nodded, his eyes unreadable.

"When Shay invited me to his Campus Bible Study, I went with her for the free donuts. After a few weeks, I went because I really wanted to hear what he had to say. He taught me so much about the Bible, and that's funny, because I've been in church my whole life. But the more I learned, the more I realized that the whole party scene would get me nowhere."

Leah licked her lips and looked at his eyes, trying to gauge his reaction, but his face showed nothing.

"Besides, I was sick of waking up feeling like I'd been beaten with a stick. Anyway, I told Shay I wasn't giving up my music, so she found some groups with a good beat and a good message. It took a while, but by senior year I was pretty much back on the 'straight and narrow' much to my parents' relief."

Michael laughed, "I'll bet. I get the feeling your Momma doesn't put up with too much nonsense."

"You got that right. That woman gets her prayers answered. If the prayers don't work, she'll get you another way. Momma will win in the end. Besides, I needed to get myself together because that CPA exam is no joke. What about you?"

Michael smiled, his brown eyes shining, dimples etching deep lines in his tanned cheeks. "I had my wild days, too. I've always loved to build things, but was never very interested in school. Math was okay, but the rest was so boring, I could barely stay awake."

"Don't mention that to Shay. She's an English teacher."

He grinned and pulled onto I-10, and the wind tried to tear his words away. "I skipped out a lot, partied with my friends. Then my folks died when I was 14."

Leah forced herself to close her mouth. She really wanted to ask how they died, but couldn't put together the right words.

Michael just shrugged, glanced over at her, and continued, "I had no real family, no place to go, so I ended up in Mobile with my Dad's old friend, Gator. He had this great little houseboat on Fowl River. I want you to meet him, a refugee from a Louisiana bayou. He's a wild-lookin' old thing, goatee, long gray braid down his back, earrings—a pirate without the eye patch. You'd never believe how many tattoos this fella has."

Leah forced a smile, unease creeping into her throat. She hoped they weren't going to his house for dinner. Her days of longhaired guys with tattoos were far behind her. She'd promised her parents when she moved back home that she wouldn't date anybody that Phil had arrested. Gator sounded like one of those guys.

Michael smiled at her, "He is the best carpenter I've ever known. He taught me a trade and got me started in the business. I was better off with him than most, I guess. Speaking of family, why didn't you become a cop?"

"In college I took a couple of criminal justice classes, thinking maybe I should go into the 'family business'. One of my professors read a paper that I wrote on ways to dispose of a dead body. I'd done it as a joke for my creative writing class, but the professor didn't see it that way. Professor Gronkowski advised me not to bother trying to get into the police academy because I'd never pass the psychological evaluation. I thought about it, and he was right. I knew I couldn't stand there with a gun on the bad guy and be sure I wouldn't pull the trigger, especially if he'd hurt a child. Weirdly enough, Professor Gronkowski had only written one comment on my paper, complimenting me on my 'creative mind'. So I changed my major to accounting, with a minor in music, and now I'm a somewhat-highly paid professional, at least during tax season. Most days I can work from home, and my boss is a good friend of my parents."

"Did you ever think about teaching music?"

"I haven't played much since Sammy left, but I do get small comfort from singing in the church choir. Our music director is so talented. It's almost like the days when I performed with my brother. I love it when the harmonies fill the building and make my blood dance in my veins."

"There's a poet in there, Leah. No wonder your best friend teaches English."

Leah sat quietly for a few moments. She didn't know what to say. Thankfully, the radio spared her.

"Oh, I love this song," Leah gushed, as Eric Clapton's *Tears In Heaven*, came wailing through the speakers. "Tragic and beautiful, one of those squeeze-your-heart songs. Do you ever notice how the worst things lead to the best songs? Anyway, I wish I could write like that."

"Oh, you're a songwriter, too?"

"Not exactly. I have all these songs in my head. One day I'll write them down."

"I'll be sure to get your first hit CD." The dimples were back, and Leah wanted so badly to hold his cheeks in her hands.

"I'll autograph it for you."

They spent the rest of the trip singing along with the radio. Michael was tone deaf—so much for the Josh Turner voice—but Leah didn't mind. She wasn't auditioning him for the choir, after all. It wasn't very long before they were pulling up to a graying, weather-beaten wood shack on stilts, with the name "Thornton's" splashed across the front in huge bright neon hot pink letters.

Leah smiled at Michael, grateful they weren't going to meet the "Gator" on their first date. She wanted to get to know Michael better first.

"I just have one more question for you. Hunter doesn't seem like Sheanna's father, and she calls your dad Uncle Phil, so–"

Leah laughed, a tinny sound that wasn't quite convincing, "No, Michael. Sheanna is my cousin Brinne's child. She's just, just not able to care for her right now. Aunt LouAnn was doing a great job, but there's something with her health, so we went and got them. I don't know how sick she is, but I'm sure going to find out."

"I believe you will, and I believe that we are going to eat really good tonight."

"With no crashes or other tragedies allowed."

"You got that right." Michael held out his hand, and Leah took it. The waves smashed against the breakers as they climbed the winding staircase toward the tantalizing smell of fresh yeast rolls and grilled seafood.

They spent the rest of their evening staring out at the moon's glittery diamond reflections on Mobile Bay, listening to Blues and eating delicious surf-n-turf, talking like they'd known each other for years. Michael loved the same music, hated the same movies, and laughed at all of her jokes. It was after 11 o'clock when they noticed that they were the only diners left. She felt the waiters' eyes on her as they took the antique brass candles off the other tables.

"I think they want us to go," she whispered.

"Would you like to drive along the bay?" he asked, as he rose to pull out her chair.

She nodded, afraid her voice would break the spell, and she'd be kissing some handsome prince that was about to become a toad.

But she kept searching for the warts, and there didn't seem to be any. How could this man be single?

The drive along Mobile Bay seemed to take only a few seconds, and then they were home. He walked her to the door, slowly as if he didn't want to leave. Michael brushed his lips lightly across hers, then grabbed her hand and held it to his heart, looking at her earnestly. Emotion danced in his eyes.

"Can I trust you with my heart?" he asked her.

"I have to confess something first."

He looked at her for a long moment, his eyes as dark as the night, and nodded slowly.

"I still listen to Rock sometimes, especially when I'm really behind at work. It helps me focus when it's crunch time and Skynyrd or Boston is blaring in the background. I hope you'll forgive me for leading you to believe I was completely reformed."

Michael's eyes jumped to life again, and the dimple-smile was back.

"I suppose I could forgive you, if you promise to let me take you out again."

She'd nodded and kissed him lightly on his chin, as electricity raced through her, and her heart thumped against her chest like never before. She had to admit that she was completely intrigued by this tough and tender man. But he wasn't getting off that easily. She'd been fooled before.

"If you want to see me again, you can take me to church Sunday morning," she said, using the line that had scared off many would-be suitors. "The service starts at 9:00, so you can pick me up at 8:30. The choir has to be early for one last practice before church starts."

"I'd love to hear you sing."

He looked into her eyes for one more lingering moment, smiled a strange half-smile, and walked back to his car.

Leah tried to ignore the thudding of her heart, as she turned and walked into the house. She wondered whether he'd show up, and she shot a quick prayer up that he would.

Chapter 9

Prov. 1:13 We shall find all kinds of precious wealth…

    Cullen hadn't boosted a car in many years, but it was surprisingly easy. He waited until just before dark, when the old folks in the complex were busy inside, and he just strolled up to an older model car and had it started in less than thirty seconds. Easy. He drove to his first target, a cash advance business that would be closing soon. The girl who worked inside usually had her very large, well-built boyfriend meet her to take the bank deposit to the night drop, but Cullen would get there first.

    It was the first of the month, and people had been paying on their loans. He figured he would get a couple thousand dollars and be on his way south. His artist's eye had worked well for him, as he checked his make-up in the rearview mirror. He would actually make a very pretty old woman—if old ladies could be pretty. He straightened his gray wig and slid the cane from the passenger side of the car. He made himself walk slowly, leaning heavily on the cane, but he licked his lips in anticipation. He couldn't wait to get his hands around that old bat LouAnn's throat. Sheanna would watch her die, of course, and then she wouldn't give him any more trouble. Or she could watch him loose his frustrations on Brinne. That always got her attention. He pushed open the door and smiled as the little bell announced his arrival.

Chapter 10

Prov. 8:19 My fruit is better than gold, even pure gold...

Michael did pick Leah up for church on Sunday, early. When she got to his car, there was a red rose sitting on the seat surrounded by baby's breath and shimmery green tissue paper. Next to it laid a new CD by one of her favorite bands, "Skillet".

"Thank you," Leah forced herself to say quietly, squashing the happy squeal that tried to slip from her chest. "I love everything they write."

She didn't want to rush anything, but Michael just seemed to know how to get his hands around her heart. She couldn't believe how fast the time went when she was with him, or how much they had in common even though they had been raised completely differently, and he was five years older than her. Why wasn't he married? Was there something he was hiding, or was he just a workaholic like her?

She watched him from the choir loft as she sang, and he seemed completely at ease with her brother and parents. Then Beth got up to sing, and Leah flashed a grin at Michael. She watched as the petite woman lowered the microphone, and her rich sweet voice floated through the church, "A place called grace, where Christ met me, lifted my face and set me free. Oh bless that day when he reached down, and raised me up, gave me a crown."

Leah looked at Michael and saw his eyes shining with emotion. Was that joy in his eyes? She couldn't tell. When the choir finished and she was next to Michael in the pew, she could barely concentrate on the sermon. He was too close, and Leah worried that he could see her heart pounding in her throat. Was he there only to impress her, or because he wanted to be? Only time would tell.

After the service, Phil shook Michael's hand and said, "Glad you could join us. Would you like to come back to the house?"

Leah stared at him in utter surprise. Was Daddy trying to get rid of her? Happy butterflies danced in her stomach as Michael nodded and slid his hand into hers.

"Can I bring anything?"

Phil smiled. "If I know my wife, we'll have more than

enough. LouAnn went to the early service and has been cooking for hours. Maybe next time."

Michael gently squeezed Leah's hand, and Leah tried hard not to let her mouth drop open. *Next time?*

They took the long way home, riding along the Gulf shoulder to shoulder, watching white foamy waves crash against the shore as the pelicans rested on dock pilings that had survived the last hurricane.

"Did you like the song that Momma sang?" Leah asked.

"It was beautiful. I know where you get your love of music. I never heard it before, but it seemed like it should be on the radio."

"Sammy wrote it. We sing a bunch of his songs at our church."

"I hope I get to meet him soon."

"Me too," Leah said, though she hadn't seen her brother in five years.

Michael looked so happy at lunch afterward, grinning at the teasing banter as they feasted on Momma's fine, buttery homemade biscuits and LouAnn's thick sausage gravy, cheese grits, scrambled eggs and crispy bacon. He helped clear the dishes from the table, and then took Phil and Hunter for a ride along the Gulf in his "hot rod".

"You should keep this one," Hunter teased after Michael left. "He's better than any of those long-haired losers you dated in college."

"Well, I'm so glad you approve. What about you? I notice you been spending a lot of time with that sweet little tennis star from USM."

"She's a nice girl," Hunter flushed slightly and looked at the floor.

"And?" Leah couldn't resist teasing him. After all, she was twenty-five and he was nearly twenty-one, and she'd overheard her mother on the phone talking to one of her friends about how she would 'never have any grandchildren at this rate'.

"She's a nice girl. I'm not as old and decrepit as you. I don't have to rush into anything."

"Huh, you're afraid she won't have you. I wouldn't want some skinny little thing like you either. I don't even think the police academy will have you when you graduate. You'll get beat up the first day."

"You talk so big and bad when Daddy's around. I'd like to see you in an honest throw-down like when we were kids."

Leah grinned. She knew all his tickle-spots.

"You'd get whipped, just like when we were kids. You know I'm stronger than I look."

Leah glanced over at her father, dozing in his chair as the Saints kicked a field goal on an ESPN2 rerun. Leah tried not to excite Daddy unless absolutely necessary. He'd always liked to be constantly working on something, and rarely sat still. It had been years since he'd flipped his motorcycle, but the wreck had taken the lion out of him in many ways, and Leah feared all the stress would make him sick again. That kind of trauma was nothing to mess with. Was Daddy happy to see her with Michael? He seemed to like him. Only time would tell, and Phil wouldn't go too long without telling her what he thought. There was plenty of time to talk to him. Besides, she wasn't sure that she wanted to admit that her heart was quickly being won by the quiet man with the calloused hands.

Chapter 11
Proverbs 4:17- For they eat the bread of wickedness and drink the wine of violence.

"Wake up! It's Black and Gold day at Preston's Bayou! Wake up everybody! We're burning daylight. Time to go swimming with the college kids," Hunter announced as he banged on doors and gleefully made a nuisance of himself.

Leah groaned, "Isn't there a verse in the Bible about people who call loud greetings early in the morning?"

"Wake up, sleepyheads. Time to go play in the sand. Wake up," Hunter stuck his head in every door, flipping on the lights. In one motion he pulled off Leah's blankets. "You weren't up gabbing with Michael *that* late last night Medusa-hair. Get up."

Leah followed her brother into the kitchen, unwilling to let him insult her and get away clean.

"Hey, that was the first time we talked yesterday. He owns a business, remember? Maybe someday you'll get some business and find a girl who will like spending time with your skinny tail."

Sheanna padded into the kitchen and Beth, Leah and Hunter broke out in a rousing rendition of "Happy Birthday" complete with 2-part harmony.

LouAnn's rich alto rang out from the hallway as she carried a tiny cake that looked like an Oreo cookie. Five hot pink candles blazed from the middle of the cake.

Sheanna's eyes reflected the flickering candles, and her cheeks were pink with joy. Her lips made a perfect pink oval as she readied herself to blow out the candles.

She only left one burning, and Hunter quickly reached over and pinched it out.

"No boyfriends for you, Princess," he teased.

"I like you, Cousin Hunter," Sheanna said softly, staring at Leah's hair.

Leah caught her astonished gaze and rummaged in her pocket for a ponytail holder. Her hair must be really bad it if got Sheanna to stop looking at her pretty cake. That little thing had seen it all.

"I got the jet skis charged up, fueled up and ready to go," Phil gently flipped Sheanna's pigtail. "You are going to learn how to go tubing, girl."

"Grab a biscuit and we'll bring the cake with us. Go put on your new swimsuit, Sheanna," Beth said. "Leah, you have five minutes to get ready. You know you don't want to miss this."

"I'm almost ready—just putting my hair up, Momma."

"Oh, we don't have time for all that," Hunter teased. "Just throw a hat over that mess and come on! Toby Lipschitz is waiting to give you a ride on his jet ski."

Leah threw a wet washcloth across the kitchen at her brother, who easily caught it. He twirled it between his hands and snapped at Leah's leg. She jumped back just in time.

"Quit, you two. We're going to have a good day with no fussing, do you hear me?" Beth used her sternest voice, but Leah knew there was a laugh hiding in there somewhere.

Sheanna came out of her room in her new, bright yellow swimsuit with the Tweedy Bird on the front and matching sunglasses.

"Aunt Beth, I don't know how to swim," Sheanna said softly, a tear dribbling down her cheek.

"You'll learn soon enough. Besides, you don't have to swim, Honey. You'll have a life jacket on, and Leah or Hunter will be with you all the time. We rented the game room for your party and I've got a purse full of quarters with your name on it. This will be your best birthday ever, if I have anything to say about it."

"I'm going to take you on the wave runner, gal. I'll drive just fast enough so it will be fun, but not too fast. Okay, Sheanna?" Daddy scooped her up onto his shoulders and she held tightly to his chin. "When we get home, you can help me burn some chicken on the grill."

"Okay, Uncle Phil," she squealed, planting a tiny kiss on the top of his head.

Leah smiled, glad that Sheanna had finally warmed up to Daddy. She was so quiet around strangers, and usually cowered around men, like a completely different child. Leah remembered all the times she'd been carried around the same way, especially at the beach. She'd never liked having wet sand stuck to her feet when it was time to leave, and Daddy always made sure she got to the truck with clean toes—when he was there. Before the wreck she didn't remember much family time; he had usually been working a reunion or funeral or a parade. Funny how almost dying had cleared out his schedule.

Aunt LouAnn followed, her arms piled with towels, beach toys and sunscreen. "You'll be an expert swimmer by the time this crew gets done with you, She-she."

"That's the truth," Hunter said. "I've been swimming at Preston's ever since I can remember, and we've never had a bad day yet. Except for when I saw that 'gator."

Sheanna almost toppled from her uncle's shoulders, "What? A-alligator?"

"You have never seen a 'gator over there, Hunter, and you know it," Leah said, stuffing a handful of files into her beach bag. "Don't listen, Sheanna. He's just trying to make excuses for hitting a tree stump and messing up our old wave runner."

"I did see a 'gator, and he came right for me."

"You quit, Hunter," Momma scolded. "Sheanna, I've been going there a lot longer than my son has, and I have never seen anything but minnows and ducks at Preston's. It's perfect there."

"You're right, Momma," Leah agreed. "Preston Chantel must have some kind of special blessing on his family. The breeze is always just right, and I've never been stung by a fire ant or even had a mosquito bite. It's like a little piece of heaven over there."

"It's gorgeous, child," Aunt LouAnn agreed. "I forgot how much I loved it there. We've had so many church picnics and parties. I always came back kissed by the sun and stuffed like a tick!"

"I hope we do see a 'gator, and some 'gator hunters, too," Sheanna piped up.

Everybody laughed and headed toward the kitchen table, where a heaping bowl of biscuits and three different kinds of homemade jam waited.

"You stay close to us," Beth reminded the child. "No wandering off like at Ted's."

"I just wanted to see the baby," Sheanna stuck out her lip.

"I would've taken you," Leah soothed.

"You were with Ms. Shay," Sheanna said.

"Well, I'm old enough to go off by myself, little lady. You're not."

Sheanna dropped her head and put her thumb in her mouth.

Then she seemed to change her mind and asked for another biscuit.

"Don't eat too many biscuits," Momma warned. "I have a huge lunch packed, and I don't want to bring home all of this food. Plus, Uncle Phil is cooking out tonight. A few of his friends are coming over, too. We're going to make a party out of the whole day."

Phil slid Sheanna off of his shoulders and took the towels from Aunt LouAnn.

"I'll bring these to the truck. Don't eat all the strawberry jam before I get back!"

Leah picked up one of the buttery biscuits and smothered peanut butter over the top of it. She wished she could invite Michael, but he'd already told her he had a big job to finish, so he could join her for church on Sunday. In all their conversations since the Oyster Buoy, they hadn't run out of things to talk about. That was a good sign, and the blues band at Thornton's hadn't been bad either. Leah wondered if he'd bring her a rose again before church, or if that was just for the first impression. She also wondered how many hours she'd have to work on Sunday afternoon to make up for slacking off today.

"Hey, Leah, quit daydreaming and pass me the jam," Hunter said. "I'm starving."

A loud thud against the window made them jump, and Leah ran to the front door and flung it open. Hunter raced past her out onto the road, with Trooper right on his heels. Somebody had thrown a jar of what looked like a mixture of ketchup and red Kool-aid onto the porch and it shattered, leaving glass and red goop all over the steps.

An old rust-colored pickup truck full of screaming, laughing teens was putt-putting its way down the street.

"That's the killer's house. That's for Bobby Max, Killer Phil!" one of the girls in the back screamed.

Leah just shook her head, and quickly shut the door before Sheanna could see.

"Our 'friends' are back, Momma. Hunter is chasing them down the street like a dog. Guess they thought stealing and skipping out of school is a good idea, too. I'll get the broom."

Nothing was going to ruin her good day, Leah resolved, as she carefully corralled the glass shards into the garbage can at the edge of the porch.

Leah looked up to see their neighbor, Dr. Sandra Daschle, standing in the yard, staring at them. Leah tried not to stare at her face, but the woman looked like a geometry project. Her head was perfectly oval with a completely pancake-flat face. Her nose was a perfect triangle jutting out from the plane. Her thick silver hair was cut in a straight line above her bushy eyebrows and directly below her earlobes. If she had been created by a computer program, she couldn't be more angular.

"Good thing they didn't hit my porch this time," the elderly woman observed in her uppity nasal twang. Her many layers of silver and turquoise jewelry shone in the sunlight.

"Have they hit your porch, Ma'am?" Leah tried to keep her voice even.

"Not yet, but yo' daddy isn't exactly the most popular man in Ocean Shores. It's only a matter of time before the hooligans start to destroy more than just your front porch," the woman observed, wagging her twig-like finger at Leah.

"We hope this will all be resolved quickly," Leah said as calmly as she could. "Those punks will move on to another victim soon enough."

"It wasn't the silver truck this time," the older woman muttered.

"What silver truck?" Leah asked.

"The one that sits outside your house early in the morning. At first I thought it was one of your Daddy's police officer friends, watching out for you. But the man had unruly hair and a plethora of earrings in his face, and he drove off when I tried to speak to him."

Leah stared at the eccentric woman. "Have you mentioned this to Daddy?"

"I'm telling *you*. He's lurking here almost every night, you know— sometimes for merely an hour, and sometimes until dawn. He parks in different spots and camouflages his car tag with mud, but I know it's him. He's got an unusual dent in his door. It resembles a bullet hole to me."

"Ms. Sandra—"

"You know I have a doctorate. I worked hard for it. Please address me correctly, young lady, or not at all."

The woman turned and marched back into her house,

slamming the front door behind her.

"Does that old witch ever sleep?" Leah asked Hunter as he came around the side of the house with the hose. "I thought you were chasing that truck down the street."

"I got the tag number."

"I'm impressed. You finally had a good idea."

"Ha, ha. Daddy will take care of the rest. Trooper almost got one of them in the shorts. It was pretty comical to watch them scream and run to the front of the truck bed with their behind hanging out."

"That would've been worth running down the street for."

Hunter shrugged, and adjusted the spray. He managed to hose the goop off without dousing Leah too badly. Trooper jumped around, trying to drink from the hose.

"Nice try, Hunter, but I have some things to tell Daddy. Daschle just gave me an earful, and I'm not letting those little punks wreck our picnic."

At least my life is never boring, Leah decided, as she went to find her father.

Chapter 12

Joshua 1:9 Have I not commanded you? Be strong and of good courage; do not be afraid, nor be dismayed, for the LORD your God is with you wherever you go.

They had gotten home from Preston's just in time. The storm was rolling in quickly, and the lightning tore like blinding threads against the inky sky. Thunder shook the house, and Leah watched from Momma's favorite rocking chair on the porch, enjoying the cool breeze that came with the furious booming, trying to figure out how to broach the subject of LouAnn's failing health as gently as possible.

Aunt LouAnn rocked next to her, crocheting a fluffy pink baby blanket for the church mission's closet. She was so like Momma, always doing something for someone else, but was much more brash. LouAnn said exactly what she thought. Her voice was still soft, though it had lost much of its southern lilt from years of living up north. But her strength was that of a much younger woman, until recently anyway. Momma had told Leah proudly how she'd had the guts to stand up for Sheanna many times against Brinne's sadistic boyfriend, and now even risked going to prison to keep the little girl safe.

Heat lightning crackled across the sky, followed by the deep rumble of thunder.

"Do you think the storm will scare Sheanna?" Leah asked.

"I don't believe so. She never complained, bless her heart. Maybe I'd better go check on her."

"Keep working on that blanket, Aunt LouAnn. I'll go peek in on her. She's probably still napping. I heard her get up a couple of times last night, and she stayed in that water for hours today. I thought she'd fall asleep in the truck on the way home, instead of trying to make us go get snowballs."

"That's a sweet girl, Leah. Thank you," LouAnn said, and patted her hand. "I know we've spoiled that child here lately, but I can't help it. She could use a little meat on her bones."

"Well, we've certainly done our best to help her there," Leah grinned. She took one more deep breath of cool, fresh air. "I love thunderstorms."

"I'd forgotten how refreshing they are. I've stayed away too long, I'm afraid."

"Well, it wasn't exactly an easy drive, and Momma said that Uncle Red couldn't sit still for very long with his blood clots. It would've taken you a week to get here!"

"Red's been gone for two years. I should've come sooner. It would have been better for all of us."

"You did what you had to. No one else looked out for poor She-she. I'm so glad you brought her to us. I love her bunches."

"That girl is my heart. I can't imagine life without her."

Leah nodded as fat raindrops started to pelt the roof.

"I'll go check on her before the power goes out."

LouAnn shook her head and chuckled. "I'm sure you all have plenty of candles around here."

Leah grinned at her great aunt and slipped inside the house. She swiftly made her way up the stairs, hoping to get to Sheanna before the thunder woke her. She didn't want to hear the girl's screams if she awoke alone in the dark with a storm crashing all around her. She had only heard a couple of stories of how the child had been starved and beaten by those who were supposed to protect her, and the thought of it burned in her chest. Leah really hoped her sorry cousin and that Cullen had the guts to come down and try to take Sheanna from their house. Daddy's gun wasn't the only thing they had to watch out for. Everybody in the family was skilled in self-defense, and Leah knew she had a mean streak. She'd hit low and dirty if she needed to. Momma often tried to appeal to her tender heart, but the fire in Leah's gut usually won easily. The whole "love your enemies" thing was the hardest part of Christianity for Leah. It was easy to sing praises and pray and serve, but forgiving the people that attacked those she loved most was almost impossible for her.

Leah walked from bedroom to bedroom, looking for Sheanna. Her little bedroom had been empty, but she'd fallen asleep in her swimsuit, so Leah wasn't alarmed at first. A growing dread built in her belly as she looked in both bathrooms, then under the beds, in closets, and behind doors. No Sheanna.

"Come out, Sheanna! Come watch the storm with me and Granny LouAnn. It's really beautiful. Don't be afraid, She-she."

Silence was her only answer. Leah knew that Momma had

taken Hunter to Biloxi for some big appointment, and Daddy had run to the station with his red notebook to retrieve some report that he'd forgotten about, so they couldn't help. With all the stress Daddy had been under since the wreck, Leah wouldn't add to it for anything, so she pushed her phone deeper into her pocket. Then she pulled it out, and slid it back in. It had been a good day so far. She wasn't going to bother him at work, especially since he was cooking out that night. That left him only a couple of hours to do whatever needed to be done. Phil had ribs, chicken and steaks marinating since early that morning, and Leah's mouth watered as she thought of her dad's skill with a grill.

    She returned to Sheanna's room and looked around for some clue as to where she could be. The only thing that seemed different was her little change jar lay on its side, empty.

    Think, Leah. If you were afraid, where would you go? Where would she *go?*

    Then Leah had an idea. Gulf Park was only a couple blocks away. Sheanna had loved to run up and down the huge ramp that led to the concession stand, and had begged to go back there for a "Blue Raspberry Splash" snowball almost every day. Maybe that little fit she threw on the way home from Preston's wasn't over, or maybe she'd scraped up her change and decided to go for an adventure and got lost in the storm. She was such a tiny little thing, and used to running the roads with her hot pink backpack purse slung over her shoulder. The purse! Leah searched the room looking for it. Then she ran to the laundry room and tore through the pile of towels and wet swim suits. No bag, hot pink or otherwise. Spot was sitting on Sheanna's pillow, and Leah was pretty sure if Sheanna was hiding from the storm Spot would be with her.

    Leah hoped she could find Sheanna. She opened her cell phone and started to dial Phil's number as she sprinted out the side door and through the neighbor's back yards on her way to the park. It was the quickest way there, and she didn't want to frighten Aunt LouAnn. Her poor, weak body had been through enough lately.

    Leah impatiently waited for his voice to finish the voice mail message.

    "Daddy, call me when you get this message. Sheanna's missing. I'm near Gulf Park looking for her. She's still in her swimsuit, and I think she might have gone for a Snowball. Please get your buddies out looking for her, Daddy. I'll call you if anything changes."

She snapped the phone shut, and shoved it into her pocket as horrible thoughts occurred to her. What if the silver truck belonged to Cullen? What if Brinne and Cullen took her? What if they were on Highway 63 right now, headed north?

Please, God. Don't let them take her. They love their crank more than her. They don't deserve her. Please, God, keep Sheanna safe. Please, she prayed, hoping she was just imagining things. Druggies didn't spend good drug money on gas, did they? Who would loan them a car, with their history? It's not like LouAnn had called and told the welfare office to stop sending the checks. Brinne had no good reason to come get Sheanna, not when she could just stay put and get high.

As she neared the park, Leah screamed Sheanna's name, her voice fighting the howling of the wind and crashing of dozens of waving tree branches. She squeezed water from the legs of her denim cargo shorts, which were soaking wet and heavy.

"Sheanna, it's Cousin Leah. Come to me, baby. Aunt LouAnn is looking for you. Come out, She-she. Sheannnaa!"

Leah slipped out of her flip-flops and raced up the ramp to the concession stand. The padlock was fastened, and no one answered her pounding at the door. She sprinted toward the pavilion as rain pelted her face, but she was too far away to see if Sheanna was crouched under one of the picnic tables.

Well, it's not like I can get any more wet, she thought as she slip-slid her way back down. She sprinted toward the playground, but it was completely empty. Only one more place to look. The bathroom was a block structure in the middle of the park, and Leah ran for it with all her might, screaming Sheanna's name. She could barely catch her breath, but she forced her feet to keep going forward, and willed herself not to slip in the wet grass. Finally, she reached the ladies' side, and she pushed open each door. No one. She went around the men's side, hoping she wasn't about to embarrass anybody, especially herself. Her family probably wouldn't be too pleased, and Hunter would never let her live it down, but she had to search everywhere. Besides, how many four year-olds paid attention to signs six feet in the air?

"Sheanna. Sheannnna!" Leah yelled as she once again

stormed through the bathroom. There was only one stall to push open here, but it was empty.

Leah jogged over to the concession stand ramp and slid back into her flip-flops, trying to imagine where Sheanna could have gone. Leah crossed the road, and walked out onto the pier, hoping it would give her a better view down the beach. She saw the volleyball nets flapping in the breeze, and waves crashing against the shore, but no little girl. She walked to the covered area where the fishermen cast their nets, and looked under the bench. Nothing. Then it hit her. Maybe Sheanna was *under* the pier, hiding from the storm, or looking for hermit crabs.

Leah jogged back to the front of the pier and vaulted over the railing. She crouched down in the sticky wet sand and noticed a small hot pink purse. She grabbed it, and pawed through the few belongings—a hairbrush, two tiny seashells, a few coins, several rocks and nothing "girly". Sheanna's treasures. Leah hugged the purse to herself as if it was the child. Where could she be?

Leah slid her phone from her pocket and shielded it with her body as she pushed the buttons.

"Sheanna's been to the pier, Daddy. I found her purse. I'm walking toward the Point now. Maybe she just got lost. I'll keep looking for her."

Leah jogged as fast as she could, pressing her hand into the stitch in her side, calling Sheanna's name as loud as her hoarse voice would allow. She noticed something small and yellow huddled on a bench next to the concrete breaker.

"Sheanna? It's Leah. Come to me, Sheanna."

Slowly, the bundle straightened, and began to run toward her.

Leah shouted, "Be careful!" as the tiny shoes slapped on the wet concrete abutment.

A wave crashed, and then Sheanna was snatched from her sight. The Gulf had taken her. Leah shrugged off her heavy jean shorts and dove toward the huge slabs of concrete, hoping she wouldn't bash her brains in trying to reach the little girl, who was nothing but a light blue piece of tennis shoe in the midst of roiling gray foam. Her head was under the churning surf, and Leah knew it was just a matter of time. She had to pull her up. Leah swam with all her might toward the tiny shoe, her arms straining to grab the child before a rip current took her far out into the Gulf. But as her hand closed around the shoe, she realized it was empty. Leah threw it toward the abutment, and spun around, pushing off from the bottom to keep her head above the waves. Leah prayed furiously as she strained, looking for a head, listening for a scream. The sound of sirens and the bright blue and red of flashing lights roaring down the Old Beach Road toward her gave her strength. Daddy came through again! The posse was coming.

Leah pulled herself further into the Gulf, toward something small and white bobbing the distance. If it was a crab trap, she was done. It had been too long. That had to be Sheanna, or she was a goner. Leah prayed Sheanna's doggy paddle, learned just that morning, would be strong enough to keep her head above the waves. She forced her tired arms forward against the waves, which assaulted her mouth with salty slaps. Then a skinny white arm reached toward her, and the coughing scream of a child frantic with terror reached her ears.

"Sheanna," Leah croaked. "I gotcha, babe. Quit fighting. I got you."

Leah slid her arm under Sheanna's and flipped the girl so her head would be above the surf, so she could tow her in without being within her reach. Even the tiny panicked child had incredible strength, and Leah was terribly tired, and still far from the shore. She concentrated on kicking her legs and pulling with her free arm toward the flashing lights, which inched closer in a painfully slow march. Then someone else was in the water, taking Sheanna from her.

"I got her, Leah. Just get yourself in. I got her," Officer Billy Martin yelled, sliding a white flotation device onto her arm.

That skinny kid? He'll be lucky to make it to shore himself, Leah thought, snickering in spite of her exhausted muscles and the crashing waves.

She slid herself fully inside the buoyant circle, thankful for the help. Then she realized that they were pulling her toward the pier with the buoy. Of course; it was sandy there. There was no way to climb the concrete breakers in this storm. As tired as she was, she'd be smashed to bits on the concrete by the waves. Leah made herself concentrate on getting there. Pull, pull, and kick. Pull, pull, and kick. Keep moving, girl.

Leah barely felt the sand under her arms and legs, or the

blanket that one of the officers wrapped around her. She was fixated on Sheanna, who was lying on the beach, flailing against her blanket, retching and crying. Leah pulled the girl into her quaking arms and said, "Don't you ever go the park without me again. Do you hear me? What were you thinking, baby? Losing you on your birthday would be the saddest day ever. We love you!"

Sheanna looked up at her with those huge, green, tear-filled eyes as another siren roared closer.

"I just wanted a Snowball. Don't send me away to the police station. I want to stay with Aunt Beth and you and Granny LouAnn!" She began to wail inconsolably.

"You silly girl. We will never send you away. You're one of us, and we will never let you go. Now I won't say LouAnn won't tear up your bottom for this little stunt. It's dangerous to go out in a storm, and it's twice as dangerous to go out alone. Don't ever scare me like that again!"

Sheanna's head fell back, and her gaze went blank. The child's lips were blue, and she shivered uncontrollably, even though she was tightly wrapped in a blanket. Leah held her closely and rocked her back and forth as she watched the ambulance squeal to a stop and waited for the EMT's to come take care of Sheanna. Billy walked up, swinging her jean shorts on his finger.

"I think you might need these," he said with a wolfish grin.

"One word to Hunter, and the penalty will be unbearable," Leah growled. "Oh, and thanks for pulling her in."

The ambulance attendant, a slender, freckled brunette with dozens of tattoos, and short, spiky hair, slipped Sheanna from Leah's arms and soon had her strapped onto the gurney.

"Mom, help me!" Sheanna cried as they whisked her away.

Leah swallowed the lump in her throat and snatched the shorts from Billy's grasp. She held the blanket against her and turned away from her brother's friends, affectionately known to her as "the rookies", as she slipped her sandy, soaking wet shorts on. Then she limped to the ambulance.

I can't believe she'd call for Brinne. Guess a sorry Momma is better than no one at all, she thought.

"I'm coming, Sheanna," Leah said, giving the EMT a look that left no doubt of her intentions. She was riding along. Period.

"Billy, I don't want to try and call Daddy with my wet phone.

Would you let him know I'm okay?"

"Sure, Leah. He's probably halfway here now."

Leah grinned. Billy had grown up, and he was so handsome he was almost pretty. His thick lashes twinkled with raindrops and his ice blue eyes drew her attention to his high cheekbones and perfectly touchable jaw. Billy had turned out to be a heartbreaker.

"Tell the guys I said 'thanks', okay?"

"Hurts you to say it, doesn't it, Leah?"

"You know it," she said, giving him the thumbs up before she pulled herself into the ambulance with the last of her strength.

Chapter 13
Prov. 15:1 – A gentle answer turns away wrath, but a harsh word stirs up anger.

Momma had just gotten Sheanna all bundled up on the couch next to Aunt LouAnn, and their favorite movie was loaded in the DVD player. Leah had taken a hot shower, and was in her room, putting her hair in its customary ponytail, occasionally peeking out the window at her Daddy grilling steaks and barbeque chicken in the back yard under the giant oak tree. The rain had stopped and the breeze off the Gulf smelled fresh and clean. That smell mixed with the barbeque made the whole nightmare of that afternoon seem like a bad dream. Except that she had several very painful scrapes, and her lungs and arm muscles still hurt.

Leah bounced down the stairs, and snuggled up next to Sheanna.

"Promise me you'll never do that again, She-she," she whispered, as she stroked the little girl's silky golden hair. "You have to let us know if you want something."

"I won't, Leah. That water tasted nasty! It just snatched me right up!"

"Little girls don't go by the water in a storm. What if lightning had hit you? Then you'd be a crispy critter."

Sheanna squeezed her cousin's arm, "Oh, you're teasing."

"Not really. And as long as we're talking about health issues, when are you going to go see a doctor, Aunt LouAnn? You don't look so good."

LouAnn started at her open-mouthed. "You just called me ugly?"

"No, you look sick. You've looked sick ever since you got down here. I'm not going to lose anybody I love, so I want you to go see Dr. Mendez. He's a great guy, and Momma just loves him."

"Child, I don't think my health is any business of yours. Besides, I'm still adjusting to the heat, and that long trip didn't do me any good either."

"You were healthy as a horse when we got to Milwaukee."

"I'm still healthy as a horse. I just need to get back on my vitamins. Now stop worrying this little girl, and let's watch the movie." Her glare stopped Leah cold.

Oops, why did I say that in front of Sheanna?

"I'm sorry. I guess that little swim today has me all twitter-pated, just like Bambi."

"You're twitter-pated about Mr. Michael." Sheanna grinned a shy grin.

"Maybe one day he'll be Cousin Michael, and if I get my way we'll move right down the block, so he can come tickle you every day."

"He can't catch me," Sheanna bragged, covering a yawn.

Leah stroked the girl's silky hair for a few minutes until Sheanna fell asleep, then Leah laid back and let the drowsiness overtake her.

The loud crash seemed to be a part of Leah's dream. She was back at the Oyster Buoy and a large truck was sliding toward her. The squealing of the metal along the floor was like a thousand fingernails on the world's biggest chalkboard. Leah fought to open her eyes. She knew something was wrong, and she forced herself awake.

Momma was bent over, sweeping some broken glass into the dustpan.

"What happened, Momma?" Leah rubbed her heavy eyes.

"Our friends again," she whispered softly, pointing at the sleeping forms of Aunt LouAnn and Sheanna.

Leah felt the blood rush to her face. Why did some people have to be so hateful? Hadn't they suffered enough?

Leah walked over and slid the dustpan close to the broom.

"Are the police coming again?"

"No, Daddy just put the rock in a lunch bag and he'll take it in when he goes back to work tonight. Or Dan might take it. He should be here for the barbeque any minute. Daddy's pretty sure it's the same kids that we saw last time, and he hopes they'll find some prints on the note."

"What note?"

"Another 'killer' note."

"You're kidding me."

"No, I am sorry to say I'm not."

"I've been wanting to talk to you for a while about Aunt LouAnn, Momma. There's something very wrong with her. She's so weak and tired compared to when we went up to get Sheanna. I wish you'd get her to go see a doctor."

"She's already seen doctors. That's why she called me, and had you girls come and get them."

"Cancer?"

"No, Parkinson's disease. The medication wears her out, but she takes it because her head and hands are so shaky. That's what gave her the nerve to take Sheanna. She knows she's getting weaker. The doctors don't know how long she has, and from what I understand there is nothing anybody can do. Except pray, of course. And we've been praying. Aunt LouAnn wanted to make sure that Sheanna had someone to love her when she leaves this earth. LouAnn will be eighty years old next month, you know, though she's always looked much younger than she is. She's had a good, full life, though I hate to lose her again. You were too little to remember when she ran off and married your Uncle Red twenty years ago. He was a famous saxophone player in Chicago, and left it all for her."

"Musical people are so weird," Leah whispered, "like Sammy."

"Don't worry about Sammy. Daddy says he has a friend in New York looking out for him. We're hoping he'll come back one day soon, when he's done running wild. Your daddy's very different than he used to be; he likes to be home grilling burgers more than chasing criminals. When Sammy was little he—well, he never spent much time with him. He got so consumed with his job that it was like we didn't exist. It hurt Sammy, made him bitter. I hope they can patch things up, and we can have our whole family together again."

"That would be so nice, Momma. I miss him a lot."

"I know you do, Leah. You're both such passionate people. Just don't let that be your undoing. Let the Lord guide you, girl. Don't just jump in without looking first."

"What do you mean, Momma?"

"I mean don't get yourself all into this mess with those hateful people and your daddy. Don't expect Michael to be perfect. Don't be so hard on Hunter."

"You know I'm just joking with Hunter, Momma."

"I know it hurts that Sammy left you. I think you're afraid to love Hunter too much. But Hunter won't leave. He's happy here.

You can let yourself love him, instead of teasing him all the time. I know that every time you and Michael go out you're looking for a hidden flaw, waiting for the axe to fall. But he looks at you like your Daddy looks at me. I pray for you, that your heart will have peace."

"I am happy, Momma."

"Just don't let those old hurts wreck your future. Let Michael make mistakes. Your daddy made his share. He wasn't here much when Sammy was little and needed him. He didn't realize it until it was too late. He's worked hard to make it up to you younger children, but I know it hurts his heart."

"But Sammy never said anything about that, Momma. One day we were in school-- working together and happy. The next, he just left us."

"There were clues. We just didn't want to see them. Now with the death of that Holmes boy, all the hurt has been multiplied over and over. Pray for your daddy, Leah. I know that you know in your head that prayer works, but I promise you from my heart that God will work this all for good. Trust Him."

"I'll do my best. I promise."

Leah heard the roar of an engine pulling into their driveway and peeked out of the window, looking for Michael's truck. He had promised he would be at the barbeque unless something terrible happened, and she wanted to see him so badly. Although they texted back and forth several times a day, she wanted to hear his voice and look into his gold-flecked eyes. She loved the feel of his strong hand at her back, and the little half grin he kept when they were together. But it was only Daddy's partner, Dan.

"Michael will be here soon. You'd better get ready," Momma said, as if reading her thoughts.

Leah sprinted for the bathroom to check her hair and makeup. Then she changed into a silky new blouse she'd found on their shopping trip. She was definitely a 'winter' and the cranberry color complemented her. She touched up her matching toenail polish and slipped into her new sandals, just as she heard Sheanna squeal with joy.

"Mr. Michael. You haven't been here for so long! Did you bring me a treat?"

"Yes, little doll. I brought your favorite, Reese's."

"The little ones?"

"Of course. Here you go."

Michael made the candy appear as if by magic from behind Sheanna's ponytail and handed it to her. Then he turned to Leah in the hallway.

"I have something for you, too," he said.

"Candy?"

"Not exactly."

"Roses?"

"No."

"A new car?"

"Come here and give me some sugar," he said, curling his finger at her.

Leah glanced at Dan, sitting in Daddy's chair, as she loped toward him. He had the strangest look on his face, but Leah wasn't too concerned.

Maybe Dan is lonely, she thought.

Leah slipped a kiss on his lower lip, "Now do I get my treat?"

Michael slipped a small white bag from the back of his waistband.

"Oh, how pretty," Leah said, as she pulled two sparkling barrettes from the bag. "Where did you find them?"

Michael just shook his head. "Why don't you put them on?"

Leah rushed into the bathroom. When she came back out, she noticed an uncomfortable silence in the living room. Dan was staring at Michael, and Michael was breathing too hard. His face was red, and his eyes were black with emotion.

"What's going on, guys?" Leah asked, looking from one to the other.

Dan rose from the chair, "I think I'll go out and help Phil with those burgers."

"Is there a problem?" Leah asked Michael.

"Not really. I don't think your Daddy's friend is ready to see you grow up."

"Oh, is that all? Actually, I used to have a mad crush on Daddy's old partner, Rob. Maybe Dan is jealous that I'm not partial to redheads."

Michael forced a laugh and folded his arms around Leah. "You look very pretty today."

Leah kissed his lips lightly, "You, too. So would you rather stay in here and kiss, or do you want some of Daddy's great cookin'?"

"Both," Michael said, stealing another kiss.

Chapter 14
Prov. 2:12—To deliver you from the way of evil, from the man who speaks perverse things.

Leah watched her father pull out of the driveway early the next morning, and wondered if she should follow him. He had been under so much stress lately that he had actually taken a leave of absence from work. The media had painted him as some sort of irresponsible monster, but Leah knew that something else was working on him. His evasive answers had made Leah very uneasy, and she wondered if he was doing something dangerous. Maybe he hadn't been cured from the call of the adrenaline rush.

The kitchen phone startled her. It sounded incredibly loud in the quiet house, and Leah grabbed it before the shrill ring woke everyone up.

"Daddy?" she said softly.

A cruel laugh sounded on the other end of the phone.

Oh no, more prank calls, Leah thought, as she glanced at the caller I.D. "Listen you sick little—"

"No, you listen," a male voice slurred, "I wanna talk to that little witch Sheanna, or LouAnn. Either one will do."

"Who is this?" Leah demanded, cupping her hand over the receiver so she didn't wake the whole house.

"I'm Sheanna's dad, so you better put her on the phone before I have you locked up for kidnapping."

"Kidnapping? You sick, twisted psycho. I know all about you. You're not Sheanna's dad, and you're the one going to prison!" Leah couldn't keep the shriek out of her voice.

A stream of profanity was her answer; then the phone was taken from her hand.

"Leah, go check on Sheanna. I'll handle this," Momma's eyes seemed to be boring through her, and her tone left no room for argument.

Leah took her hand from the phone and walked slowly toward the stairway.

"Cullen," Momma's voice was steady but firm and she spoke as if she knew him. "This is Beth. You can ask Brinne about me later, but I am telling you that you can take my word to the bank.

Right now I'm going to offer you a deal. One time only."

Leah heard a slight pause; then her Momma spoke again.

"Just listen, and then I'm going to hang up and give you time to think about it. You have a choice. You can go back to prison for a long, long time. Or you can keep the welfare money you've been getting for that little girl and let me take care of her. So here's the deal, Cullen. You are going to let me keep Sheanna and raise her in a decent home with people who will care for her and feed her, and I won't call your parole officer and let him know about the scars you put on that little girl's body. I have a husband who is a police officer. He looked up your record; it was easy for him to find your P.O. I have Mr. Haberman's fax number, and I have plenty of pictures. You're not the only one who knows how to operate a camera. So either you just let things be, or you can go back to living with large, smelly men who hate you. Your choice."

Another pause.

"That would not be a real smart choice, Cullen. Comin' down here would be very expensive, and extremely bad for your health. Do you hear me?"

Momma hung up the phone with a resounding smack.

Leah wanted to clap and cheer, but she was so shocked to hear Beth lie that she was frozen to the spot. Maybe it was to keep him off guard, let him think he was safe until the authorities could pick him up. Leah knew that all the information they could gather had already been faxed to Mr. Haberman, social service agencies in Milwaukee County and Andrews County, and everybody else Daddy thought of who could intervene. The fact that Cullen was still a free man made her even happier that they had gone to get Sheanna. Why wouldn't they keep him in a cage when he'd proven himself an animal? Leah quickly tiptoed up the steps toward Sheanna's room. She opened the door as silently as she could. There was Sheanna, all twisted up in her sheets, thumb in her mouth, looking like a skinny cherub with disheveled golden hair. Leah walked to the bed, bent down and brushed a light kiss across her cheek, happy she was finally feeling at home. It had been two nights since she had last crawled into Aunt LouAnn's bed, and she looked one hundred percent better than when they'd picked her up in Wisconsin. Sheanna's pale skin had been bronzed by the sun, and her cheeks held a healthy pink glow. The veins no longer stuck out on her forehead, and her beautiful aquamarine eyes had lost their sunken appearance. Her hair was thicker and shone like gold. Sheanna's arms and legs no longer looked like twigs. She was still thin, but Leah could look at her without thinking of a TV commercial begging for money to feed third world children. It hurt Leah's heart to think of all the days that little girl had spent alone with no electricity or food, waiting fearfully for Brinne's return, knowing that with her mom came a cruel, hateful man who loved to make her cry. It brought tears to Leah's eyes, and she quietly backed out of the room, vowing she would do everything she could to see that Sheanna had a happy childhood from here on out. Leah tiptoed quickly to the kitchen.

"Momma, do you know anything about this case Daddy is working on with Robbie Colazzo?"

"Did you ask him about it?"

"Yes, and he doesn't want to tell me anything."

"Then you'll just have to trust him. I know it's important if it made him take off of work. With all this harassment lately, Daddy said he wanted to make sure those people knew he wouldn't be intimidated, that he wasn't responsible for a neglected teenager's bad choices. Then he just up and takes time off– which he doesn't even do when he's sick. I'm sure there is a good reason. That's all I can tell you."

"Momma, what if that Cullen comes down here and snatches Sheanna?"

"He is the kind of man who would snatch her just to be cruel, but he won't come down here if he's got any sense. Besides, LouAnn has an ace up her sleeve."

Leah leaned across the table. "What is it?"

"LouAnn has a custody order with her name on it. Brinne spent sixty days in jail last year because she was shoplifting sinus medicine to cook her drugs with. She gave LouAnn temporary custody, but when she got out of jail, Brinne swore that she would do right by her child, so LouAnn gave Sheanna back to her mom. We have a copy of the order; it has never been revoked. With Brinne's record and the scars on Sheanna, we will have a good case when we get to court. It's only a matter of filing at the right time."

"So what are you waiting for?"

"Just waiting. The phone records will show that Brinne knew

Sheanna was here, and did nothing about it. Cooper's call came from a cell phone with a '414' area code– Milwaukee area. We have a court order, coupled with the fact that Brinne is receiving welfare for a child that is not living with her. Once Sheanna has been here six months, we'll file for full custody for abandonment."

"Momma, I always knew you were smart, but you amaze even me."

"I'm glad you don't think I'm old and slow, Honey-girl."

"I never will make the mistake of underestimating you, Momma. Now I'd better get ready for church. There's a good looking guy who will be pulling up in less than an hour and I want to look great."

"You do look great, dear," Beth said, kissing the top of Leah's head. "I'm so glad you're finally happy."

"Momma, I've been wanting to ask you something."

"What's that?"

"Dan doesn't seem to like Michael. Do you know anything about that?"

Beth had a truly surprised look on her face. "I honestly didn't notice. I can't think of anything. Except maybe Dan's just being protective. I'll talk to your father about it, okay?"

Leah kissed her mother on the top of her head. "Thanks, Momma."

Chapter 15
Prov. 4:24 – Put away perversity from your mouth; keep corrupt talk far from your lips.

Yes, ma'am, this is Officer McPhillen from the Ocean Shores Police Department. We're following up on a cold case from August, 2005, and I'd like some information from the Attendance Officer for the school district. Is she available?

"You've got the right number, Officer McPhillen. How can I help you?" the warm voice calmed him.

"I'm investigating the disappearance of two females, approximately twelve years of age, both with red or strawberry blonde hair, who may have disappeared from your area. I wonder, do you have any records of sisters who suddenly stopped attending school, say in 2005 and 2012? Possibly these girls also have a record of unexplained injuries as well?"

"Well sir, as I told the other officer, I've been the attendance officer here for fifteen years. I have no recollection of such a family."

"Other officer?"

"Yes, from Ocean Shores. He just called a few hours ago."

"Okay, Ma'am. Thank you for your help."

Phil shot a text over to Robbie. "U working the case? Thot U needed help."

The answer came just minutes later. "I do need help. Find anything?"

"Not yet. Few more places to check," Phil answered, wondering who else from Ocean Shores could possibly be interested in Robbie's case. The FBI? Nobody mentioned their involvement. They wouldn't have identified themselves as Ocean Shores, though. Maybe Robbie's superior officer hadn't been blowing his ideas off after all. Maybe there was an open case, but why would they lie to him?

Phil's phone rang moments later. He smiled as he glanced at the caller ID.

"Hey, Dan. Are we still going to the football game Friday night?"

"Sure. But I'm wondering about this case you mentioned, the redheaded girl from Hurricane Katrina. Why are you dragging all that up again? We have dozens of cases that weren't closed, other dead bodies that weren't drowned. Why that case, after all this time?"

Phil frowned, "I always hated that we didn't solve that one. She was such a contrast—perfect braids in her hair, those terrible scars, and the tattoo. Something nags at me about that little girl. I'm just making a few calls while I'm on leave, that's all."

"You taking time off? That's crazy too. You're not quitting on us, are you Phil? You're not going to work for the sheriff, are you?"

"No, and I have worked a couple shifts here and there. I'm just waiting for the furor to die down and the kids to stop throwing rocks at my house."

"That reporter just won't let it die—cop-hater. I'm glad she hasn't come after me, and I hope she's never kidnapped."

"Why is that?"

"I wouldn't look too hard for that criminal; I'll tell you that."

Phil laughed. "Hey, I do need to ask you something. My wife mentioned that you didn't seem to take to Leah's new beau. Is there something I need to know?"

"I need you to keep this under your hat, but I have information that he's about to lose his business. I have a buddy who has been trying to buy him out for months. Got in over his head, and owes a bunch of money. Not much of a businessman, I guess. When I asked him about it, he got real defensive. Nasty. Something about him just ain't right."

"I appreciate the info, Dan. But now I got to go to the doctor's office, so I'll let you go."

"Nothing serious, I hope?"

"It's Aunt LouAnn. Beth doesn't think her meds are right, so we're going to see what Dr. Diaz thinks. The old girl hasn't been right since she got here."

"Okay, I'll see you Friday."

Phil hung up his phone, and walked out to the truck where Beth was blowing the horn. Aunt LouAnn was already in the back seat, looking pale and gray. He smiled at his wife.

"Sorry, Beth. Dan called about the game Friday night. Guess he was worried I wouldn't go out in public."

"You're usually the one who has to be early for everything."

"Yes, Baby. We'll make it to the doctor's office in plenty of time, and get dear Auntie here all fixed up."

LouAnn flushed. "I admit that I have felt better. I hope your doctor can help me."

"If he can't, we'll find somebody who can," Beth said. "I know that this sounds terrible, but is there any chance that Brinne took your medicine to sell and replaced it with something else? I've heard of people doing that."

"Brinne hasn't been to my house in a long time. That Cullen was real nasty after the last time Sheanna came over. Said terrible things. He wouldn't let either one of them near me after that. Of course, he was in the apartment when all that happened, but I was feeling fine until just about a week or two ago. I don't think that's the problem, but I have the prescriptions if you want the doctor to take a look at them."

Phil opened one bottle and looked at the pills. "I can't tell by looking at them. I hope it's a simple fix."

"Excuse me, Officer McPhillen, do you have a minute?" Sandra Daschle stood in her front yard, waving her straw hat. "I need to tell you something."

He looked at his wife apologetically and sprinted over to where the older woman stood.

"What can I do for you?" he asked.

"Your dog keeps defecating in my flower bed. I would appreciate it if you would keep him inside the fence. He has been stomping on my flowers, too. I have cleaned up the last droppings. They are in your back yard."

"Thank you for your help, Ma'am. We'll keep a better eye on Trooper. I have to take my wife's aunt to the doctor now. Please excuse me."

"I do not mean to be harsh, but that horse is not welcome in my yard, period. Understood?"

"Yes, Ma'am. I apologize again."

Beth giggled as he returned to the truck. "The great doggy doo-doo caper—Officer McPhillen on the case."

Phil did his best Barney Fife impersonation, "I'm going to nip it in the bud. Yes sir, nip it in the bud, Miss Beth."

"You two kids better stop goofing off and get me to Biloxi or I'm going to miss my appointment. You talked me into it. Now you're stuck with me."

"Aunt LouAnn, we don't know what we did before you and Sheanna came to live with us," Beth said.

"Yes, it's usually so boring and quiet around here. Between the vandals, the football games and the girls running here and there, I don't know how you two get up at the crack of dawn every morning. I'm tired just thinking about it," LouAnn said.

Phil gave his wife a little kiss on the tip of her chin. "That's what gives us our energy. Sugar in the morning, sugar in the evening, loving at suppertime."

LouAnn's eyes shone bright with tears. "You remind me so much of my Red, sometimes Liam. Beth did a good job picking you."

"Picking me? I had to fight both of her brothers just to get close enough to ask for a date. I worked hard for this woman. And I'm still working hard for her. See that perfectly manicured lawn?"

Beth threw her head back and laughed. "Okay, tough guy. Let's hit the road."

Chapter 16
Prov. 1:22 How long will you simple ones love your simple ways...

"Michael, it's Leah. Please call me back right away. Shay just gave me two free tickets to Summer-Slam tonight, and I need to know if you can come with me. It's got some of my favorite bands, and I really want to go. Call me soon."

Hunter snuck up behind Leah and poked her in the ribs.

"What's the big emergency?"

Leah was almost jumping up and down with excitement.

"Well, you know I had to work late the day Summer-Slam tickets went on sale, and of course they sold out in ten minutes."

"I got mine," Hunter teased.

"Yeah, but no date. Which one of the football players are you bringing?"

"I do have a *female* date, smarty. How did you get tickets?"

"Lucky Miss Shay. She got four tickets, and her sister and brother-in-law just canceled—sick kids. So she gave them to me. Tenth row!"

"I'm only two rows behind you."

"Where you need to be—behind me."

"If Michael can't go, you can give me your extra ticket. Toby Lipschitz won't mind competing with your hair for a seat."

Leah pushed her brother away.

"Fat chance. I'll take Daschle before you get my tickets."

"Huh, like she'd go to a Christian concert? She thinks we're terribly ignorant folks, you know."

"Better a snobby neighbor than a brainless jock!"

"You used to like quite a few of those 'brainless jocks' not too long ago."

"I like strength—and muscles. At least I finally found a guy who has brains and build—unlike your buddies. Any conversation that doesn't revolve around them or football is bound to fail. And I do believe that's my hunk of burning love calling now."

Hunter rolled his eyes and stalked into the kitchen, as Leah answered her phone.

"Hello?"

"Leah, it's Michael."

"I was hoping you'd call me right back."

"I would love to go to the concert tonight, but I'm not quite finished. Can you meet me in Mobile about seven?"

"Yes, Shay and I have reserved seats. How about we meet at the Civic Center? I'll be watching for you at the South entrance."

"See you in a couple hours. Love you!"

"Love you, too," she whispered, the words sounding strange to her.

Of course she loved Michael as a person, but did she really, truly love him? He did make her heart thunder like a racehorse, and she enjoyed every stolen moment they spent together, but was that 'true love'? Was there even such a thing? She sunk down into the sofa, thinking about how Sammy had been there for her all of her life, her favorite brother, her musical partner, her study buddy. Then he was just gone. Exactly like her high school sweetheart. Trey had been as close to her as anyone in the family most of high school. They did their homework together. They went to Junior Prom together, and were voted 'cutest couple'. Being with him was as easy as breathing. Then Senior year, two weeks before graduation, Trey dumped her for Jessica Petrowski, the head cheerleader. Jessica was brilliant, beautiful, and everybody liked her. Everyone except her younger sister, Patti, which was just fine with Leah. Leah begged Trey for an explanation, but one never came. He just shrugged and walked away. Sammy said she could forget an explanation because a guy can't stand to see a girl cry.

"Then why did he make me cry?" she'd raged. Why do they all end up making me cry?

Sammy had wrapped his arms around her and held her while she cried. Sammy, who was always there when she needed him, had similarly abandoned her just two short years later.

So Leah had decided that she didn't need a man. She needed a career. That would never break her heart. She threw herself into her studies, and graduated magna cum laude. Her momma had known Mr. Alexander since first grade, and he'd hired Leah the week after graduation. Now she had a great job, and a healthy bank account. But she wasn't sure if her heart was healthy yet. Daddy's motorcycle wreck had shaken her to the core just when she'd thought she was over losing her high school sweetheart and her brother without any warning. If he had left her, she didn't know what she would do. But Daddy didn't die. He came back better, more *there.*

Was Michael the man he seemed to be? Or would he break her heart at the last minute like the others? Leah hated the raw ache, way deep down, that never seemed to leave her. Why couldn't she trust? Was she supposed to be alone forever? Why did Michael say he loved her after only a few short weeks? Did he, really? Or was it another temporary love that would fly away just as she embraced it?

Leah's phone rang again. It was Shay.

"Hey, girl. Are you gonna ride with us, or is Michael coming to get you?"

"I'll ride to the Civic Center with you and Landon if you don't mind. I'm supposed to meet Michael there."

"Sounds good. We'll pick you up in fifteen minutes."

The phone clicked off, and Leah looked at her watch. Fifteen minutes! She hurried to her room to get ready.

It seemed only moments later that Landon's purple low-rider truck was in the driveway, beeping his obnoxious horn that played some old trumpet tune for the whole neighborhood to hear. Leah ran out of the front door, and slipped into the back seat.

"Wow, you look great, Leah," Landon purred. "If I wasn't engaged to Shay, I'd be givin' you a call, you hear me girl?"

As if you'd have a chance, Leah thought, a toothy smile plastered on her face. *Why do you waste your time with this creep, Shay?*

"You're so funny, Landon," Shay whispered. "You do look good, Leah. That royal blue is perfect for you."

"I hope Michael thinks so."

"He will," Shay said. "I have a feeling you won't be riding home with us after the concert."

"It'll be going until midnight. I don't think we'll be able to go anywhere afterward. I have a staff meeting at work tomorrow. It's almost time for the yearly audit, and you know what that means."

"Yeah, I won't be seeing you for a couple of weeks."

"So we'd better enjoy tonight."

"Oh, I plan to. There's only one band I don't like, and they're playing second. That's when I'll stock up on the junk food."

"I'm with you. I hate that rap music; it's so NOT musical."

"You girls are crazy. That band's the only reason I'm going

to this thing."

Leah bit her lip, knowing that Shay had paid for their tickets. She really wanted to say something to put Landon in his place, but knew that Shay would be hurt if she did.

Landon turned up the radio, and they rode in silence for a few minutes until they reached the exit.

"Wow, it's packed already. We're never going to find a parking spot," Leah complained.

"I know a good spot, "Landon said. "All the news trucks park back there, and there's usually a few extra spaces."

"Don't you need a pass?"

"I have one, from when my brother was a courier for the NBC station in Mobile."

"Where's he working now?"

"Delivering pizzas up at Hattiesburg. He says he makes a lot more in tips, but I think he just wants to meet college girls."

"Doesn't he have enough? The guy has a new girlfriend every two weeks."

"Well, he says he won't be able to play football forever, so he'd better get as many dates as he can now."

Leah bit her lip hard, praying she wouldn't blurt out something that would wreck the whole night.

"Here's a good spot," Shay announced. "Hey, look at that."

Two people were leaning up against the WWMS-TV news van, a tangle of lips and arms.

"Get a room!" Landon yelled.

"Drop dead," the girl answered, untangling one arm long enough to flash a rude gesture.

Leah recognized the childlike voice of Patti Petrowski. What was *she* doing at a Christian concert? Was she here to smear the good name of the musicians? Leah took out her cell phone, and decided to snap a few pictures.

"Hey, give me that phone!" the man screamed, swinging his arm toward Leah.

"Private property, Bud. Patti loves to smear my family; I'm just trying to return the favor."

"There's no law against kissing," Patti sneered.

"Tell that to Buddy's wife, Patti," Shay growled. "I'm sure she'd be interested to know how he spends his spare time."

"They're separated!" Patti screeched.

"Then why were they shopping together at the Food Tiger on Saturday?" Landon said casually.

Patti glared at them, her slimy pale skin glistening in the twilight. "Don't you have somewhere to be?"

"There are plenty of Pastors inside, Patti. Maybe you could go find one of them and get some counseling."

"I don't need a man to tell me how to live."

"Somebody should," Leah answered. "You do nothing but hurt people, and the scariest thing is, you probably think you're a pretty good person. How can Jessica be so sweet when you're such a disaster? You're like a giant oil slick."

"I'm not a killer like your Daddy, if that's what you mean."

"You know that's a lie," Leah was itching to slap Patti's smug pasty face.

"Let's go, Leah," Shay soothed. "We don't need to be a part of this."

"Your day is coming, Patti. You'll reap what you've sown, believe me."

"Huh. I'll believe it when I see it," Patty huffed, and then slipped her hand on the back of Buddy's neck.

Leah shook her head, and secretly snapped several more pictures with her phone as she slowly walked behind Shay and Landon. The girl had absolutely no shame, but maybe the pictures could be useful one day.

As they neared the south entrance, Leah was thrilled to see Michael waiting. He was early, and he looked so handsome in the fading light. He was leaning back against the building, his tanned muscular arms contrasting starkly with his white polo shirt. A slight breeze rifled through his silky hair, which had blonde highlights from the sun. He seemed to be daydreaming and Leah wanted nothing more than to kiss that half-smile on his face, but Landon would have complained half the night about "ridiculous displays of affection". Landon, whose idea of showing Shay affection was picking her momma's flowers to give her a Valentine's bouquet.

As if he felt her stare, Michael met her eyes, and his grin widened.

"Hey, beautiful. How about going out tonight?" he called.

"Any time, big boy," Landon called back. "If you don't mind

that I already have a date."

Leah ran up to Michael and threw her arms around him. "I was hoping you'd ask. You're the best looking thing here."

"So, you've been looking. I guess I'd better be more careful when we go out."

"Yes," Leah grinned. "I always make sure I'm with the best guy possible, and you definitely fit the description."

Landon just had to cut in, "Even with me here, Babe? I know I'm quite a catch, but it would probably make your best friend a little jealous if we hooked up."

Shay slapped Landon's arm. "You're terrible."

"I'll try to control myself," Leah said, keeping her voice as steady as she could. She'd love to slap him, but not his arm.

I wouldn't date you if you were the last male on earth! Leah thought. *Shay's too good for your sorry tail, and I wish she'd dump you like girls dump your loser brother!*

Michael slipped his arm around her waist and Leah hugged him.

"Tonight is going to be so fun. Thanks so much for the tickets, Shay. I owe you one," Michael said, ignoring Landon's comment.

"This is the best concert of the year. I'm happy to share," she answered.

"Oh, so we're back to the sharing thing," Landon said. "She's so physical. I'd better marry her soon and make an honest woman out of her."

Leah's mouth dropped open, speechless. Did Landon really love somebody beside himself? He'd been dating Shay on and off since high school and he'd never mentioned anything about making it permanent. This night just kept getting more interesting.

"Shay, I think the pod people got your date. Landon just said the word 'marry' without choking."

Shay flashed her left hand at her friend. A tiny diamond glinted in the last rays of the sun. "We were going to have a party and announce it. But now you know. Will you be my maid of honor?"

Leah screamed and threw her arms around her friend, though her insides churned with concern. "I'll do anything you want! Have you set a date?"

"July 5th, because most of the families have the 4th of July weekend off. We've already met with Pastor Alan, and the date is on the church calendar."

"Boy, you miss choir for one week, and everything changes!"

"I've got more news for you, too. Rose is expecting again. That's another reason we wanted to get married early. In case she's put on bed rest again. I'm just having two attendants—you and her."

"Oh, Shay. It'll be so fun to plan the wedding. What did your Momma say?"

"She already has the hall booked at Preston's Marina. We'll have an elegant waterfront dinner with all her friends, and then my friends get to eat cake and dance until our feet hurt."

"Only bad thing is no alcohol. I'll have to sneak it in," Landon complained.

"What do you mean?" Michael asked.

"Preston's doesn't allow alcohol at all. Not on the beach, at the marina, in the restaurant, nothing. But since Gemma is paying for the whole thing, I wasn't going to argue. We'll have good eats anyway," Landon said.

"Gemma?" Michael asked.

"Shay's momma," Leah answered.

Shay beamed and leaned against Landon's arm. "I guess we'd better get inside. I hear the crowd starting to scream and we don't want anyone to take our seats. We'll have plenty of time to talk about this later."

You bet we'll talk, Shay, Leah thought. *You can do so much better than this.*

Chapter 17
Prov. 17:4 A wicked man listens to evil lips; a liar pays attention to a malicious tongue.

Phil turned off his cell phone and threw it down on the bed. His voice mail was full of hateful venom, and he was tired of being beaten up for something he couldn't change. He didn't know how the unstable folks had managed to get his cell phone number, but unlike his wife, he didn't care if everyone had to learn another number. It was time to get a new phone. The one message he had kept was from Robbie, thanking him for trying to track down the family of the tattooed girl. Phil had found no matches on the strange tattoos, though he'd faxed every tattoo shop in a two hundred mile radius, and found only three missing-endangered reports in a hundred mile radius from 2005. None of the girls had been strawberry blondes. It was a puzzle that his mind kept trying to solve. Who would torture and kill two beautiful young girls, and why? Why were there no records of them being missing? Didn't they go to school? If not, how did the parents hide them? Was it just two dead children, or were there more out there? Now that he was back at work full time, maybe he could find out.

Phil tiptoed out of the room, trying not to wake his wife and Sheanna, who had crawled into their bed sometime during the night. Dr. Diaz had admitted LouAnn immediately and said she would likely be in the hospital for several days until they could straighten out her medication. Sheanna had not taken the news well, and had clung to Beth like a sand burr ever since they'd returned from Biloxi.

Phil bit his lip as he took one last look at the little girl curled up next to his wife. What had she endured in her short life? He knew there were families who flew completely under the radar; he had dealt with a few of them in the past twenty years. Usually the parent—there had never been two—was an addict, living in vacant houses or camping in small stretches of woods in untended lots. The children often became small versions of their toxic caregivers by the age of nine or ten, looking for their next easy buck and subsequent high. Often they were brain-damaged or permanently scarred, in body and mind. The laws were written so they'd be quickly returned to their abusers, and he often chased the same kids over and over again, until they had kids. Once he'd helped deliver a baby, born to a thirteen year-old mother in a falling-down shack affectionately referred to as the "Manatee cottage", named after the pleasant street it sat on. The city had been trying to demolish it for years, but the owner was a lawyer who kept the yard cut, and who was determined that the rickety trash heap would one day be declared a historical monument. She kept litigation going from several angles. Each time the city won a victory, another court order appeared. Every year, the house sagged more, drug dealers moved in and out, and the police walked more carefully on the rotting floorboards as they chased derelicts and passionate teens from the crumbling ruin. Phil walked to the driveway and mounted his police motorcycle, as thunder rumbled ominously in the distance. He was glad Beth was sleeping, since he could see the worry in her eyes every time she knew he wasn't in the safe confines of a police car, but working at night on the 'cycle he was relatively anonymous. It was the only way he could do his job, and just a few days off had left him bored and restless beyond belief.

    Thoughts of the Manatee cottage kept swirling through his mind, and he decided to do a little walk-through. It had been a while since the neighbors had called, but for some reason his mind kept returning to the house, and he decided to act on it.

    Phil pulled his motorcycle into the driveway, and looked intently at the dark windows. Nothing moved, and all was quiet. He called his dispatcher and relayed the address out of habit, then carefully walked past huge oaks draped with moss up the front steps onto the wide porch. The house dated back to the 1850s. There were two doors in front, from the days when masters and servants didn't enter through the same place. He turned the knob on the left, and the door squeaked open. As Phil turned on his flashlight and stepped inside, a chill inched down his spine. For some reason, he felt like he was entering his own tomb. Every nerve tingled, and his ears strained for even the tiniest sound, but all he heard were his own footsteps on the creaking boards. Upstairs he heard a sudden crash, then the sound of running feet. He ascended as swiftly as he dared; hoping it was just kids playing around.

    "Police officer! Come out where I can see you," Phil shouted.

    Glass crashed; someone cursed, and several thuds sounded both above him and in the overgrown back yard. Phil decided to go upstairs and look around first, hoping again that it was just kids. He moved stealthily, hoping there were no surprises at the top of the stairs. The burned plastic marijuana smell wafted toward him and he tried not to cough.

Something knocked him hard on the back of the head. As he fell, he heard more running feet. His flashlight flew through a hole in the floorboards and disappeared. The splintered floor tore into his knees as he scrambled to his feet, his senses on hyper-alert watching for another attack.

"Police officer," he called out again, holding his pistol against his leg and sliding his back tightly against the wall. "Is anybody there?"

A faint sob was his answer. He walked faster, thankful for the lightning, which illuminated the hallway as he stepped around several holes in the hardwood floor. Thick clouds of marijuana smoke filled the hall, burning his eyes.

"Help," a small voice said. "I cut myself."

"Are you alone?" Phil asked.

"Yes sir, I'm bleeding bad. I think I'm gonna throw up."

Phil rounded the corner into the room where a short chubby boy about ten years old sat on the floor holding his arm. It had a large gash on it, and there was plenty of blood, but not the pulsing stream of a sliced artery.

Phil looked closely to ensure there was no glass in the cut, pulled his handkerchief from his pocket, and pressed it against the wound.

"Hold it tightly here," he told the trembling child. "I'm calling you an ambulance."

Phil called his dispatcher and relayed the request.

The boy looked up at him with huge eyes and said, "I'm not going to jail?"

"Did you do something wrong?" Phil asked gently. "You didn't break this window, did you? I heard the others running away. And you're not tall enough to have knocked me in the head."

Tears of relief clouded the child's eyes. "You right. I didn't do it."

"What are you doing, smoking that junk at your age? You guys shouldn't mess around in here. One day somebody's going to fall through the floor and really get hurt."

"I didn't want to, Sir, but my brother and—"the child bit

back the words that tumbled from his lips.

"Okay, Son. Let's just walk downstairs, okay? Do you think you can walk?"

The boy stood, wobbling slightly as his bare feet picked their way across the rough floor. "My name's DeJuan. I can get downstairs okay."

Phil noticed lights flashing across the windows. "Your ride is here, DeJuan."

The child peered fearfully out at the ambulance. "Momma's gonna kill me."

"We gotta get that arm fixed up."

He helped the child down the stairs, and out onto the front porch where his favorite EMT, Lani Randall, waited with her first aid kit open.

"This is DeJuan, Lani. He cut his arm on some glass."

She lifted the handkerchief and blood oozed onto the porch step.

"You're gonna need some stitches for this one, DeJuan. Didn't you just have a broken arm at Christmas time?"

The child's eyes rolled back into his head, and he fell into Phil's arms. "You really have a way with kids, Lani."

She grinned, "That's what they tell me. C'mon, let's get him on the gurney."

As Phil carried the boy back to the ambulance, the sky turned ominously dark, and thunder and lightning crackled around them.

"Let me take a look at that gash across your ear. You have a knot right above it, too. When was your last tetanus shot?"

"After the wreck, but I'll probably get another one when Beth sees that gash. Hey, I've got a question for you. Do you remember seeing a family with two or three red headed girls? Strawberry blonde, not ginger with tattoos on their wrists. It would have been some kind of abuse case, a strange injury or domestic violence. Somewhere off the beaten path. Have you heard of anything like that?"

"No, I can't say that I have. I've patched up a few red headed kids, but nothing unusual. Why?"

"Oh, it's an old case I've been thinking about. Abuse always gets to me."

"I know what you mean," Lani whispered. "Speaking of

abuse, Dad told me what you did. You know, about those kids and that wreck. Thanks for taking that bullet for him."

"Oh, those nasty vultures in the press didn't need anyone else to ruin. I'm just glad he let me know the kids were coming. They could've done a lot more damage than they did, racing around at lunch time like that."

"Too bad they didn't report the truth. That boy was doing 85 in a school zone! Of course you needed to stop him. I don't understand why nobody's asking why he's listed as being from Saucier, but was skipping school in Ocean Shores. Why was he so far from home? Who was taking care of him? Where was Momma when he was out terrorizing the streets? She's all over the news now that there's money in it for her."

"It's okay, Lani. I'm sure the truth will come out soon enough, and we can put this all behind us," Phil said, but he was glad to hear that someone knew the truth. He was tired of thinking everyone hated him for simply doing his job. He didn't mind being cursed at by criminals, but when regular people did it, he lost sleep.

"I bet there's a lot of interesting information about that family in Saucier, if somebody wanted to look into it. She's Daddy's stepsister you know, the Momma. That's how Daddy knew Bobby Max was up to no good."

Phil nodded as they loaded the child into the ambulance, mentally making a note to text that information to his attorney's office. It was a lead, and he couldn't afford to miss even one.

Lani waved a small ampoule under DeJuan's nose, and his eyes snapped open.

"Stinks," he said, making a face. Phil noticed he was missing his two front teeth.

"Welcome back, kiddo. Let's get you to the hospital."

Phil stepped out of the ambulance, and his heart sunk to his feet. In front of him stood Patti Petrowski, flashing a blinding light in his eyes, as she gave yet another live news report that featured Officer Liam McPhillen.

She stuck a microphone in his face. "Officer McPhillen, how is that you and injured children seem to always appear together?"

"Young lady, I have no comment for you. Find someone else to harass."

"Did you hurt that young boy?"

Lani was at Phil's side in a flash. "For your information, Patti, Phil probably saved that boy's life—as he's saved many lives. Go hunt for some real news, will you?"

Patti turned and faced the camera "man", a large woman with short spiky rainbow hair. "In Ocean Shores, it seems officer McPhillen and wounded children go together. For WWMS news, I'm Patti Petrowski, live on the case in Ocean Shores."

Thunder boomed, and the sky opened up. It seemed buckets of water were falling from the clouds. Phil hoped the expensive camera would be ruined so Patti would be fired and quit stalking him. He rushed to his motorcycle, and pulled his slicker from the storage compartment under the seat. He hoped to get it back to the station before he was completely drenched, but it didn't look promising. For once, the paperwork looked inviting. He waved at Lani; then he sped away.

Chapter 18

Song of Songs 2:13—"…Arise, come, my darling; my beautiful one, come with me.'"

"Will this phone ever stop ringing?" Leah said as she snatched up the receiver. "Hello?"

"Leah, this is Gator. What time do you get off work on Friday?"

"Four o'clock, why?"

"It's Michael's 30th birthday, and he's helping me at that Shrimp Boil for that little boy with leukemia. I'm hoping you'll help me surprise him."

"Sure. What do you want me to do?"

"Just show up. Invite your family, and those two friends of yours Michael likes, Shay and her boyfriend."

"Easy enough. Where's the shrimp boil?"

"Fowl River Marina. It starts at seven, so if you could be here at six, we can have a little pre-party for Michael in the pavilion before the crowds get here."

"Good. My parents aren't much for crowds, these days. Is it okay for a little kid to be there? I'd like to bring my cousin, Sheanna."

"She will love it. Wear black, and look for the black balloons."

Leah snorted. *Gator had to be close to sixty, and he was having everybody wear black for Michael's 30th?* she thought. *It will be nice to meet some of their other friends and the guys he works with.*

Leah went to the chalkboard on the refrigerator and wrote a huge note: Michael 30th Birthday Party Friday @ 6—Fowl River Marina. Wear black. ALL are invited!

"What does that say, Cousin Leah?"

"We're invited to Mr. Michael's birthday party. Wanna go?"

"Yes. Will there be cake and ice cream?"

"I know there will be cake, and if there isn't any ice cream, Daddy will get you some on the way home, okay?"

"Let's go."

"It's not until Friday. I have to talk to Momma and Daddy, too."

"What about Granny LouAnn?"

"She's invited, if she wants to come. But she may still be weak from all those tests in the hospital."

Hunter walked in. "If I know her, she'll want to go. With Gator being from Louisiana, it may just feel like home to LouAnn. She loves a party, as long as the food is good."

"Don't we all—I think it's in the blood."

Beth called from the living room, "We're coming!"

"We who?"

"Daddy, LouAnn and me."

Leah swung Sheanna up into her arms and carried her into the living room, swinging her side to side.

"Cool. Can you all ride in Daddy's truck, and I'll bring my car in case I want to stay late?"

"What about your truck, Hunter? Is it coming out of the shop any time soon?"

"I get paid tomorrow, and that's when I'll have it back."

Leah snorted. "Maybe we'll get to know the tennis star a little better. Hey, I forgot to call Shay."

Sheanna kicked her legs over her head and flipped to the floor.

"I'll go get your phone." She took off running, her usual mode of transportation, with Trooper loping behind her.

"It's in the car," Leah reminded her. "I forgot to bring it in after work."

Sheanna zipped out the side door. "Got it."

A few moments later she walked in, chatting with Shay on the phone.

"And Leah says they'll have cake and we have to wear black. I don't think I have anything black. Guess I'll wear my Tweedy swimsuit."

"You cannot wear your swimsuit every day. I'll find you something black. Now give me my phone, little monkey."

"I am not a monkey. I'm a cheetah like Spot, and Trooper is my elephant."

She handed Leah the phone, patted Trooper on the head, and ran out into the back yard. Trooper galloped behind her like a puppy.

"Hey, Shay. You got plans for Friday night?"

"I do now. I can't wait to see all those fine construction workers you've been telling me about."

"I do not ogle construction workers. That was one conversation, last April. And I only have eyes for my man. You finally dumping Landon's skinny tail? Because there are a couple of guys at the office who would love to take you out to a real restaurant and a movie that does not star Sylvester Stallone."

Shay laughed. "You are so funny. Actually, Landon is going to some wrestling thing with his brothers, so I'm a free woman. What are you wearing?"

"Jeans, and that black shirt we got at FashioNation last week."

"Oh, I like that one. Are you wearing your black boots with all the buckles?"

"It'll probably be my flip flops, but I'll get back to you on that one."

"Okay, I'll meet you after work. Say, 5:30?"

"Sure, that sounds good. Now I don't have to get another lecture from Daddy about driving with that headlight out."

"Girl, when are you going to get that fixed?"

"The next time Mr. Alexander lets me off early enough. Which may be never."

"Let Hunter take your car in."

"That boy is not driving my car. He'll probably let his jock friends drool all over it, and then I'll have to have it cleaned, or worse, somebody will take a baseball bat to it like they did his truck."

"Okay, keep driving it until you get a ticket. Then your daddy will really have something to fuss about."

"Yes, dear. I'll see you on Friday, dear. Goodbye." Leah turned and flicked her hair out of her eyes. "Okay, Momma. I'm off to choir practice. See you later."

"Aren't you going to ride with us?"

"No, I feel like walking. After the day I've had, I need some fresh air and sunshine. But I will take a ride home."

"Okay, I'll meet you in the back of the church."

The next two days passed quickly, and before she knew it, Leah was in Shay's car, pulling up to the Fowl River Marina pavilion. She had Michael's present in her lap, a pack of sleeveless t-shirts, a Saints cap and his favorite treats—homemade caramel brownies, chocolate chip cookies, and a four-pack of energy drinks. She threw in a bottle of Centrum Silver in keeping with the "old age" theme, and packed it in a black and gray camouflage duffel bag with a huge black bow.

Shay had gotten him a $25 movie gift card, which Leah thought was a great idea. It was even black.

Gator had black balloons tied to each corner of the pavilion and black tablecloths on the picnic tables. A chocolate sheet cake with black candles sat in the middle of the first table, and black plates, cups and plastic utensils sat neatly piled next to the cake. There was also a huge bowl of crawfish, with little red potatoes and corn on the cob pieces interspersed between them. The other bowl was piled high with shrimp. Both bowls were black, of course. Gallons of sweet tea sat in a cooler filled with ice, and Leah was grateful that Gator had held off on the beer until her parents left. Daddy had dealt with enough drunks over the years that he wasn't much fond of alcohol, except an occasional toast at a wedding or retirement party.

Leah looked around for Michael, and saw him sitting off to the side, looking embarrassed.

"Happy Birthday," Leah said, placing his gift in front of him. Her family came behind her, and soon Michael had a stack of gifts in front of him.

"Now that you know I'm an old man, do you still want to go out with me?"

"You really think thirty is old? My brother Sammy is 28. You're not that much older than him. Plus, I like the idea of you being older. Now you can never call me your 'old lady'."

Shay laughed. "Leah always fusses at Landon for calling me that. Funniest thing is, Landon's only three weeks younger than I am."

"And you're much better looking than he is," Leah added.

"Where is Landon?" Michael asked.

"Some wrestling thing with his brothers. He said to tell you 'hi' and he hopes you have a good one."

"It's already good. I'm glad y'all came."

They sang "Happy Birthday" and cut the cake, and soon everyone was stuffed from eating too much food. Then more people started to arrive for the shrimp boil, and Momma and Daddy said their goodbyes. They had to pry Sheanna off of Michael's lap, and even Aunt LouAnn seemed to have a great time.

"Okay," Michael said. "Now that the sprite is gone, you can sit in my lap." He flashed a devilish grin at Leah.

"I'd rather meet your friends. You know, the guys you work with. Gator's buddies, too. I feel like there's so much I don't know about you."

"Okay, come meet my much-less-better-looking crew."

He grabbed Leah's hand and reintroduced her to Chase and several men whose names she would never remember. Shay kept busy handing out plates of shrimp and playing 'the hostess with the mostest' as Michael called her.

Leah smacked him in the arm. "Are you flirting with my best friend?" she asked. "You heard she's engaged."

"Of course not. Just complimenting her on her wonderful serving skills. But if you would have sat in my lap, I may be lavishing you with wonderful compliments right now."

"Like what?"

"Well, I'd start with that gorgeous mane of black hair, and then your beautiful chestnut brown eyes, and then your sweet little pointy nose."

Michael kissed Leah on the end of her nose, and then Leah heard a resounding slap right next to her face.

"Michael, what are you doing?" an obviously drunk girl with dirty blonde hair shrieked.

"Renee, I'd like you meet my girlfriend, Leah."

"Your girlfriend? You jerk! How could you bring a girl here?"

Michael grabbed Renee by the arm and walked toward where Gator was cooking, about ten yards away.

Leah just stood there watching, the shock numbing her from head to toe.

She couldn't make out the voices, but then she heard, "You don't love her. You can't love her. You love Rachel!"

Leah turned, and hurried away to find Shay, her heart sinking to her feet. He loves Rachel? I knew he was too good to be true. He loves Rachel? Who is she?

Leah felt the hot tears running down her face, blurring her vision. Where was Shay? She needed to leave. She needed to leave now. This was too much. How could he lie to her? Why did he lie to her?

Somebody had grabbed her arm, spinning Leah around.

"Leah, please don't cry. Please let me explain. Please, Leah," Michael said. "Come sit in the truck, and let me explain."

"I can't let all these people see me like this. I have to find Shay."

"She's getting more shrimp for Gator."

"Then I'll wait in her car."

"You got a key?"

"No."

"Then you're better off sitting in the truck, right? Come with me, Leah. I've been wanting to tell you about Rachel for a while, but I didn't know how. There is no other woman."

Leah followed him to his company truck, willing herself to stop crying, but it was no use. The hot tears continued to stream down, no matter how she tried to control her breathing, she couldn't stop the tears from burning salt trails down her cheeks. When she got to the truck, she slid into the passenger seat, and wiped her face with the top of her shirt.

"So who's Rachel?" she asked, ashamed of the misery in her voice.

"She was, she was my wife. She died eight years ago. Her sister Renee, that girl you saw, was her sister. She never got over it. She thought I never should either. And I almost never did."

The tears were still coursing down her face, and she wiped them away with the back of her hand.

"Why didn't you tell me, Michael? You were married? Don't you think that's an important piece of information?"

"She's dead, Leah. I haven't spoken of it. Even Gator and I don't talk about Rachel. It wasn't pretty, Leah. She was a drug user, needles. She contracted Hepatitis, and her liver just gave out. She couldn't fight it. Her little body was just too weak. She killed herself with that junk. We tried to get her help so many times, but she killed herself."

Leah looked into his tear-filled eyes, and felt the anger and self-pity melt away. She touched her finger to the side of his face, catching a fat tear.

"I'm so sorry, Michael. It was just such a shock. I couldn't believe that you'd been married and you never told me. I don't like surprises, and I, I'm sorry I wrecked your birthday."

Michael kissed her lightly on the cheek. "You didn't wreck my birthday. I should have told you. I honestly didn't know how."

Leah kissed his jaw softly. Then Michael was pulling her toward him, his kisses searing her lips, burning through her body. Her blood felt like lava in her veins, and it took every ounce of her will to push him away.

Chapter 19
Prov. 11:10- ...When the wicked perish, there is joyful shouting.

Cullen pulled into the driveway. It was well hidden among the trees, but he had good directions. He could tell that this guy was used to sending people down this bumpy country road and somebody made sure it was passable. He had ditched the old lady's car for a truck in Memphis, the stolen car capital of the USA, and it handled the rutted road well.

Soon Cullen pulled up to a group of three small shacks, each painted with a garish ménage of colors. Two other trucks stood in the yard. One was a new red F-150 and the other looked like something ransomed from a junkyard. As he pulled up, he saw a greasy haired kid of about sixteen walk out of the mostly-pink building and climb into the red truck. He gunned the engine and spun the tires as he made his way down the road. A young redheaded girl stood in the doorway, a look of confusion on her face. Somebody quickly pulled her back into the shack and slammed the door.

Cullen walked up to the mostly blue building as he'd been instructed and knocked at the door. He'd never worked with a partner before, and he hoped that he was making the right choice now.

Chapter 20
Prov. 13:19- Desire realized is sweet to the soul...

"I'm sorry. I've gotta go. I'll find Shay before everybody sees me looking like this. Goodbye, Michael. Happy Birthday."

"The bathrooms are right over there. I'll find Shay and send her over there. Please don't leave. It won't be the same without you."

Leah sprinted to the bathroom and ran cool water over her face until the burning stopped. She felt a hand on her shoulder and turned to see her best friend looking at her with the strangest look on her face.

"What?"

"Why are you trying to chase Michael away? Do you have something against happiness, Leah?"

"What?"

"So he was married years ago. So what? You've only gone out a few times, and it's not something a guy is going to send you a text about. Now you're going to run away because you didn't get the full life history? Didn't Sammy teach you how much running away hurts others? That man is miserable, and you did it, Leah. He's the best guy you've ever had, and you're going to leave him like this on his birthday?"

"Shay, don't you think that was an important piece of information? I told him about Trey, and Sammy. I just thought—"

"You think a high school boyfriend and an ambitious brother are the same as losing the woman you love? Have you forgotten about Rose?"

"About the babies? No, I haven't forgotten, but--"

"Having somebody die is light years worse than a break up or a brother that doesn't call. I thought watching my sister have all those miscarriages would have taught you something about death."

"I know about death."

"Who? Two uncles and grandparents you never knew? You've never lost anyone close to you. Not really, Leah. Why do you have to be so hard-core all the time? Give Michael a break. He told you about his parents. That was probably all he could handle. He's lost a lot more than you have, and you're acting like he purposely tried to hurt you. Why are you throwing happiness away with both hands?"

"Why are you going to marry that loser?"

Shay began to pace. "Oh, now I have a problem? Landon is my best friend. He has a good job, and he loves me. He's the only guy I ever really cared about, and we've been dating for seven years. It's time."

"He isn't very good to you. Why do you want a guy like that? He's so stuck on himself!"

"That's just an act. He does love me, Leah. You'll just have to trust me. They don't give teacher's licenses to idiots, you know."

Leah splashed water on her face and thought about Michael's story. She knew about hurt too deep to mention. Maybe Shay had a point. She forced herself to smile a tight little grin and said, "Actually, sometimes they do. Mrs. Finley was a teacher."

"Now I'm like crazy old Mrs. Finley? You are really losing it, girl! That was fifteen years ago, and her daddy was on the school board. Now she terrorizes everybody who comes to the library. What does that have to do with Michael?"

"You need to leave Michael alone! He'll never love you like he loved Rachel!" Renee stood there, all four foot six of her, with her hair a tangled burgundy-with-blue highlights-mess and black makeup trails running down her face. The alcohol on her breath almost knocked Leah over.

Shay just stood there, her mouth hanging open in shock.

Renee sucked deeply on her cigarette and threw it down at Leah's feet.

"My sister gave him everything, and this is what she gets. He was her first love, you know? There never was any other guy for her but Michael. And now he's stomping on her grave. Stomping on her grave!"

"I'm so sorry for your loss," Leah whispered. "I didn't know."

Renee pushed past Leah and Shay and ran into the first stall. She began retching into the toilet, and the girls quickly walked out.

"Please, Leah. Take this mirror, go fix your make-up and rejoin the party. Michael looks like he just lost his best friend."

"Well, maybe he did," Leah snapped, but she took the mirror from Shay and walked toward the river.

She could still feel the heat in her face as she walked, so she slipped off her flip-flops and put her feet into the cool river water. Frogs croaked and mosquitoes buzzed around her as she tried to put her feelings into some kind of order. As disgusting as Renee was, she had confirmed Michael's story. She was all upset over another woman who happened to be dead. So what if he'd been married before? She had kept asking herself why this wonderful man wasn't married, right? Of course he had been married. But now he was widowed, and he loved her. She could see it in his eyes. So why was she so upset? It wasn't that he'd lied, just that he hadn't trusted her with the whole truth. Was it a trust issue? Or was it just too painful to speak about like Michael had said? Who was she to decide what was and was not too painful to share? Leah suddenly felt like a completely selfish person. She was ruining Michael's birthday and had thrown a temper tantrum over what? Because she didn't know his whole life story after two months of dating? How dare he?

Leah stared at the sunset, a strip of blazing orange and gold with inky clouds broad brushed above it. How small she was compared to the sky and the universe beyond.

Why do I matter? I'm such a wreck, Lord, and so easily thrown into a quivering mass.

Leah absently kicked the top off a fire ant mound and watched the ants pour out, quaking from side to side, *just like her insides.*

Leah's eyes searched the sky as if looking for an answer to be written in the gilded swirls of gray. "Can I trust him, Lord? You know I hate secrets."

Leah knew that Shay was right about one thing. She was throwing away happiness with both hands, but maybe that was the best thing for her poor, scarred heart. She dug through her purse until she found her mirror.

"What are you afraid of, girl?" she asked her reflection.

Well, her face was rather scary at this point. Leah removed a tissue from her purse and quickly wiped the black mascara trails from her cheeks. She splashed some cool water on her face and gently dabbed around her eyes, willing the swelling to go down, then blew her nose and reapplied her lipstick. Leah shot up a quick prayer.

"Lord, don't let me hurt him, and don't let him hurt me. Show me if he's the guy for me. I'm falling hard and fast, and I don't want to be heartbroken again. Show me the way."

Leah slipped her feet from the river and dried them in the grass. She slid into her flip-flops and carefully made her way back to the party. Jason was making a birthday toast, his glass of sweet tea raised high.

"Happy 30th birthday, Michael. You have great taste in cars and women, and I hope you have many more happy birthdays to come."

The crowd laughed and applauded. Leah walked up to Shay and bumped her arm.

"You're right. I'm an idiot. Forgive me?"

"Sure. Sorry I had to be so rough on you."

"No, I needed it. Can I borrow your glass?"

"Of course."

Leah raised it high. "Happy Birthday, Michael. You have great taste in music and women, and I hope you have many more happy birthdays to come."

The smile on his face said it all—she was forgiven, and Leah's heart felt a little lighter. But the unease in the pit of her stomach stayed, and Leah hoped that she'd made the right choice.

Chapter 21
Ps. 17:26 It is not good to punish an innocent man...

The court clerk looked at the crowd over the top of her computer. It was 11 a.m., and they had been sitting there for two hours waiting for the plaintiff and her counsel to show up. "Is Officer Liam McPhillen present?"

"Yes, Ma'am," Phil stood and answered in his booming voice. His hands were sore from clenching and unclenching them as he waited.

Phil's lawyer, Chandler Lee, was shuffling through papers in his briefcase. Several police officers sat in the row behind him. Some were witnesses; others were moral support. His family sat at the back of the room with friends from church. He could feel them praying, and it calmed him somewhat.

Finally, Miss Holmes appeared, her bosom falling out of a two-sizes-too-small sequined blue shirt-dress, with her impeccably-coiffed attorney striding behind her. Her heels clicked a staccato rhythm on the marble as she walked, a bemused grin on her face as if she had just heard something funny—until she noticed the media. Then her face melted into a mask of sorrow.

As the grieving family's very young lawyer began a booming oratory on police abuse of power and began flashing gruesome pictures of the deceased boy, Phil forced himself to look at the judge, not at the glaring family, or the media members sitting behind his friends.

"Your Honor, permission to approach the bench," Chandler said, when it was finally his turn to speak. "We have some new information which is relevant to this case."

"Your Honor!" the young lawyer tried to object.

"Both counsels approach," Judge Sharkey grunted, waving them forward.

A fiercely whispered conversation ensued, and in the end the counsel for the plaintiffs stalked to his seat red-faced. Phil looked down and tried not to show any emotion. His friends had provided him with a copy of the court order from Saucier that had ordered Robert Maximus Holmes to be at school every day. The teen had multiple unexcused absences, and there was a report from the

Harrison County Department of Human Services, which showed they were in the process of reviewing the custody placement of Robert. His father had been recently released from prison, and had sued for custody after a drunken party at the mother's house had resulted in several arrests for underage drinking and narcotics use— and it wasn't the first time this had happened. In fact, the mother had several open cases with human services in four different counties, and had already lost custody of two of her children. It seemed that she had a penchant for grabbing the closest child and beating him or her to within an inch of their lives whenever she drank tequila, which was pretty often. Chandler had reams of evidence showing that the grieving family wasn't much of a family.

Not that any of this information would matter to the media, Phil thought bitterly.

"I'm ordering a continuance," said Judge Sharkey. "Chandler says you two can work this out on your own?"

Both attorneys nodded, and Robert's mother stifled a shriek of rage.

Phil stood up to leave, and the scurrying of feet told him that he once again was going to run the gauntlet through the microphones and cameras.

"Give me strength, Lord," he prayed. "I'm afraid I'm going to say something really rude today."

Chandler patted his arm, "It's almost over, Phil. There is no way you are paying off on this one. Just keep this stuff quiet for now. It's got to come from me, and there are still more possible open cases we haven't located. This lady moves around a lot."

Phil gave him a grim smile, and sat back down. If the reporters wanted him, they were going to have to wait until after the Noon broadcast. He was staying put. Leah gave him a small wave as she rushed out the door before they could badger her with questions. She had promised Mr. Alexander that she would finish up several reports before the end of the month, and it was the end of the month.

Just moments later, Hunter walked into the courtroom, holding a handkerchief over his face. Liam stood as he recognized the blood stains on his son's shirt. A small cry escaped from Beth's mouth and she rushed forward to her son.

"What happened, Hunter? Where have you been?" she gasped.

"In the parking lot. You should see the other guys. There were a few," Hunter mumbled, as his legs collapsed from under him. "I called 9-1-1 already."

Several uniformed officers hurried out of the side door toward the back stairs. Liam knew that if the boys were still around, they'd be arrested quickly, but all he could do was stare at the blood streaming from a gash in his son's swollen lip onto the marble floor. Beth grabbed the boy's scraped hands and began to dab at them with a Handi-wipe from her purse, while Phil applied direct pressure to the split under Hunter's right eye.

The sound of an ambulance getting closer helped calm the rage in Phil's heart. He kept praying for his son's safety, trying to shut out the red-hot anger that raced through his brain.

Chapter 22
I waited patiently for the LORD; he turned to me and heard my cry. Psalm 40:1

"Leah, do you and Sheanna want to come to Preston's with me? I want the check something out, and you two can go swimming while I tie up some loose ends," Daddy said.

Sheanna jumped into his arms. "Thank you, Uncle Phil. Thank you! I have been waiting forever to go back to Preston's Beach!"

"Forever?" Leah teased. It's only been a week, Sprout."

The family had stayed close to home, bringing Hunter pain medication and sweet tea, and pointedly ignoring the ringing phone. Squad cars were parked in front of their home morning and night, and the bullies had shied away from certain arrest.

"Get your suits on, girls. You have five minutes."

Sheanna's little feet pounded against the floor and she let out a whoop of joy as she ran to her room.

"I guess that means 'yes', Daddy," Leah said. "I'll be ready in a flash."

"Just a second, Leah. I need to ask you something. Alone."

Leah's eyes narrowed. "What, Daddy?"

"It's about Michael's business. Dan told me he's in trouble. I checked into it, and the threat is real. That's why he's been working six days a week. He's been sued by a business he worked with, and it looks like the guy might get Charbonneau Woodworks."

Tears filled Leah's eyes. "What are you saying, Daddy?"

"I'm saying that you need to know that Michael is in financial trouble. I see the way you look at him, and I don't think you should go into this without knowing that it's not going to be easy. The debt against his business is substantial."

"Oh no, Daddy. That's terrible."

"I'm not saying you need to do anything. I just wanted you to know."

"Why wouldn't he tell me this?"

"No man wants to be shamed in front of the woman he loves. It wasn't his fault—more of a hostile takeover situation—but it's going to be a tough row to hoe for quite a while. Are you ready for that?"

Leah sat down, her head swimming. She knew Michael worked too much, but she'd gotten it into her head that he was just trying to show off a bit, to be the big successful businessman that came up from nothing. Her heart filled with anger as she realized that somebody was trying to steal what Michael loved away from him.

"Why are people so rotten, Daddy? Don't they know it will come back on them one day?"

"Honey, if I could answer that, I'd be a rich man. It doesn't seem fair, but this isn't heaven. We shouldn't expect it to be—and it doesn't always 'come back' on them. Sometimes the most rotten people seem to have it the best. But you just can't worry about them, or it'll eat you alive. Believe me. I've learned that the hard way!"

"I know you have. Thanks for telling me. I'll talk to Michael tonight, and see what he has to say about it. But one thing bothers me."

"What's that?"

"How did Dan know? It's not like he's the king of carpentry in Mobile, for goodness sake."

"The guy that sued Michael is his brother-in-law. His version of the story is a little less flattering, I'm sorry to say. But everything I've found out points to the guy trying to steal Michael's business and reduce his competition."

Leah gritted her teeth. "So that's what Dan and Michael were discussing at the barbeque. I thought he was just being overprotective or something."

"He can't help who his sister married."

"He could accidentally shoot him. He is a cop."

"You're very funny. Go get dressed before Sheanna does terrible things to you for wrecking her trip to Preston's."

"What are you 'looking into' at Preston's, Daddy?"

"One of the log cabins may have a clue that I need for an old case. Remember, the one I'm helping Robbie on? Something jogged my memory the last time we were there. I remembered the old campground, further back in the woods. It may have the answers I need, but if I show up there alone, it may look suspicious to some folks. You two are my attractive decoys."

"I feel so special."

"Get dressed, Girl, or I'll sic the little tyrant on you."

Chapter 23
Prov. 14:10 Each heart knows its own bitterness...

"Cousin Leah, Mr. Michael is on the phone," Sheanna called from the sandy shore.

"Don't tease me, Sprout, or I'll dunk you," Leah laughed.

"It is him, really. Here." Sheanna waded into the water with the phone in her hand.

Leah heard Michael's voice as she gingerly took the phone into her wet hand.

"Hey, where are you? I'm at your house," Michael said.

"We're with Daddy at Preston's Beach. Want to come swimming?"

"Sure, I'll be there in fifteen minutes. I finished early, and there's something we have to talk about."

Leah's stomach twisted into a knot. "What?"

"Uh-uh. You'll have to wait until I get there. See you soon."

Leah tossed the phone onto her sandy towel and turned to her little cousin. "Mr. Michael is coming to swim with us."

"Yeah," Sheanna clapped, spraying sand all over Leah's swimsuit.

"Let's work on that swimming so we can show off when he gets here."

"Where's Uncle Phil? I want him to help me swim."

"He'll be back in a few minutes. You'll have to settle for me, Squirt."

"I'm not a squirt. I'm Sheanna," the little girl asserted. "And there's Miss Shay!"

Leah shaded her eyes with her hand, and there was her friend, piling bags on a nearby picnic table.

"Hey," Shay called. "I came to crash the party."

"The more the merrier. My life is going to get very busy next week, and I have to work on my tan while the sun shines."

"You are tan enough. How are the swimming lessons going, Sheanna?"

"She's not as good as Uncle Phil," she pouted. "He buys me ice cream."

The carnival tune told them the ice cream man was near, and Sheanna never missed an opportunity to jockey for a sundae cone.

She usually got one too, because the family was trying to make up for all the treats she'd never gotten from Brinne.

"You win, tyrant. Here's a dollar," Leah sighed as she snatched one from her purse. "So how'd you get a day off, Shay?"

"I'm sick. Sick of work. My principal actually dressed me down yesterday in front of a group of kids. I stopped an argument and he made it look like I had instigated it. So I took a mental health day, and when I saw your Daddy drive by with all that junk loaded in the truck I knew y'all were coming here. So here I am. Let's get us a sundae cone too."

"Sure, why not? If I had to teach those mean middle school kids, I'd eat sugar by the handful and I'd probably be bald-headed too. Plus, I owe you one from the concert the other night, anyway. Those seats were awesome, and we had such a great time! I wish Michael and I could go to one of those every weekend. Even the rap group was pretty good."

"You're right. They need to do more concerts like that. Spread the gospel every which way they can."

"You got my vote. Where's your man?"

"At work. It's my own personal mental health day. I need to relax and soak up the sun all by myself. With you and Sheanna, that is."

"You won't get much quiet around that little chatterbox. Look at her talk to that poor ice cream man."

"Hey, we'd better get over there. You know about the ice cream man, don't you?"

"What about him?"

"He's a career criminal, in and out of jail. The kids in my class make jokes about him. His whole family is a bunch of thugs."

"So what is he doing here?" Leah hurried toward her young cousin, terrified that he'd snatch up the little girl and disappear.

"Looking for victims, probably. His dad is worse; he was the first ice cream man, but he'll never get out of jail now."

Leah looked at the slight man with the huge red beard as Sheanna's pointed and waved her money at him. He didn't look threatening, just hairy.

"What are you girls up to?" Phil asked from behind them.

"We're hoping my daddy will buy us some ice cream," Leah teased. "How did the search go?"

"Nothing, the one building that hasn't fallen down is locked up tight."

Leah's face turned serious. "Do you know about the ice cream man's record?"

"He sells over-priced ice cream. Is that a crime?"

"Oh, it's much more than that," Shay whispered. "My students tell me that you never want to be caught alone with the ice cream man."

Phil stood still, looking over the wiry, red-headed man and his face paled.

"Take your time ordering your ice cream, girls," he said under his breath. "I need to look at the tattoos on the man's arm."

Leah and Shay gave him a strange look, but they hemmed and hawed for several minutes before ordering their sundae cones. Leah watched her daddy as he carefully inspected the man's arm as he handed out the treats. He seemed enthralled by the blacked-out hearts on the man's arm, and seemed to be reaching back for his pistol, even though he was only wearing his swimming trunks and a dark tank top.

"Daddy, what is going on?" Leah hissed as they walked toward the water.

Sheanna chattered excitedly to Shay between bites of melting ice cream. "Mr. Michael is coming. I got the phone call."

"He's coming here?" Shay asked.

"Yes, he said he has to talk to me about something," Leah explained.

"Shay, can you take these girls home later? I need to follow that ice cream truck," Phil said in a low tone. "I need some answers, and that guy just may be able to give them to me."

Phil hit a few buttons on his phone, and called in the license plate number on the ice cream truck.

"You weren't kidding about him," Leah said to Shay.

"I didn't really think my students were serious, but I guess they weren't pulling my leg."

"Pulling your leg about what?" Sheanna wanted to know.

"The man in the ice cream truck. He's not very nice. You don't go around him unless we are with you, okay?" Shay said.

Sheanna shrugged. "I thought all ice cream men were nice. He didn't even take my dollar."

The older girls exchanged a look.

"So did I. But I was wrong," Leah said. "Let's get in the water before Michael gets here. I want to teach you how to stand on your head."

"Oh, I can do that. I used to do that on my mattress all the time. I got up to three minutes once."

"Well then you'll have no problem doing it under water," Leah said.

Phil waved to the group. "Thanks, girls. The old cabins didn't help me, but this ice cream man thing may be big."

"Sure, Daddy. Make sure Officer Cutie knows we helped you crack the case."

"I'll tell Robbie, you flirt. Gotta go."

He sprinted to his truck and followed the winding road the ice cream truck had taken. Moments later, Leah heard the squeal of tires as a gray truck spun out of the gravel driveway and down the road, with Phil's F-150 hot on its trail.

"A gray truck," Leah whispered to Shay with a shudder. "I hope it hasn't been following us."

"Why? There are dozens of gray trucks around here," Shay said.

"Yeah, but Daschle says there has been one parked down the block almost every night since that kid's wreck. Daddy's been looking for him."

"What does that have to do with the ice cream man?"

"I honestly don't know."

Sheanna squealed, "Mr. Michael! Come swim with me."

Michael walked up to the shore in his sawdust-covered jeans. "I gotta change. Give me a minute."

"One minute," Sheanna yelled back.

Michael walked over to Shay and Leah. "Not to be rude, Shay, but can I borrow Leah for about thirty seconds? I have a little girl waiting for my services."

Shay laughed. "Thirty seconds. Okay, Michael. I'm getting wet."

She ran toward the water as Sheanna followed her, squealing with delight.

"What's going on?" Leah asked, her heart pounding in her throat like a tennis ball.

"I just talked to your dad's friend, Dan. He thinks I'm doing you wrong, and I wanted to give you the whole story before it wrecks everything. I'm not trying to bring up my birthday, but I learned you have a hatred for surprises."

"What surprises?" Leah asked, barely able to breathe.

"I took a large job with another company, a competitor. I thought I'd make a huge profit, but the guy was crooked. He made sure I couldn't fulfill my part of the deal, and then sued me. He's trying to get my business, and I need a large amount of money, fast. So I've been calling in favors, working like crazy, anything to keep ahead of the game. I still think I can do it. But I need you to know because I, because I want you to know that if I had my way we'd be together every single day. I'd buy you dozens of roses, and we—"

"Michael, stop. I understand. It's okay. I love the time we spend together. I know about the business. Dan told Daddy, and I decided this morning that I'm in. Whatever happens, I'm in. If you own Charbonneau Woodworks or not, you're the man that makes me happy. And that hasn't happened in a long, long time. Okay, never. I've never been this happy."

Michael grabbed her hands and pulled them to his chest. His eyes were black with emotion and he whispered, "Then have dinner with me Saturday night. In Pensacola. Just me and you."

"I will," Leah whispered back, her heart pounding in her throat.

A small, wet hand tugged on Michael's jeans.

"Are you coming swimming or what?" Sheanna whined.

"I'm getting my trunks on right now, Ma'am," Michael said.

Leah scooped Sheanna into her arms and announced, "I'm dunking you first!"

Sheanna squealed and kicked her legs and Shay splashed water in their direction.

"Hurry up. It's my only day off, and I want to get wet!"

Chapter 24
Prov. 16:27—A scoundrel plots evil, and his speech is like a scorching fire.

Leah had been up since dawn, first making sure Aunt LouAnn and Momma got off to the doctor's office okay, and then frying up a big platter of French toast. She sprinkled a little powdered sugar on the top and set it on the table next to the syrup. Her mouth was watering. French toast was one of her specialties, and Sheanna's new favorite breakfast. Leah couldn't wait to see the look on her face when she saw it. Leah thought she's never seen anything as beautiful as those pretty little cat eyes shining with joy.

Trooper got to his feet and let out a growl, an evil sound that made her blood run cold.

"What is it, boy?"

She followed him to Sheanna's room and opened the door.

"Sheanna, time to get up," Leah said softly.

Trooper raced past her and jumped out the open window.

The open window?

Her mouth dropped and she ran to the window, calling for her dog. The screen was missing, and the pillow lay on the floor. Leah snatched the sheet off the bed, hoping Sheanna was just playing a trick on her, but there was nothing there except Spot. The hot pink bag lay on the floor next to her dresser, and Leah rifled through it. Everything was there. She looked through the open window again. Only a blast of heat met her. The screen lay off to the side, leaning against the house unmolested. There was no blood that Leah could see, no sign of a struggle. But something in the pit of her stomach screamed that this was very wrong.

"Daddy!" Leah shouted. "Daddy, Sheanna's gone. You need to take a look at this. I'm not kidding."

He was at her side in an instant, his eyes running over the scene.

"Her pink bag is here, and it looks like everything's in it," Leah whispered. "Look at the screen. It doesn't look right."

In a moment he was radioing the sheriff's department.

"This is Sergeant Liam McPhillen, Ocean Shores Police Department. We have a missing endangered child, Sheanna LouAnn Jakes. She's four years old, about 3' 8" tall and 35 to 40 pounds, with blonde hair and green eyes. May be traveling with a middle-aged male, 5'8", thin build, bald, with several missing teeth. Male may be armed and dangerous. I believe they're heading north on 63, or could be on I-10. Can you get an Amber alert out ASAP?"

"I'm going to drive around the neighborhood and make sure this isn't just another 'Snowball run', Daddy," Leah said softly, her stomach churning with fear.

Hunter called from the hall, keys jangling, "I'll call it in to O.S.P.D. check the road to I-10. Maybe they're not too far ahead of us."

As Leah sprinted to her car, she spied a large shoe print in the dew and pointed.

"Look, Daddy," she said through the open window.

"I see it Leah. That's why I called for the Amber alert. Go on and drive through the neighborhood. I've got some friends on the way to collect evidence around here. Make sure you have your phone on you. I'll call your momma."

"Oh, Daddy. Don't worry Aunt LouAnn now. Let's wait until they come back. There's nothing they can do, and it may send the poor woman right to the emergency room."

He nodded grimly, pulled a card from his wallet, and handed it to her. "Hey, get on your phone and send a picture of Sheanna to this web address. Then stop by and see what our dear neighbor has seen. Daschle doesn't miss a thing that goes on around here. I'm surprised she didn't catch Cullen in the act. Lord knows she's told me everything you kids ever did wrong in excruciating detail."

"Maybe this time her watchful eyes will do us some good."

"I'm going to jump on the 'cycle and see if I can catch up to them; surely he's headed north. I'll meet Robbie and his buddy at the George County line, and we'll go from there. I wish I knew more state troopers."

"Daddy, once those cops see her little angel face, Cullen will have nowhere to go. We'll get him."

His eyes turned stony. "Sometimes beautiful little girls die, Honey. I hope we're not too late. Now get over to Daschle's."

Leah prayed as she sprinted past the perfect flowerbeds toward Sandra Daschle's front door. She knew she was about to get a lecture about waking her up in the early morning hours, but for once Leah didn't care.

She knocked sharply on Mrs. Daschle's front door, an oversized oak, stained dark brown with an oval of leaded glass that sprouted three perfect magnolias in green and white. It had been many years since she'd been inside the house, but she remembered it was very clean and quiet, like a museum. The house had smelled of sickness then, since Mr. Daschle had been bedridden after the boating accident that had crushed his legs. The man had never gotten over their loss; he just sat and stared at the television until the day he died from an infection in one of his bedsores. It had eaten to the bone, and he never even seemed to notice. As much as Leah had tried to be compassionate to his widow, her abrasive manner was more than Leah could take, so she left the neighborliness to saints like her mother and the rest of the prayer group. Not that Daschle appreciated it.

"Dr. Daschle, this is urgent. I need you to answer the door. I know you're here."

Leah pounded for several more minutes, and then tried the door. It was locked. She walked around to the side door, and gasped. It wasn't closed all the way, and there were brown smears on the handle. Leah used her elbow to push open the door. On the kitchen floor laid a pitiful form, curled up and mangled, smelling of vomit and human excrement. Her hands and feet had been duck taped tightly together behind her back, and she'd been beaten to a bloody pulp. In fact, the beautiful hardwood kitchen floor was smeared with blood from one end to the other. The old girl had put up quite a fight. Leah leaned down next to Mrs. Daschle to see if she was still breathing. A small groan escaped the woman's mouth, and Leah slipped her phone from her pocket. When called Lani Randall, knowing she could get an ambulance there faster than 9-1-1 ever could.

"Lani, it's Leah," she nearly screamed. "I'm next door at Daschle's house and I need an ambulance here yesterday. She's dying!"

"I'm on my way," her friend chirped. "See you in five."

Leah dialed her daddy's number. She knew that he'd check his messages every few minutes, and figured it was the best way to let him know what was going on. She waited impatiently for the beep.

"It's Leah, and I'm at Daschle's. Somebody beat her half to

death. I'm calling Dan, and Lani's on the way with an ambulance. It's pretty bad."

Leah hung up, then put the phone on speaker and dialed 9-1-1. She didn't want to wait any longer, or leave any messages.

"This is 9-1-1 emergency. How can I help you?"

"I'm at 1110 Vista Bonita, and I need officers here right away. There's been a-a murder. Please, hurry."

Leah swallowed hard. It wasn't quite a murder, but she wanted cops here, and fast.

Besides, they're probably already next door, checking out Sheanna's room, she told her conscience. *It's only a little lie.*

"Please remain on the line," the voice said. "They're on the way."

"Tell them to come in the side door," Leah added.

She took a tissue from her pocket and gently wiped some of the saliva and dried blood from around the old woman's mouth.

"I'm so sorry Ma'am. Do you know who did this? Was it a bald man?"

Mrs. Daschle opened her mouth to speak, but only a soft groan came out. Leah noticed that her front teeth were pointed backward at a strange angle, and her face and neck were so puffy and bruised that the woman barely looked human. Her nose was smashed and swollen, surrounded by crusted blood.

Leah grabbed her pocketknife and sliced through the tape at the woman's wrists and ankles. She knew that she was probably destroying evidence, but her heart ached to see the pulp that had been her irascible neighbor. She went to the sink and poured some water into a glass, then gently dribbled it over Mrs. Daschle's lips.

She whispered something, and Leah put her head right next to her lips.

"Say it again?"

"Tattoo face and neck. Silver truck," she wheezed out the words haltingly, the pain obvious. "He's gotta place for her."

Leah wiped her mouth with the wet tissue again and stroked the woman's purple fingers gently, trying to get the blood moving in them.

"Help will be here soon. Don't talk anymore. I know it hurts."

The woman opened her mouth to speak again, then her eyes

rolled up into her head, and her face went slack. She looked ghastly pale, but Leah could still hear slight wheezing breaths. Thankfully, she also heard sirens, and the sound of footsteps running up the front stairs.

Leah shouted, "Come to the side door. It's open. There's blood all over, though. Side door!"

"Gotcha," Daddy shouted. "Lani's here, too."

"Please hurry."

Leah slid back as her dad and a few of his officers stepped gingerly through the door, trying to keep from disturbing any evidence.

"Has she said anything?"

"He has a tattooed neck and face, Daddy. I'm betting it's that no-good Cullen. Who else would beat an old woman like this?"

Sergeant McPhillen crouched down and wiped a solitary tear from his daughter's cheek.

"Dr. Daschle, can you tell us anything else? Anything that would help us catch him? He can't be too far ahead."

Silence was his only answer, and soon they heard the welcome sound of Lani urging her partner to 'hurry up with that stretcher'.

As soon as the elderly woman was loaded in the ambulance, Leah kissed her daddy's cheek and sprinted through the back yard.

"I hear Trooper barking. Sounds like he's getting closer. Call you later, Daddy."

"Don't go anywhere. I left a message for your momma, and she'll want to know what's going on."

Leah didn't answer; she was already half way to the next block calling her dog's name as loudly as she could.

Chapter 25
Prov. 8:17—I love those who love me, and those who seek me find me.

Leah racked her brain, trying to imagine what "he gotta place for her" meant. She held tightly to Trooper's collar and walked her dog toward the house. She watched as the ambulance raced down the street, thankful Lani had gotten there so quickly. There were over a dozen officers collecting evidence around the two homes, and several others working the neighborhood, looking for information.

"One more time," Daddy prodded. "Everything you know."

"She told me a couple weeks ago that there was a silver Chevy truck with something that looks like a bullet hole in the driver's side door parked down the block. She thought somebody was watching us, but she said it was a young guy with a bunch of piercings. I knew that's not what Cullen looks like, and I kind of thought maybe it was Gator or one of Hunter's buddies watching over us. When I found her today, she told me 'he' was in the silver truck. I'm not sure if it's the young guy or Cullen, just that it's the same truck."

Leah listened as Daddy radioed the description to the dispatcher.

"Honest, that's all I know. I can't even tell you if it has a Wisconsin tag or not. She never mentioned the license plate. Of course, he could've stolen the truck. Aunt LouAnn said the man never could keep a vehicle. We never dreamed he'd have the guts to come down here. Where did he get the money for gas? He never had a dollar to his name, from what I hear."

"It's June 3rd. I'm guessing he got Brinne's welfare check. But a man like that will find money when he wants some—no matter how he has to get it."

"But Mrs. Daschle saw the truck parked down the block weeks ago. Could he have a friend down here?"

"No tellin'. Those kind of people seem to always land on their feet. If we can track down the friend, we can probably find little Sheanna."

"So you don't think he's on his way back to Wisconsin?"

"Not in that truck. I think we'd have caught him by now if that were the case. You don't know how many cops are out looking for that little girl right now. Every minute we don't find her, well, you know the statistics. Even if he stole another vehicle, it would help us to trace his path—if it's been reported stolen."

"I think I'm going for a drive. Who knows? I may stumble onto something."

"Bring Trooper with you, and keep your phone handy. I know your Momma and LouAnn will want to know where you are. If you see anything, call me first. Don't put yourself in any danger, girl."

"I won't. I'm not the daredevil I used to be."

Daddy's partner, Dan, laughed wryly. "Sure, I noticed that about you. At least you're done with the pranks. Folks still haven't gotten over that time you filled the gym with boats."

"It was our senior class prank, over six years ago. Why can't people just move on? Besides, I wasn't the only mastermind of that one."

"I know. But in case you didn't notice, there were several students who were forbidden from ever speaking to you again."

Her mind shot back to that terrible day when Trey stopped returning her calls. *Was it all about our Senior prank? Why didn't he just say so? I would've apologized to his parents for moving their boat, and everything would've been just fine. I lost the love of my life because of my great imagination? How silly!*

"I didn't notice. I never noticed."

Dan patted her back, and said, "Please just drive around the neighborhood like you said, and make sure this isn't a wild goose chase."

Daddy added, "And keep out of trouble!"

As she drove through the streets, Leah kept one ear open for Sheanna, and one ear on the police scanner. The Amber alert was functional, and every road sign between here and Canada would contain the information. Missing endangered: five year-old female. How could Cooper get away with this? Suddenly, her phone chimed with several voice messages. She shook her head, wondering why people always called when she was in a dead spot. She pulled over and checked them.

"It's Momma. Aunt LouAnn has several blood clots in her right leg and some other side effects from her medication, so they're admitting her to the hospital. I'll be home in a few hours; be good."

"Hey, Sis," Hunter whispered, "Stop checking the neighborhood and head north. We just heard that Cullen cut off his monitoring device three days ago. He's suspect number one. It wasn't Sheanna running off after all. Thought you needed to know."

"Leah, it's Lani. We got Daschle here just in time. Broken ribs pierced a lung and they got her in surgery now. Just saw your Momma downstairs in admitting. I'll fill her in. 'Bye."

Leah snapped her phone shut, and closed her eyes. Momma was going to be hot as a live coal when she found out from Lani what had gone on that morning. She didn't want to be Daddy right now. Hell hath no fury like a Momma kept in the dark! Leah lowered her head to the steering wheel, and started to consider her options. What kind of people would Cullen know? Criminals. Where could she find them? She thought of all the times her Daddy complained about drugs fueling ninety-five percent of the crime in their city. Where did all the high school stoners go for their drugs? She knew two places, and she was going to go drive through them, looking for the silver truck.

"Please, God. Don't let anybody kill me before today is over—especially Momma and Daddy. I hope you have a couple of huge, tough angels riding along with me because this could get hairy."

She started her car, and turned up the music on the Christian radio station, and headed for the apartment of the one drug dealer she knew. If he still lived there, and if he would talk to her, maybe he could give her some direction.

It was only a few minutes until Leah pulled in front of the largest housing project in Andrews County. Tony was well known to the kids in town; the party always started at his house from what she remembered. Sure enough, there in his window hung the same tattered black P.O.W. flag. He hadn't moved, but would he remember her? She looked at her watch, only 9:30 a.m. He'd be mad when she woke him, but it couldn't be helped.

"Tony, it's Leah. Open up!" she yelled before banging on the door. She didn't want to scare him off. It's Leah McPhillen, Sammy's sister. Open up!"

She heard footsteps shuffling to the door. When it swung open, she hardly believed what she saw. Tony's hair was matted, and smelled like it hadn't been washed in weeks. His face was so sunken in that his eyes bulged like a frog's. A garbage can smell assaulted her nose, and her eyes stung.

"Tony, do you remember me? I'm Sammy McPhillen's sister, and I need your help."

He limped back from the doorway and let her in. The house smelled even worse than he did, like cooked Drano mixed with old shrimp. Leah put her hand over her mouth until the nausea passed.

"Tony, have you seen any strangers around here? He's a skinny bald white guy. He has a friend with a silver truck that has a bullet hole in the door. Do you know him?"

Tony threw back his head and laughed. "Sammy's not here."

"I know. Sammy's in New York. I'm asking about a guy with a silver truck. Do you know anybody with a truck that has a bullet hole in the side?"

Tony's eyes were unfocused and he seemed to be trying to figure out where Leah had come from. He touched her ponytail, "Pretty hair."

"Thanks, Tony. But can you help me out? I really need to find this guy."

Tony just threw back his head and laughed again. "Trucks are for red necks."

"You're saying that nobody here has a silver truck?" Leah pressed.

"No trucks. No trucks," Tony repeated in a sing-song voice.

"Thanks, Tony. If you see one, would you call me?"

Leah slipped one of her business cards out of her purse, and circled the cell phone number. "Call me if you see anything."

Tony laughed again, and Leah let herself out, gratefully gulping in the fresh hot air as she ran to her car.

Leah drove across town to the other hot spot for kids seeking a good time. It was affectionately known as the "Roach Motel", and students could get anything from booze to weed from "Han", the guy at the front desk. She drove around the building slowly, looking for the silver truck. She hoped the guy at the desk remembered her from her occasional college beer runs, or she'd be stuck in another dead end.

"Han, do you remember me?" Leah asked as she breezed into the entryway. "I used to come here for beer a few years back, and I need your help."

She tried not to focus on the impossibly long hairs that streamed from the large mole on Han's chin or his yellowing eyes and skin, or the thousands of wrinkles that lined his face. She willed her smile to look friendly and un-cop-like.

"I don' know what you say. Get a room or get out," he grunted.

"I'll pay for a room, if you can tell me something. I am looking for a silver Chevy truck with a bullet hole in the driver's side door. Have you seen that vehicle? It's worth fifty bucks to me."

He spat on the floor. "No trucks. Get out or I call the cops!"

"No, you won't call the cops. I know where you keep your stuff. So just tell me. Are you sure you haven't seen a silver Chevy truck with a bullet hole in the driver's side door? It's not about you. There's a little girl who's missing."

"No trucks," he roared. "Leave now or you Daddy will be takin' you to jail!"

Leah gulped, "If you know my Daddy, you know that it's best to tell me what I need to know."

"You a killer like him, little girl?" the man snorted. "No trucks. Just cars. Now go, and don't come back!"

Leah sat in the parking lot for a moment trying to think of anywhere else she could go to search for the silver truck. Then a memory tickled the back of her brain. The other day at Preston's Bayou, Daddy had started out following the ice cream man's van, but ended up tearing out of the parking lot after a silver truck. He hadn't caught it, and he was pretty angry when he finally did come home. Leah tried to picture the back of the truck in her mind. Did it say, "Chevrolet"? She couldn't recall. Why hadn't she asked him about it before? She'd just assumed that the ice cream man had changed vehicles and ran, but that didn't seem probable. How would he know that somebody at Preston's would want to ask him a bunch of questions? He wouldn't. So what had happened to the silver truck? Would anybody at Preston's remember it? She had to ask.

Chapter 26
Prov. 17:28—Even a fool is thought wise if he keeps silent, and discerning if he holds his tongue.

Leah drove slowly past the entrance to Preston's Bayou and parked next to the marina, in full view of the office. She walked back to the man at the entrance, digging through her purse for the parking fee.

"Have you seen a small bald white man, about 5'9" and 130 pounds? I'm supposed to be buying his truck, and I'm a little late," Leah said to the elderly man in the window.

"Can't say that I have. What's the truck look like?"

"Just an old work truck, a gray Chevrolet two-door with a dent in the driver's side. See it?"

He turned back to an even older man who ran the concession stand that faced the beach.

"Does that sound familiar to you, Joe?"

"Nope, can't say that I've seen either one around here," Joe replied. "You're welcome to look around, young lady. No charge."

She fished a business card out of her purse. "My cell phone number's on there if you see him. It's really important y'all. Thanks."

The younger man smiled and slid it into his front pocket. "No problem, Sugar."

Leah turned and walked through the marina, looking for anything that looked suspicious or out of place. She quickly walked through the crowd on the beach, and along the shaded side that her family favored. She sat down on the edge of brick grill, thinking. *Was the gray truck that Daddy chased away really Cullen? Would Cullen bring her here, where there were crowds of people? If I wanted to hide a little girl, and I didn't know the area well, where would I put her? The old campground entrance might look deserted to a stranger.*

Leah decided to walk through the woods where Daddy had gone searching for clues. Maybe there was something along the trail that sparked Cullen's interest—if indeed, he was following Daddy around. Leah passed the log cabin that held the restrooms and the nearly empty campground, a tiny RV park and the boat launch. She walked through the grove of live oaks and pine trees and followed the trail to the old campground. Leah noticed that there were still a couple of buildings partially standing back in the trees, and suddenly she felt her heart beating in her throat. Leah took her cell phone out of her purse, set it on "silent" and slid it into the crook of a tree. She slipped around behind the cabins and stepped carefully through the underbrush, keeping an eye out for snakes and other creeping things. The first cabin had a caved in wall, and was littered with empty beer cans, cigarette butts and booze bottles. The second cabin was almost identical. But Leah smelled smoke coming from further in the woods, and she continued to pick her way through the brush until she saw a large shed with a tin roof, and several smashed cigarette butts smoldering in a coffee can in front of it. She made a wide circle around the back, but there was only one door, and the windows were small and covered in dirt.

Something like a brick hit her on the side of her head, and everything went black.

Water was dripping on her face, and Leah swiped it away with her hand. The pain on the side of her head made her nauseous and the sniffling noises weren't helping. Sniffling noises? Leah forced her eyes open, and tried to focus. It took a few seconds before she saw Sheanna handcuffed to the other side of a small rusted metal cot with no mattress. There were bruises on her neck and arms that looked like fingers, and a red palm print marred her tiny cheek. Her pretty blonde hair hung in sweaty strings, and her eyes were filled with tears.

"Are you okay, Leah?" she asked shuddering despite the heat.

"I'm fine. Are you okay Sheanna?"

Leah looked around the dark room that reeked of cigarette smoke. There were several rakes, a shovel, and her purse dumped all over the floor.

"Yeah, he doesn't want to make any noise. Is Uncle Phil coming?"

"I hope so. I left my phone where they could find it. You didn't see Cullen come back with a phone, did you?"

"No, but he just left a few minutes ago. Don't make him mad, Leah. He will hurt you. Just do what he says, okay?"

Leah pulled at the handcuffs that held her to the bed frame.

"I have to get to my purse. I can get us out of these if I can get a barrette. I'm going to slide this as quietly as possible. You keep an eye out for Cullen."

Just then the door opened.

"Thanks for the info, Leah. First your dad shows me this great hideout, and now you tell me just how to keep you here all safe and sound. I heard of southern hospitality, but you folks take it to the next level!"

He kicked her purse out of the door, and picked up her car key. "I can just drive right out of here with this little darlin' and nobody will catch me now. Thanks for the wheels."

He kicked Leah in the ribs several times and punched her in the mouth. Each blow felt like an explosion of pain. Cullen knew his business when it came to inflicting pain.

"That's for not respectin' your elders. If I ever see you again, it'll be the day you die, you hear me? And I will take my time. He reached over and grabbed her shorts, slipping them off almost effortlessly, and tucked them into his pocket. I'll give you plenty to remember me by, you hear me, *Cousin* Leah? You're lucky I like mine skinny."

She forced her lips together and nodded, her brain feverishly trying to work a way out of there, as Cullen tied a smelly rag around her mouth.

"Be nice and quiet until we get away-- like a good girl," he spat.

He unlocked Sheanna's handcuff and tucked her under his arm like a football.

"Don't give me any trouble or I'll throw you in the river," he threatened. "There are 'gators who would love a bite of a little girl like you. Then you'll never see your mom again!"

When he turned away, Leah made doggie paddle motions with her hands. She hoped the man would throw Sheanna in the river. She'd be safer with the fish than around a monster like him.

"Oh, I almost forgot," Cullen sneered. "Your phone."

He threw it down and stomped on it until it was in several pieces. He picked up the battery and threw it into the woods.

"Guess Daddy won't be able to find you today, will he?"

He flicked his cigarette at her face and kicked her viciously once more on the side of her head. Leah slumped against the bed, feeling nauseous and watching black blotches dance before her eyes.

He stomped out the door, giggling. "We're taking Leah's car on a nice long ride."

Leah waited until she couldn't hear his voice any more before she lifted her head. The pain was almost unbearable, but she wasn't about to let Cullen get away with Sheanna. He'd put enough marks on that baby for one lifetime, and he deserved to have a large, scary roommate do the same thing to him. She inched across the floor, dragging the bed frame toward a large nail she'd spied near the iron rake. It would do nicely. Years of playing with Daddy's handcuffs had left her quite an expert and popping open the lock. All she needed was to move a few more feet without throwing up from the taste of the rag and the blood in her mouth.

She didn't know how many times she slipped in and out of consciousness, but she knew that the room had cooled a little. There was a breeze coming in through cracks in the door, and it smelled like campfires and rain. She hoped it would be a real southern thunderstorm that would slow Cullen down. Was he stupid enough to head straight north? She hoped so. There were plenty of people watching for him, and most of the locals would know her car right away. Plus, she had a headlight out. Somebody would stop him sooner or later, wouldn't they? They had to. But now he had access to a police scanner. Why hadn't she put it away?

She needed to focus on moving toward the nail. One more inch, then just one more. She was so close. She stretched her arm out as far as it would go. She was almost there. She pulled herself a little closer and reached again. There! The nail was hers. Leah sat up panting, willing her fingers not to tremble and she worked at the lock. She was free in a matter of seconds. Leah ripped the stinky rag from around her mouth, rubbed her wrist and moved her fingers. Now, all she needed was to find a way out of the shed. She pushed against each board, looking for rotted ones, for rusty nails. Something told her to push against the door. She was able to push it open about two inches, but no farther. There was something blocking it, but it wasn't the padlock. Cullen must have ruined it when he broke in. Leah looked for something heavy to beat against the door with. She thought she saw a log in the corner of the shed.

"Please, God, don't let it be a rat," she prayed. "And please let us get Sheanna back. Don't let him hurt her any more. Please."

She stumbled gingerly toward the corner of the shed. It was a log. She picked it up, ignoring the screaming of her ribs. Leah tossed it toward the door, crying out in pain as she released it.

"Is somebody there?" she heard a male voice outside the wall.

"Help me," she yelled as loud as she could. "I'm locked in."

She heard something crashing through the brush, and a strange hissing sound. Soon the wind was whipping at her hair and fat raindrops were flying through the doorway. A teenage boy looked up at her through the semi-darkness.

"What are you doing in here?" he said. "Who broke the lock? My grandpa's gonna have a fit when he sees this mess."

Then the teen noticed that she was standing there in her panties, covered in crusted blood and bruises. He flipped open his phone.

"I'm calling 9-1-1."

Leah sank to the floor, grateful. Her head had never hurt so terribly, and now the room was spinning and black, yet full of white pinpricks of light. She spat blood from her mouth, and then there was nothing.

******

Leah heard the roar of an engine and the screech of sirens. Thoughts kept running through her mind, but as hard as she tried, she couldn't get her eyes to open. Was Sheanna okay? What would Michael think when she missed their date? Did somebody find her Sim Card? Her phone was smashed! How could she call him? Please forgive me, Michael. Forgive me, Sheanna. I tried my best. How could she let down the people she loved most?

Chapter 27
Ps. 141:10— Let the wicked fall into their own nets...

Liam McPhillen was impatient. He was sure he would have caught up to Cullen by now if he'd taken Highway 63. He studied the map, trying to ignore the thunder rumbling in the distance. The sky was black, and he hoped he would still be able to see when the storm hit.

If I were a criminal with limited resources and a little girl to hide, which way would I go? I know he is an addict, and very arrogant. I do not know whether he is even driving the silver truck; stealing a car would be easy for him. He wouldn't count on us having the manpower to cover all the roads out of Mississippi, and he wouldn't take a chance on getting lost and losing the child. If he cuts over to Alabama or Louisiana, we're sunk. But will he use an extra tank of gas for the sure escape?

He traced his finger along the highways and looked for the straightest route that wasn't an interstate. He kept coming back to 49. It wasn't the most obvious route, but it wasn't some country road a stranger would get lost on either. He sent a text message to Leah, the family in Sardis, and Hunter that he was headed north toward 49, and got onto his motorcycle. He hit the redial button.

"Rob, would you let the state troopers know that I'm going to keep heading north to Jackson? I just have a hunch about this guy. I'll keep y'all posted."

"I got your back. Good luck."

I'll need more than luck, he thought, as he pulled out his phone again.

"Beth? It's me, Honey. I need you to get your friends together and start praying. We haven't caught him yet, and I have an awful feeling in the pit of my stomach that something is terribly wrong. If he gets out of Mississippi, I'm afraid we'll never see Sheanna again. Have you heard from Brinne?"

"No, I couldn't even leave her a message. The mailbox was full," Beth answered, a tremble in her voice. "I haven't heard from Leah either. I've left her so many messages, but nobody has called me back. We've been praying—got half the church working on it. But you're right. Your guys should've caught up to him by now. Somebody should have found something by now."

"Okay, I've got another call coming in. I'll call you soon. Love you!"

"Be careful. I love you."

"McPhillen, here."

"It's Lani Randall. I thought I'd let you know that we found Leah."

"Leah? Since when is Leah missing?"

"It's a long story, but it looks like she's going to be okay. She wanted me to tell you that the silver truck is at Preston's Bayou. She said to tell you that Cullen has her car, and it still has that headlight out."

"Cullen has her car?" he almost roared. "Is she bloody daft?"

"Well, she was pretty beat up. They've admitted her, and they are still running some tests determining the extent of the internal injuries. Do you want me to tell Ms. Beth?"

"Yes, Ma'am. Thanks, Lani," Phil growled, snapping his phone shut, and gunning the engine.

He fought the urge to throw his phone, and slipped it into his pocket instead.

Leah found Cullen and tried to take him on herself? What was she thinking? Just wait until I see that girl! I'm going to beat her myself.

He radioed the tag number and description of Leah's Mustang to the state police and made sure they knew that her passenger-side headlight was out. This bad weather was actually a blessing in disguise. Cullen had to turn his lights on if it was raining. It was state law, and posted all along the highway. He wouldn't take a chance on getting pulled over for something so small, or he would get pulled over for not having his lights on in a storm. Either way it was good news. That should make it much easier to catch Cullen Jeffrey Beal, escaped parolee. Something still nagged at him to hightail it to Jackson. So he turned on his lights, and headed north as fast as he dared.

He flew through Hattiesburg and Okatoma, hoping he didn't dump his motorcycle on the wet roads. He was going so fast that he almost missed it-—an officer had pulled over a blue Ford Mustang in front of a little church just outside of Richfield. It had a passenger side headlight out, and a "PETA-- People for Eating Tasty Animals" bumper sticker in the back window. There was no way he could safely stop quickly enough, so Liam slowed and pulled to the side of the road just in time to see the car door open quickly, knocking the county sheriff into the road, and then the car sped straight toward him. Liam let his motorcycle roll to bottom of the steep ditch and prayed that Cullen wasn't crazy enough to follow him. He picked up his radio.

"Officer down, officer down. Highway 49, just south of Richfield, near the Assembly of God church. Be on the lookout for a dark blue '11 Ford Mustang carrying missing-endangered child. Suspect is dangerous and likely armed. Off-duty officer in pursuit."

A shower of gravel rained down on him as the Mustang hurtled past. Liam scrambled up out of the ditch to check on the fallen officer. The young deputy sheriff was dusting himself off and running toward his cruiser, so Liam turned and jumped back into the ditch to get his 'cycle. Seconds later, he was covered in clumps of grass and mud spatter and weaving in and out of traffic, hoping to catch a glimpse of his daughter's car. The young deputy had cleared a path, and soon they were right behind Cullen. Liam shot up a prayer that Sheanna wouldn't be hurt when he crashed the car, or that the car would stall or he'd run out of gas. He was sure the little girl was not in her safety belt, and he was also positive that Cullen would not stop on his own. He heard the radio call; there were Stop-sticks ahead. They were going to take out his tires before he made it to Jackson and endangered more drivers. Phil backed off a little, and Cullen seemed to sense that something was coming. He swerved, and only one of the tires was hit. It didn't slow him down. He just kept driving as if he had four good tires instead of three. The deputy got on his loudspeaker.

"Cullen Beal. Stop the car. You can't get away. Stop the car."

Cullen swerved into oncoming traffic and hit the brakes. The car spun 180 degrees and bounced off a light post, and then it accelerated across a grocery store parking lot, headed for the plate glass windows in the front. Phil was closing fast, not sure what he would do when he actually caught up to the vehicle. He knew that Cullen would run him down and not even think twice. Suddenly, the driver's side door opened and Sheanna was pushed into the 'cycle's path.

"Good thinkin', Cullen," Liam whispered and he screeched to a stop, laid down the motorcycle and jumped to scoop up the little girl.

"Are you okay, Sheanna? It's Uncle Phil. Are you okay, baby?"

The little girl shook and cried, clinging to her uncle so tightly that her fingernails drew blood.

Several police cars raced past, hot on Cullen's tail. Phil only glanced at them. He was busy checking Sheanna for injuries.

"Baby, I have to take you to a hospital. They have to look at these injuries on your leg. They look pretty bad."

"No, don't leave me! Don't leave me, Uncle Phil. We have to find Mom. He said she might be dead. Please!"

"I promise I'll be right next to you the whole time, and we'll get your momma to safety too, if she's here. I'll be there. Even in the ambulance, okay Sheanna?"

Phil heard an ear-splitting crash, and he knew that Leah wouldn't be driving her car any time soon. He scooped Sheanna up and went back to radio for an ambulance. Thunder rumbled ominously nearby, so he retrieved his slicker and put it over them like a tent while they waited. Sheanna had her thumb in her mouth, and her crying was like a knife in his heart. Phil held her close and rocked her, humming "Hush, Little Baby" as best he could remember it.

As the ambulance pulled in front of the grocery store, Liam looked over at the line of police cars exiting the little gravel road next to the store. He noticed that there was a man in the back of the first car banging his head and feet against the side windows. He jumped as a spider-web crack appeared in one window. The officer squealed to a stop, and soon Cullen was lying on his stomach across the seat with flex cuffs around his ankles.

That was worth waiting for, Phil thought, as he climbed into the ambulance.

Chapter 28

A wife of noble character who can find? Proverbs 31:10

"Cousin Leah, Mr. Michael is here," Sheanna yelled, as she pounded on the bathroom door.

Leah watched as Michael walked to the side of the house and shook Daddy's hand. The two men walked together, talking as if they had known each other for years. It warmed Leah's heart to see them together. They yelled at the TV together after Sunday brunch; they commiserated about the economy and the price of gas and wood.

Leah put on a glimmery new eye shadow that would complement her outfit and touched up the polish on her nails and toes, spraying them with a special quick-dry liquid that Shay's sister Rose had found. Rose was the queen of all things beauty. She was the only one Leah trusted to trim her hair or do her eyebrows, and she stared into the mirror at the highlights Rose had talked her into. Nothing dramatic, but the subtle brown streaks at her temples did make her hair look more civilized.

"Hurry, Leah. Mr. Michael is waiting!" Sheanna said with a giggle.

"I'm going as fast as I can, Sprout."

"Everything okay in there?" It was Michael this time.

"Two minutes, I promise."

Leah quickly twisted the top of her hair into a ponytail clip and crunched up her curls. Then she snapped her new barrettes over a few wispy stray hairs at each side of her head. She put on some glossy cranberry lipstick and a quick smudge of eyeliner. Then she got out her "super-chunky" mascara and finished with a few quick strokes. The silky pink shirt had been a gift from Momma on their last shopping trip for Sheanna. It was light and soft and somehow made her curves look attractive over her faded jeans and favorite silver flip flops. Plus, it almost made her forget all the yellowing bruises that covered her ribs.

Leah bounced out of the bathroom almost knocking Michael over. "I'm ready!"

"Good. I'm hungry and we have a long drive." Michael let Sheanna down from his shoulders gently.

"Where are we going?"

"I told you; it's a surprise."

"What were you and Daddy talking about?"

"You, of course. Now kiss your momma goodbye so we can go."

Leah bent down and planted a kiss on Sheanna's head, then another on her momma's cheek.

"Mmmn, you smell like apple pie," Leah whispered.

"There will be a couple of pieces left when you two get back," Beth said with the strangest sparkle flickering in her eyes.

Leah stared for a moment, trying to figure out her expression, and then gave up and followed Michael to the car. He waited for her under the oak tree in the front yard and she stared into his dark, dark eyes for a moment. He pulled her close, and then he was kissing her. His lips burned their way into her and her blood began to boil. She undid the buttons on his shirt and slid her hands along his skin, wanting nothing more than to be close to him, as close as two people can be. His tongue was driving her crazy, and she rubbed his back and tried to pull him into her. But her cracked ribs would have none of their embrace. She cried out in pain, and Michael jumped back.

"I'm so sorry, Leah. I just……it's hard to keep my hands off of you. I look at your lips and they make me ache to kiss you."

Leah put her hand on his cheek. "I know how you feel. But I hope we didn't give Sheanna the show of her life."

Michael chuckled softly and went around to open her door.

"Are you going to leave your shirt open like that?"

"Only if you want me to," Michael said.

Oh, I do. I wish I could kiss you for days.

"So now will you tell me where we're going?" she asked instead, as he closed her door.

"Well, since you stood me up last time we were supposed to go to Pensacola, I thought we'd go there."

"I had a little help. Some crazed psycho that is now in a jail in Jackson, I believe."

"I'm glad he's locked up, so Gator can sleep at night instead of watching over your house at night."

"I had a feeling it was him, but Daschle said he was young, with a bunch of piercings Then she said the guy who almost killed her was in the gray truck, so I didn't know who we were looking for."

"He may look young to her, and I don't know how she mistook one earring for a 'bunch of piercings' but it was Gator. He confessed it to me when you were in the hospital. Strange that Cullen stole a gray truck to come get Sheanna in."

"Even stranger that Gator would come all the way over here when he knew we're surrounded by cops."

"I know the media attacking your daddy had him pretty hot under the collar. It happened to a friend of his once. The reporters had the guy branded a killer, and even after they found the real murderer the man's life was ruined. He lost his wife, his job and ended up moving to Alaska where nobody would bother him. It's unbelievable how much power they have."

"At least the final court date is next week and this mess will all be over. Don't even get me started. Nothing makes me madder than watchin' somebody get hurt and knowin' the guy that did it will get away with it."

"I noticed. I always wondered why you didn't become a cop like your daddy."

"I don't trust myself with a gun. It would be so easy for me to be judge and jury—especially when kids are abused. I never want to know what prison feels like. When I saw those scars on little Sheanna I just wanted to turn that truck around and go put Daddy's pistol in Cullen's mouth. But Momma always says that God would've taken the bad guys out a long time ago if He wanted him gone. I trust Momma; she knows what's what. So there must be a reason that piece of garbage still lives. I can't imagine what it is, but there must be a reason."

"So why don't you trust yourself with a gun?"

"Because in the heat of the moment I know what I'd do. It took me a couple weeks to work through my anger at all that little girl went through, and I just know a little piece of what my cousin Brinne let that man do to her. Momma hinted that he wasn't the first abuser she'd hooked up with either. I don't even know if I could look her in the eye. Much less hug her."

"And what about the guy that hurt you-- your high school sweetheart? I heard a little of it from Shay, but I'd like to know what he did that took you six years to get over. Not that I'm complaining. It took me a long time to find you; I'm just wondering."

"Well, you don't have to worry about him. He doesn't even live in Ocean Shores anymore. It was just that he took me so off guard. One day we were as close as any two high school kids could be, and the next day he was telling me that there was another girl. I never saw it coming, and it hurt. Plus, I lost my best friend that day. We were best friends since second grade or something like that."

"Well, there is something I have to tell you."

Leah felt her heart fall out of her chest. *Here comes the 'just friends' speech.*

Michael closed up the convertible top and pulled onto I-10, heading east.

"I am sorry I didn't tell you about Rachel. It was wrong. So I understand about old hurts. When your preacher was talking about grace the other day, it just hit me. I always expect God to forgive me right away, but I haven't forgiven some things. I guess I didn't forgive God for letting Rachel die. I always knew that He could have healed her from her addictions, so I thought it was my place to tell Him that He should have healed her. I knew in my head that she made her own choices-- she had free will, but my heart just hurt too much. Before I met you, I never really went to church. I was never baptized, and I think it's time that I talk to your preacher about it."

"Since you've been coming to church with us for months, wouldn't you consider him 'our' preacher?"

"You're right, Leah. It just sounds strange. Anyway, we're going to eat good tonight."

"Now are you going to tell me where we're going?"

"I told you, Pensacola. They have a seafood restaurant on the Gulf that makes Thornton's look like fast food. They can cook a steak like you wouldn't believe."

"I'm not dressed for a fancy restaurant."

"You look great. We're not just going there for the food. There's the view. And the good company."

"I thought you were saving your money for your business. You shouldn't be spending it on me, Michael."

"I think of you all week long. Texts and short calls aren't enough. I only get to see you on Saturday nights and Sundays— and your Momma does the cookin' on Sunday. So let me take you to a fine dinner with a view almost as lovely as you."

Leah fought the tears that stung her eyes.

"Yes, sir," she whispered, knowing that her face was anything but beautiful with all the faded bruises and steri-strips around her eyes.

It didn't take long to get to the Pensacola exit. Leah smelled the salt water and saw the restaurant with the glittering white Christmas lights along the roof and the rope lights along the rails. A quartet played softly in the background, accompanied by the clinking of silverware, soft voices, and the pleasurable grunts of people enjoying their dinner. Wait staff in black carried huge trays of delicious-smelling seafood.

"We have a reservation. Charbonneau," Michael told the hostess.

"Right this way," she nodded, grabbing two crimson and gold menus.

Michael grabbed Leah's hand and led her through the tables on the outer deck. As soon as she was seated, he dropped to one knee next to her chair, his hands holding hers gently.

"Leah McPhillen, I know that if God ever made a woman just for me, she is you. I love you. I love your mathematical brain, your friends, and your passion for life. I love your family. Your Daddy gave me permission to ask you to be my wife, and I can't even wait until dinner is over to know your answer. Will you marry me, Leah?"

Leah laughed and cried at the same time. She threw her arms around Michael and said, "Yes, yes I'll marry you, Michael. You've made me so happy!"

Michael hugged her to him tightly, then planted a warm kiss on her lips. People murmured around them, and Leah pulled back into her seat, suddenly feeling very self-conscious. She gently touched one of the steri-strips next to her eye.

Michael took a small black box from his pocket and opened it, now on both knees.

"This ring was my mother's, and her mother before her. I never thought another woman would be able to wear it, but you deserve the greatest treasure my family could give."

Leah held out her trembling hand and Michael slid the huge ruby-and-diamond ring onto her finger. It was a little tight, but Leah wouldn't dream of taking it off. Michael slid into his seat, and an elderly man at the next table gave him a thumbs-up.

Chapter 29

Acts 8:37 "Look, here is water. Why shouldn't I be baptized?"

The next Sunday morning before church Michael didn't bring Leah a red rose. Instead, there was a long rectangular box on the seat, and Leah opened it carefully. Six creamy white roses tied in a red ribbon lay in the box.

"Oh, Michael. You shouldn't have."

Leah threw her arms around him and planted a kiss on his lips. Once again, her blood turned to lava as his lips crushed hers, and her hands were all over his back, his arms, his face. He whispered her name, and the sound of his voice sent electricity through her.

"Leah, it was only a few flowers. What will your parents say if we're out here making out in the driveway? And the good Dr. Daschle?"

"She's still in the hospital, and since I have this ring on my finger, I think I have the right to kiss you whenever and wherever I please."

Michael held her with such tenderness and strength that she felt out of breath and energized at the same time. He ran his fingers through her fat, unruly curls and for the first time in her life Leah didn't hate her hair. Her heart was finally at peace. She could tell that her parents adored him almost as much as she did.

Did we get engaged too quickly? The random thought tore through her brain.

She looked into his eyes, and went through each date, each time they were together. They had truly been soul mates since the day they'd met. He was her best friend, and she believed she could tell him anything. Michael was a truly nice guy, shared her faith, and they had had some great discussions as he studied his Bible in depth for the first time. Daddy had given him a men's study Bible for his birthday, and she could tell he was reading it. He had everything she wanted in a man with none of the heartache. Of course they weren't teenagers anymore, so why wait? Michael was going to have a lull in business after Labor Day weekend, so Leah hoped they could get everything arranged before his next big job started in October.

"Come in you two and get some breakfast," Momma called from the porch.

"I'm not going to argue with that," Michael whispered.

"You don't know how many questions she's been cooking up since we showed her the ring last night."

"And what about you? Do you have any questions?"

"I don't just want cake and punch reception. I want a whole dinner, and dancing. I was thinking about having the reception at Thornton's? I'll call this afternoon and be sure the date is open."

"Which Saturday in September are you shooting for?"

"How about the first one they have open?"

"You're letting a restaurant manager pick our wedding date?"

"Not exactly. But I'm pretty sure the church won't have any other weddings that soon. I haven't heard of any new engagements."

"So you'd let the Pastor pick our wedding date?"

"Well, we do have to meet with him before we can get married. So it kind of is in his hands."

"So what if Pastor Wes won't let us get married? Then what?"

"He will. Unless you're some closet pagan or something."

Michael laughed. "No, I'm not. I know that Jesus paid the whole price for my sins, and I'm finally ready to let Him be Lord of my life. But I think Pastor's going to counsel us about more than faith. There's finances, raising the children, stuff like that."

Leah lowered her head, "Oh, I'd forgotten you've done this all before."

"Not exactly. Rachel and I weren't married in a church. I just heard about it from one of the guys at work. Not all construction workers are wild bachelors, you know."

"So how did you get married?"

"Justice of the Peace did it. We were married in Alabama, so I don't even know what we have to do to get a marriage license in Mississippi."

"I can call the courthouse at lunch tomorrow and find out."

"That's a good idea. We'd better get inside before your momma comes back out here."

Hunter leaned out the front door, "I'm hungry. Are you two comin' or what?"

"See? Momma's waiting for us. Why'd you keep me out here

so long?" Leah teased.

Michael tugged at her hair and ran for the door.

"You can't beat me," Leah yelled.

"Already did," he said, holding the door open for her.

Hunter rolled his eyes as they walked into the kitchen. "You might as well forget about winning against her. She wins even when she loses."

"And you just lose," Leah snapped. "With that face, your chances of getting a date get smaller every day."

"Uh, my team is undefeated right now, and several young ladies have called to see how I'm recovering," he reminded her.

"Sure, it's only practice. The real season doesn't start until August, and the ladies from Momma's Bible study group don't count as prospects."

"Hey, is that a ring on my awful, man-hating sister's finger? Don't do it, Man. She's a bear in the morning, and her hair looks—"

Michael laughed, "I'll take my chances."

Leah slapped her brother on the arm. "I heard the tennis star dumped you when she saw how easy you were to beat up, so I guess it'll be a year or two before you find another girl desperate enough to go out with you."

"She didn't dump me. She has a special coaching session in Memphis and a bunch of tournaments coming up, so we're just taking it slow, for your info."

"Maybe if they let you into the police academy, they'll teach you how to be a real man. Then you can get a girlfriend who might stay."

"If you get tired of trying to control her temper, Michael, I'll be happy to arrest her for you."

"That's enough now," Momma said. "Three months isn't very long to arrange a wedding, so eat your muffins so we can start planning some of this stuff out."

"Well, I hope Aunt LouAnn will be my coordinator, since Momma already has that 'mother of the bride' job. Will you be my flower girl, Sheanna?"

"Sure," Sheanna said. "What's a flower girl?"

"Well, you walk in first, and put rose petals on the ground in a pretty, lacy dress."

"Can I just wear my Tweedy swimsuit?"

"It'll be in church, silly. You don't wear a swimsuit to church."

"Well, then I'll just wear this church dress. I don't want any girlie stuff."

Hunter laughed, "See what Leah has done to the little sprite already? You'll have your hands full. Welcome to the family, Buddy."

Michael grinned at him, his face flushed with pleasure.

"Only thirty minutes until church," Momma said. You two had better hurry or Leah will be too late to sing."

"If her voice is anything like yours, it'll be a treat. I want to get a spot right down front anyway. I need to talk to the Pastor about a couple of things."

"So it's true? You're getting dunked tonight?" Hunter asked.

"That's the plan."

"Don't worry. They usually don't hold anybody under too long."

Chapter 30
Jeremiah 16:20- *Do men make their own gods? Yes, but they are not gods.*

"Leah, wake up, Baby," Michael banged at the door early that Saturday morning. The wedding was only three weeks away, and Leah had been up late the night before addressing invitations, and trying to get Sheanna used to her frilly flower girl's dress. She groaned and rolled out of bed, as she heard her mother's slippers slap their way down the hall.

Beth opened the door, "Good morning, Michael. Who is this?"

"I'd like you to meet Gator. Remember? He did all the cookin' at my birthday party. He'll be my best man. Gator, Momma McPhillen."

"Pleased to meet y'all Ma'am," Gator replied, in his nasal New Orleans twang.

"Call me Beth, Gator. I appreciate all those nights you watched over us in your truck. Would you like some sweet tea?" she said, stepping back and opening the door.

Leah stared into her momma's eyes, looking for any sign of alarm. They were as clear and blue as if Pastor Wes was walking through their door.

Sheanna came out of her bedroom, rubbing her eyes. She stared open-mouthed at Gator for a moment, then her face lit up as she spied Michael. Leah heard him laugh as Sheanna ran up and gave him a big hug.

Leah wondered what her Momma really thought as she looked at the deeply wrinkled, longhaired, heavily tattooed old man. He hadn't been wearing a sleeveless shirt at the birthday party, so Momma hadn't gotten the full view of the tattoo art that covered his arms. Leah slipped upstairs and quickly dressed, eager to talk to Michael, and to hear one of Gator's funny stories. The man was full of them.

"We need to pick up a few more white flowers and pearls for Shay and Sheanna's wreaths today, too," Momma reminded Leah as she walked into the kitchen and placed a kiss on Michael's head. Sheanna was sitting next to him, leaning on his shoulder half-dozing.

Poor little thing still got up in the middle of the night from time to time and crawled into bed with Aunt LouAnn. She wasn't used to having a bed up off the floor, and often fell out. Other nights she woke up crying or screaming in terror. Momma had gone through a lot of warm milk and cookies in the past few weeks.

"The reason we're here so early is that Gator had a visitor yesterday, and we need to talk," Michael said softly.

Oh, no, this can't be good, Leah thought. *When do the surprises end?*

"Her name is Kat, and she is..." Michael looked out the window, then down at his feet. "She's my big sister."

Leah looked at him with wide questioning eyes, and Sheanna popped awake and frowned at Michael as if he'd somehow slighted her by daring to have another woman in his life.

"She's out in Gator's truck," Michael said softly.

"Well bring her in, silly. I can't believe you left her in the truck," Leah said, trying to ignore the knots twisting in her stomach.

Sheanna was violently shaking her head no.

"She is a little, well, strange, Leah. She's had a pretty rough time of it since our parents died. I haven't seen her in years. But I'd like to take you out to meet her. Wanna come, Sheanna?"

Sheanna ran behind Momma, and wrapped her arms around her, "I don't hafta, do I, Auntie?"

"No, baby. Go get dressed. I'll call you when breakfast is ready, okay?"

Sheanna nodded and trudged out of the room, lip poked out, eyes barely slits.

"Are you sure about this?" Michael asked.

Leah looked at Michael as if he'd lost his mind, "Of course I'll meet your sister, Michael. And we have to invite her to the wedding, too."

"She's a little rough-lookin."

Rougher than Gator? Is that possible? Leah wondered.

"Maybe she'd like to come in for some coffee," Momma coaxed. "I'll have breakfast ready in a few minutes, too."

"She's not used to being around a lot of people," Michael almost whispered.

"Okay, well, sure. Let's go out there. It's already getting hot," Leah said. "I'm not going to leave her there."

Leah followed Michael and Gator outside, where Kat was smoking a cigarette, sitting on the tailgate of Michael's old pickup truck. She tried to look friendly, but Kat's appearance caught her off-guard.

She couldn't have been much older than Michael, but her gaunt face was deeply lined, her sunken eyes red-rimmed, and her hair a stringy dirty blonde. Kat's face looked as if it had once been beautiful, and her eyes were an icy blue so stunning that Leah could barely look away. She had long dark lashes that curved up perfectly and deep dimples, just like Michael's. She was skeletal-skinny, but too tall to be considered petite. Her fingers nervously rubbed a small pendant she wore around her neck.

Leah stretched out her hand to shake Kat's and flashed her friendliest smile. "Hi, I'm Leah."

Kat barely squeezed the tips of her fingers and whispered, "Hey, girl," showing a mouth missing several teeth.

Leah glanced at Michael, who was smiling; obviously she'd passed some kind of test.

"You wanna come in for some coffee?" Leah asked.

"Sure," Kat answered. "If you got sugar."

"Oh, we do," Leah assured her, relieved. "Momma's makin' her great cheese grits casserole, too."

Kat laughed loudly, though Leah couldn't tell why.

"Does that mean we're eatin' breakfast? Are you making biscuits too?" Michael grinned and looked at his sister. "Kat, you're in for a treat."

Kat threw her cigarette down and ground it into the driveway.

"Oh, I suppose we could whip up some biscuits and gravy, since I'm already awake," Leah cut her eyes at Michael.

"Hey, you're the one who said you're leaving early to go shopping. So I'm here early."

"From now on, I'm telling you nothing," Leah teased as they walked into the house, which already smelled of fresh coffee and buttery biscuits.

"We'll see about that." Michael tried to tickle her ribs, then her neck, and it took everything Leah had not to react. Leah knew that if he knew she was ticklish, she'd never see the end of it. He tickled Sheanna mercilessly, and Leah wanted no part of that.

"That's a pretty necklace," Leah said, nodding at Kat.

"It's a special crystal. It keeps me centered." Her fingers moved over it even faster. "A holy man give it t'me and it keeps me alive on the dark days."

Leah tried to keep her face from showing her disbelief.

"Where do you live, Kat?" Leah asked, hoping to distract Michael from his evil tickling scheme.

"Oh, Slidell mostly. I travel around a lot. Don't like to spend my time in one place." Her eyes darted around, constantly on the prowl as she stirred several spoons of sugar into her coffee.

"Maybe you can give Michael some ideas for where to go for our honeymoon. It's his only job, you know."

"So the wedding's in three weeks?" Kat ran her fingers through her scraggly hair, and several thin strands drifted to the floor.

"We'd love for you to come."

"I'll try. I don't have any plans." She looked at her yellow-brown fingernails, which were chewed down to tiny nubs.

Leah stared into her eyes, trying to read what Kat meant. Did she really want to come? She couldn't tell. Then Leah felt someone watching from the hallway. Sheanna stood there, mouth agape in absolute horror. Leah looked at Momma, and nodded toward the tiny child. Aunt LouAnn came down the stairs just in time to catch her as she tried to run.

"What's the matter, child?" Aunt LouAnn said.

"She looks like Mom," Sheanna moaned, quaking from head to toe. "She looks just like my Mom."

Aunt LouAnn scooped Sheanna into her arms and walked her toward the back porch, shushing her as she went. She was strong for her age, but Sheanna was holding on so tightly it looked like she would topple them both over. At least the changes in medicine Dr. Diaz had suggested left her looking like her old self. A frail woman would be on the floor.

Leah sighed and turned her attention back to Kat, as she and Momma cooked, as they ate, as they talked. It was strange how Kat looked like an old woman, but spoke like a teenager who'd just been sent to the Principal's office. Her sentences were short and unrevealing.

Why had she returned now? Did she see the wedding

announcement in the newspaper? Where had she been? Why didn't Michael ever talk about her? He knew that Daddy could've tracked Kat down if Michael had wanted.

"I'll call you later," Michael said, blowing her a kiss as they piled back into Gator's old truck an hour later.

Leah handed him a wedding invitation through the window, "For Kat."

She beamed her best smile at Kat and said, "I really hope you'll come."

Kat smiled back weakly, but didn't answer.

Chapter 31
Prov. 17:15—He who justifies the wicked, and he who condemns the just, both of them alike are an abomination to the LORD.

Officer McPhillen wiped his face with his handkerchief for the fifth time in as many minutes. Both attorneys had argued their cases well, and he wondered if he would continue to be an officer after today. Who could resist the pleas of a grieving mother, even if she was not very organized or careful with her children? Bad parenting was not the unforgiveable sin, and she had lost her only son because of it. Just as he'd lost his oldest son because he had been too busy saving the world for the bad guys to realize that his children needed him there. Not just in body, really there, playing with them and listening to them. If Brinne was standing before that judge, what would Phil plead for? Mercy. Gentleness. Grace. The girl was raised in terrible conditions, and nobody stepped in to help; now her daughter suffered because Brinne didn't know what a real family looked like. Was this woman from the same kind of background?

"I have made my decision," the judge said, looking sternly at Officer McPhillen and the attorneys at both tables. "After considering all the evidence presented, I see no reason to continue this miscarriage of justice against a good man and a decorated officer. Case dismissed."

Ms. Holmes screamed, "No, no! You'll never be rid of me!"

She ran across to the defendant's table and slapped Phil across the face, screaming, "You killed my boy. My son! My son! You killed him. You killed him!"

The bailiff pulled her off of the startled man, and began to lead her out of the room.

"I won't press charges," Phil said loud enough for everyone to hear. "Let her go."

Leah's eyes flashed fire.

"After all the mess those people put us through? The broken windows, the trash in our yard? Hunter jumped and beaten? The fake 'news' reports trashing your name?"

He looked at his daughter sadly, and said," Sometimes grace is more important than justice, Leah. Try to remember that."

The officers met at the Los Lobos Coffee Too in Biloxi, just off of I-10, for a celebration lunch. There were state troopers from three different states, a dozen sheriff's deputies and almost the entire Ocean Shores Police Department. The whole family was there too; even Phil's father, Paw-Paw, came down from Sardis Lake for the final court date. They filled the restaurant and the air with good-natured teasing and stories of rookie days gone by.

Leah loved to listen to Paw-Paw's Scottish brogue as he told of adventures his boys had on the farm when they were young. Liam had been a daredevil, and had been sewn and patched up more times than his daddy could recount. There were stitches and broken toes and a scar on the back of his head where he fell out of the hayloft. But the worst adventure was when he'd followed his older brothers across the creek on a rope swing. He had let go too late and landed on a water moccasin that was basking on a nearby rock. He not only cracked a rib, but was bitten several times and had to be rushed to the hospital in Memphis for antivenin. Compared to the stories of Phil's youthful adventures, this court case seemed like a minor irritation.

But as happy as he was, Phil couldn't help himself from being drawn into the conversation between Robbie and Dan at the back table. They were arguing, faces red, about the two missing tattooed girls.

"You need to let this one go," Dan said. "Trust me. There are plenty of missing kids and bad guys out there to keep you busy."

"I am not going to let the third girl die. I'm going to find her sooner or later. You're wrong on this one, Dan. You've got the same strawberry blonde hair. What if she's one of your cousins? Do you know something you're not telling me?"

"You're fixin' to get knocked out, Bubba. No kin of mine would get away with such abuse. I'd take them to the jailhouse myself."

"So why do you keep trying to get us to drop the case?" Phil piped in.

"Because I had a case like this one. It almost killed me. I followed every lead, even the tiniest one. I lost sleep, and made myself sick about it, and finally, one day, I got the guy. The lowest scum of all, had raped his own daughter. I had the proof, did everything right, and guess what happened?"

"What happened?" Phil wanted to know.

"Two years later he was right back living in the same house, abusing the same girl. All that work so justice would prevail, and the pervert was only out of commission for two years. Then they let him move right back in. The momma let him stay after all that. He had a great job, and she needed the money."

Phil tasted bile at the back of his throat.

Robbie spoke carefully. "The bad guy might have won that one, but they can't win forever. I'll keep working until we find these people. I'll never give up on those girls."

"I'm with him on that, Dan," Phil said. "One tragedy doesn't change anything. We keep fighting, give grace when we can, and drop the bomb when we can't."

"What about twenty losers? Or fifty? How many sleepless nights? How many broken families?"

"As many as it takes, man."

"The good guys won one today. I'd say we've evened things up."

"For today, maybe."

"So enjoy it while it lasts, Buddy."

"Don't you ever get sick of being in the thick of the fight? Don't you ever just want to quit, say forget it all, and move out in the woods somewhere?"

"Sometimes. But tomorrow, I'm rested and ready. I've been sitting around too much."

Robbie patted Phil's belly, "I'll say."

"Hey, I'm up to four miles. That belly won't be here long."

"Famous last words. Your wife just walked in with a huge cake. You'd better run five miles tonight."

Beth walked over and slid the cake on the counter across from their table.

"Congratulations, Dear. It's over."

The cake read "Congratulations, Phil!" in huge blue letters with a replica of the Ocean Shores Police Department shield underneath.

"How did you know?" Phil asked.

"I just had faith," his wife replied. "The prayer group was on it, and God is good."

"All the time," Phil answered, his eyes shining with joy.

Chapter 32

Song of Songs 4:9 "You have stolen my heart, my sister, my bride; you have stolen my heart with one glance of your eyes,"

How fast the days have sped until September 14th, Leah thought. *This is the day I've waited for, and now it's here.*

She stretched and looked at the clock. 10:30! She hadn't slept that late in years. Probably since college. But she kept thinking of things to double check, and must have jumped out of bed a dozen times last night. It was after one the last time she looked at the clock. She now had only two hours left until she had to be at the church, so she'd better get moving.

"What's for breakfast, Momma?" Leah asked as she sailed into the kitchen.

"Don't ask me. Sheanna cooked today."

"Sheanna cooked. But she's only five. Are we having animal crackers?"

"I been working on my eggs. We're having scrambled eggs and toast."

"Oooh, gourmet cuisine. Anything else?"

"Sparkling grape juice in pretty cups."

"Sheanna, you've thought of everything. Thank you."

"So, can I wear my regular blue dress to church today?"

"Nope, it's the lacy pink one or go naked."

"Naked! You're teasing me."

"Naked or lacy dress?"

"They don't let naked people in church, Leah."

"It's a wedding. It's private. Your choice. Besides, everybody will be looking at the bride."

Momma was biting her lip hard to keep from laughing.

"Okay, I'll wear the dress. Do I get to rip up the flowers now?"

"Let's wait another hour. We don't want them to turn brown before you throw them. You do need to get cleaned up and get your slip on. Rose is coming to do our hair at Noon."

"I want to leave my hair down."

"Okay, but at least let her put some curls in your hair, and a pretty barrette."

Leah held up the clip covered in a circle of rhinestones. She knew that it was smart to have a Plan B when it came to Sheanna.

"This matches mine," Leah said. "What do you think?"

"I like that one," Sheanna said. "It's much prettier than the dress."

"I love the dress," Shay said. "It matches mine."

She turned and hung her dress up on the kitchen curtain rod.

"You'd better eat, Leah. Dinner isn't until 4."

"It was nice of Thornton's to open early and set up the buffet just for us."

"You'll fill that restaurant up easily. Your dad is going to have to take out a second mortgage to pay the bill."

"They gave us a really good price, and they're letting a couple of guys from our church orchestra play. It'll be perfect."

"Remember what Pastor said. Be ready for anything. Weddings are never perfect. I don't want to see you all stressed out today."

The phone rang, and Momma grabbed it. "Hello?"

"It's for you, Leah. It's Michael."

"The bride and groom can't talk before the wedding," Shay protested.

"No, they can't see each other. I don't see Michael anywhere around here, do you?"

"Hey, Babe. What's up?"

"Just calling to be sure you're going to show up today."

"Of course I'm going to show up today. What are you thinking?"

"No second thoughts about marrying an old widow man?"

"Absolutely none."

"Okay, I'll see you at two."

"And not a minute before," Shay yelled.

"Bye, Michael. I love you," Leah said.

"I love you, too," Sheanna yelled.

"I guess Momma should've put it on speaker phone," Leah said. "Goodbye."

It only seemed like a few minutes and Rose had their hair done beautifully—she had an up-do with just a few curls framing her face, and Shay and Sheanna had flowing curls and rhinestone barrettes. Momma wore an antique rose, tea length dress with cap sleeves, a tiny waist and chiffon skirt. Shay and Sheanna's dresses were dusty pink rose-colored lacy tea length dresses in front that cascaded to the floor in the back. Each dress had thin straps studded with rhinestones and an empire waist. Shay had beaten Leah to the altar, and asked for the style to hide her "baby bump", and Leah had been thrilled to comply.

As much as she didn't like Landon, Leah knew that Shay loved him, and that she was his best hope for a decent life. As the youngest of five boys raised by a single father, he needed a good woman, and Shay was that. Maybe she'd get that boy to Jesus one day. If anyone could do it, Shay could. Lord knew, the girl saved Leah's life after Sammy left. She'd been a sorry drunk, about to flunk out of college, but Shay wouldn't let her quit. How did she deserve to have a friend that would hold her hair when she was puking, then make her throw out her liquor the next day? Not once, but many times. Shay just knew how to love people. Leah hoped one day she could be that kind of person. It would probably come in handy when she was married. Momma had forgiven Daddy when he was an adrenaline junkie—even though it cost her the relationship with Sammy. She was a good lover, too, and Leah wanted to love people. Leah was glad she had so many examples because that was one thing she wasn't the greatest at—letting people off the hook when they were guilty. Mercy was a hard word for her.

Today's word was beauty. All four ladies had strappy silver sandals with rhinestones, and the men had white tuxedos with gray ties and cumber bunds, and a pink rose in their lapel.

The bouquets were cream and pink roses, magnolia leaves and baby's breath, and the church was decorated with a magnolia theme. The ladies of the church had done all the decorating, and the rehearsal dinner the night before had been enchanting—full of candlelight and delicious food. Michael had grinned all night, and as he helped put away the tables and chairs at the end of the night, Leah knew that she had made the right choice. He was the man for her, surprises and all.

Now she was standing in a little room, watching him and his best man, Gator, walk toward the sanctuary. Leah blew him a kiss, and Shay quickly closed the door.

"He's not supposed to see you," she hissed. "You're going to ruin it."

The music started and Leah felt her hands get sweaty. Shay handed her the bouquet. Okay, just a few minutes now.

Aunt LouAnn poked her head into the room. "We're ready for Sheanna. Come here, little flower girl."

Sheanna skipped toward the door, throwing petals high into the air as she went.

"That girl is going to have us all laughing through this whole wedding," Shay said. "I just love her."

"Me too. Did you see Sammy or Brinne anywhere?"

"No Sammy, and I'm not sure about Brinne. There are a couple of skinny girls out there who fit her momma's description, but I didn't see Sheanna staring at anybody or anything like that."

"I knew it was a long shot, but I hoped she'd come."

"Did you send her any money?" Momma asked.

"Just eighty dollars. I figured it would get her a bus ticket, and she would be staying with us, so it's not like she needed a hotel or anything."

"Eighty dollars can buy quite a high," Shay said, as LouAnn beckoned her from the doorway.

"I know. But I hoped seeing her daughter was worth more than that. It was a money order, so it wasn't like I could follow up to see if the check was cashed or anything."

Momma broke in, "Honey, let's talk about this later. It's your wedding day, and you look so beautiful."

Tiny tears shimmered in her eyes. "I'm so proud of you, Leah. You chose a good man. All your choices lately have been so, so grown up. I'm really going to miss my girl."

"Oh, Momma. Michael promised we will always live close by, and you know I've been tucking money away for a house for years. You won't lose me. Plus, I'll see you every Sunday. And I will come by to watch Sheanna every Tuesday night when you go to deliver the homebound baskets with your prayer group. I'll be around. You'll probably get sick of me."

Her mother hugged her tightly, and motioned for her husband to take his place on Leah's right side.

"Are you ready for this?" he asked, planting a tiny kiss on the top of her veil.

"Yes, sir," Leah answered, her voice catching in her throat. "I love you both."

They each gave her a gentle hug, eyes shining.

Her parents led her to the back of the church, and the three of them walked sedately toward the front of the church on the path of rose petals.

Michael stood at the front of the church, a huge smile plastered across his face. He didn't look one bit nervous—he just beamed.

"Who gives this woman?" Pastor Wes asked.

"Her mother and I do," Phil answered.

He lifted the veil, and gave Michael his daughter's hand.

Leah listened to her friends from the choir sing, and looked into Michael's eyes, shining with joy. The day couldn't have been more perfect. She was surrounded by the people that she loved most in the world, marrying the man that God had blessed her with.

It only seemed like seconds later when Pastor Wes said, "I'd like to present Mr. and Mrs. Michael Charbonneau. You may kiss your bride."

It was a sweet kiss, and she flushed as she looked out at her friends and family. She had a new name, and walked over with her new husband to sign her license and light their candle.

Leah Charbonneau. What new adventures are waiting for you? she wondered.

Michael grabbed her hand, and they walked down the aisle to their new life.

Chapter 33

Prov. 16:4 The LORD works out everything for his own ends—even the wicked for the day of disaster.

Liam McPhillen squeezed his wife's hand as they drove home. "I can't believe how much it costs to get rid of one daughter."

"I know you're going to miss her."

"It'll be awful quiet at the house."

"Yes, but I believe she chose the right man. Those two are like peas in a pod. I think they'll be a good match. They have the Lord, and I'm ready to have some grandchildren to spoil."

"Sheanna isn't enough for you?"

"I love that little girl, but she'll grow up just as fast as the others did."

The cell phone between them started to buzz. Phil ignored it as long as he could, but then he noticed the call was from Hunter.

"Son, what can I do for you?"

"Dad, pull over. I've got some bad news."

In the pit of his heart, he believed that Aunt LouAnn had just passed away. There was something in Hunter's voice that spoke of death. He quickly swerved onto the shoulder and braked in a cloud of dust.

"I'm pulled over. What's going on?"

"Cullen escaped. For some reason they transported him to the hospital in Jackson. Somehow, he got away in the parking lot—something about when they uncuffed him from the wheelchair, he hit the deputy and took off. They've been looking for him for hours, but he's gone. The sheriff said he left several messages on your machine, but I knew you haven't had time to get home yet. It's not looking good, Dad."

"You still with Aunt LouAnn and Sheanna?"

"They're right here."

"Meet me at the Magnolia Inn on I-10. Be sure you're not followed. We'll decide what to do after that."

"Should I call Leah and Michael?"

"No, let them enjoy their honeymoon. We'll fill them in when they get back from the cruise."

"I'm sorry to wreck your night, Daddy. I can't believe he got away."

"We'll get him again, Hunter. It's only a matter of time."